BEATITUDE

BEATITUDE

LARRY CLOSS

REBEL SATORI PRESS
New Orleans

Published in the United States of America by
REBEL SATORI PRESS
www.rebelsatori.com

Excerpts from *On the Road*, Kerouac on *The Steve Allen Show* in 1959, *Visions of Cody*, *The Portable Jack Kerouac* and *Mexico City Blues* reprinted by permission of SLL/Sterling Lord Literistic, Inc., copyright Jack Kerouac. Excerpts from "After the Party," "American Sentences 1995-1997," "New Stanzas for Amazing Grace," "Is About" and "A Ballad of the Skeletons" from *Death & Fame: Last Poems 1993-1997* by Allen Ginsberg, copyright ©1999 by The Allen Ginsberg Trust, reprinted by permission of HarperCollins Publishers. Excerpts from "Howl" and "Personals Ad" from *Collected Poems: 1947-1997* by Allen Ginsberg, copyright ©2006 by The Allen Ginsberg Trust, reprinted by permission of HarperCollins Publishers. "Carl Solomon Dream" and "Like Other Guys" by Allen Ginsberg, copyright ©2011 Allen Ginsberg, LLC, reprinted by permission of The Wylie Agency, LLC. "MoMA" and "I Used to Be But Now I Am" by Bob Rosenthal, copyright Bob Rosenthal, reprinted by permission. "A Testimonial" and "I Love Ph.D's" by Sparrow, copyright Sparrow, reprinted by permission. "Peeping" by Hal Sirowitz, copyright Hal Sirowitz, reprinted by permission. "Sail On," written by Deanna Kirk, Allison Cornell and William Lehman, copyright ©1996 Ivana Music (BMI)/ administered by Bug Music and The Anna Lee Company, all rights reserved, used by permission, reprinted by permission of Hal Leonard Corporation.

This is a work of fiction. Names, characters, places and incidents are the product of the author's imagination and are used fictitiously and any resemblance to actual persons, living or dead, business establishments, events, or locales is entirely coincidental. The publisher does not have any control over and does not assume any responsibility for author or third-party websites or their content.

Book Design by Sven Davisson
Cover Illustration by Anthony Freda
Cover Design by John Barrow

Library of Congress Cataloging-in-Publication Data

Closs, Larry.
  Beatitude / Larry Closs.
    p. cm.
  ISBN 978-1-60864-227-4 (pbk.)
  1. Beat generation--Fiction. 2. New York (N.Y.)--Fiction. I. Title.
PS3603.L686B43 2011
813'.6--dc23

2011040184

For John

"That last thing is what you can't get, Carlo. Nobody can get to that last thing. We keep on living in hopes of catching it once for all."

—Jack Kerouac, *On the Road*

ONLY BE READY, Buddhists say, and the teacher will appear.

"Ready?" asked Jay.

"Ready," I replied.

We were off to see the scroll. Finally, after what seemed like a lifetime of fantasizing and romanticizing, we were about to find out for ourselves whether the stories we'd heard were true, whether the tales handed down by true believers were fact or fiction. Some said the scroll was barely legible, that Time's unwavering transit had rendered the magic words all but invisible. Some insisted the Dead Sea Scrolls had inspired its extraordinary form. Some swore the scroll described potent rituals, possibly erotic in nature, deemed too incendiary and suppressed for years. And some maintained the scroll lacked an ending, that the final few feet were lost forever when a hungry terrier named Potschky came too close.

I grabbed a small leather case from my desk.

"What's that?" asked Jay as we headed for the elevator.

"A camera."

"I thought they said no pictures."

"They did."

He smiled and extracted a small leather case of his own from his shirt pocket.

"What's *that?*"

"A tape recorder. I figured we had to have *some* record of our excursion, since the rules say cameras aren't allowed."

"We'll see."

On the small plaza outside the Rockefeller Center skyscraper where we worked, we paused while Jay lit a cigarette. He took a deep draft and exhaled as we made a right and headed south on Sixth.

"Man, I am *so* excited," said Jay.

"Me, too. I could almost use a cigarette."

He offered his pack of Camel Lights.

I shook my head and smiled. *"Almost."*

We stopped at a Radio Shack so Jay could buy new batteries for his recorder and as we exited the store, he hit *record* and started speaking into the mike.

"This is Jay Bishop and Harry Charity," he began. "It's Friday, August eighteenth, 1995. Yesterday, after months of intense research, Harry Charity finally determined the whereabouts of the long-lost scroll, the celebrated manuscript, hidden away in a lead-lined vault…"

"Actually, Jay," I interrupted, "I don't think the vault has a lead lining."

Jay pretended not to hear me. " …hidden away in a lead-lined vault in a secret sublevel of the New York Public Library…"

"And I'm pretty sure it's in the basement, not a secret sub-level."

"After lengthy negotiation…"

"A single phone call."

"With a high-ranking forensic linguistics expert who agreed to act as intermediary on condition of anonymity…"

"She's a librarian! And her name is Elena Harrington."

"Harry finally managed to orchestrate a clandestine Level Six security briefing…"

"A what?!"

Jay put his hand over my mouth. " …a clandestine Level Six security briefing and we are at this very minute on our way to view the scroll. We're on a quest. And we know that when we see the scroll, something's gonna change, something's gonna spark.

It's very exciting. Spiritual, mystical anticipation. Talk to you on the other side."

We entered the beautiful Beaux Arts building through the main doors on Fifth Avenue, passing between Patience and Fortitude—the most famous pair of marble lions on the planet—and pausing just inside the magnificent vaulted entrance hall to inquire at an information desk how to get to room 316.

"Up the elevator to the third floor," said Jay, repeating the directions into his recorder. "Standing in front of the elevator, waiting, people around, they have no idea what we are about to do. Inside the elevator. First floor. Second floor. We are on the slowest elevator in the Western Hemisphere. Third floor. Door opens, we're out."

We made our way down a dimly lit hallway, passing rooms 314 and 315 before finally arriving at 316, the Edna Barnes Salomon Room, a large oak-paneled space filled with rows of glass display cases that were in turn filled with an exhibit of rare books and manuscripts.

"Excuse me," I said to a suitably bookish man sitting in an office on the far side. "I'm looking for Elena Harrington."

He picked up a phone, punched in a few numbers and announced our arrival. A few seconds later, a friendly auburn-haired woman in a no-nonsense navy-blue dress with gold buttons appeared.

"Which one of you is Harry?" she asked.

I raised my hand. "And this is Jay Bishop," I said.

"Hi, Jay. Nice to meet you. We're going to the conservation unit. Let me just give them a call so they know we're coming."

She disappeared for only a moment.

"Russell Brooks is due back at around two, which is almost… now," she said, glancing at her watch. "So, we can either wait up here and I can show you the manuscripts in this exhibit…" She pointed to the glass cases behind us. "…or we can mosey slowly to the Conservancy."

Jay and I looked at each other. There was only one manuscript we wanted to see. "Mosey slowly?" I suggested.

Jay laughed. "Sounds good to me."

"The Conservancy is on the ground floor," Elena explained, as we started up the hallway Jay and I had just come down. "Probably the slowest way is to take the elevator."

"We found that out on the way up," said Jay. "So, how long has the manuscript been in the Library's possession?"

"We don't own it," said Elena. "It's here on deposit. Oh, maybe two years, I think."

We took the elevator to the ground floor and made a right when we got off, passing a sign that said "Staff Only" and proceeding down a long passageway lined with thin metal lockers. Elena stopped in front of a glass door and tapped a four-digit sequence into a phone hanging next to it. On the other side of the glass, a man in a white lab coat turned toward us. A moment later, we were in.

"This is Russell Brooks," said Elena. "Russell is our senior conserver, and chief of..." She smiled. "...*whatever*."

"Whatever," agreed Russell, a friendly, stocky man with silver-rimmed glasses and a neatly trimmed black beard.

"Hi, Jay Bishop, Harry Charity," said Jay.

"They're here to see the scroll," said Elena.

"Sure, we're taking it out now," said Russell. "It's right over there."

I looked in the direction he indicated and then all around us. We were at the end of a cavernous room packed with paper presses and bookbinders, microscopes and magnifying lamps. The walls were lined with oak bookcases filled with fragile leather volumes and in the center of the room were several climate-controlled cooling chambers filled with texts too tender to touch. Above us, the ceiling was a complicated maze of louvered vents and fluorescent lights. Below us, the floor was an endlessly repeating pattern of tiny octagonal tiles.

We followed Elena to a massive wooden table. "Here it is," she said, pointing to a ten-by-three-inch yellow box with two string clasps. "It's a lot smaller than you think."

"Wow, it is," said Jay.

"The first time I saw it," said Elena, "I thought, 'Huh, it's much...' I expected it to be, you know, much shorter and fatter."

"That's what I expected," said Jay.

"But it's not," continued Elena. "It really looks more like a roll of wax paper."

We watched anxiously as Russell unwound the string from the two clasps and opened the box, revealing a cylindrical object wrapped in glossy white paper. Carefully, he lifted the object out of the box and placed it on a large piece of vellum spread flat on the table.

"I feel like Indiana Jones, opening the Ark of the Covenant," I said.

Elena nodded. "Russell's in the process of trying to figure out how to best preserve it."

"There's so much tape on the outside," said Russell. "We can get the tape off with solvent, but the treatment questions are the same. You can de-acidify. You can wash or maybe not wash it. You can do a lot of things with it, but you turn it into something..."

"Russell's got the surgical gloves," interjected Elena, smiling as Russell extracted a pair of clean white cotton gloves from his pocket.

"We're worried about getting our hands dirty," he joked.

"Nobody wants to touch this thing," said Elena.

"We do," I said.

"Oh, no," said Elena, laughing. "You absolutely do not want to touch this thing."

"It's more of an icon than anything else," Jay said.

"Well, that's exactly what it is," agreed Elena. "It can't be read anymore."

Gingerly, Russell pulled back the glossy paper, exposing a tightly wound roll of what appeared to be parchment. "It hasn't been examined for quite a while," he said. "Except for a few inches."

Very cautiously, very slowly, he unrolled about a foot of the manuscript, holding it flat with several strategically placed padded weights. He stepped aside and then, suddenly, there it was. Right in front of us. The Holy Grail. The legendary manuscript. The scroll. One solid single-spaced block of black type on paper that had taken on the translucent golden glow of ancient amber.

Jay was transfixed. "Oh, wow, that is *so* beautiful," he whispered.

And just then, just as Jay had predicted, something changed, something sparked—something I hadn't felt for a very long time. I should have realized what was happening but I didn't. And if I did, I refused to pay it any mind. At that moment, all that mattered was that moment, when all that was to happen between Jay and me was about to unfurl like the secrets of the scroll before us. It was the beginning of all good things. Or so I thought.

I moved in closer to inspect the type, which was, contrary to rumor, still incredibly readable after so many years. My jaw dropped when I saw the first line. "Jay, look!"

He read it aloud. "I first met Neal not long after my father died...."

2

I FIRST MET JAY not long after the end of an affair that went awry. I won't bother with the details. Suffice to say I lost my way. I fell for someone who couldn't fall for me. Tragedy was averted, but only barely, and in the days that followed, I slowly came to grips with the realization that I had spent a year looking for love from one who could never give it.

I concluded that a course of action was in order and settled on the only one that occurred to me at the time, reluctantly retreating into a wary solitude and resolving to avoid any inappropriate feelings by feeling nothing at all. Time passed, as it inevitably does. I healed, but only in the way a broken bone heals without proper treatment, eventually needing to be broken again to finally set it straight.

Meanwhile, in the absence of intimacy, I lived. My heart beat, I breathed. I exhibited the classic signs of life without actually having one. And I might have lived the rest of my life like that. I might have. But instead I met Jay.

It began as a day no different than all the nondescript days that preceded it. It was a Monday. I was on my way to my job as an editor at *Element* magazine, and, unlike so many of my fellow passengers on the crowded New York City subway, I was anxiously anticipating the week ahead. I'd made it through another weekend, and, for the next five days, I could put my personal life, or lack thereof, aside, and lose myself in a more clearly defined code of conduct that all but eliminated emotion from the equation. Truth to tell, I did my job and I did it well. In fact, I excelled. I was well liked. Respected. Respectful. But remote. Come quitting time, as my colleagues headed for a local bar to recap a litany of work-related lunacies over martinis, I invariably headed home.

That morning, as I stepped off the elevator on the fourth floor of the building that housed the magazine's offices, I noticed someone exit the elevator directly across from mine. We both turned and headed for the glass doors to the reception area. He got there first but held the door open for me to go in ahead of him. I looked at him and thanked him. He looked at me and smiled.

I remember thinking he was good-looking, struck by his thick, slicked-back black hair, dark goatee and bright brown eyes. But I also remember something else, a sudden feeling of familiarity, an overwhelming rush of reassurance, there and gone again in a heartbeat before I could figure out what it was.

I stood there awkwardly for a second, wondering whether our paths had crossed before. If they had, I couldn't remember where or when, but as I turned to continue on my way, he smiled again. I smiled back and nodded as he turned toward the receptionist. A few minutes later, he walked by my office with Ted Parrish, the magazine's art director. I concluded that he must be one of Ted's many friends, who frequently stopped by the office, and that I must have seen him on one of his prior visits.

The next day, Ted mentioned to me that he had finally filled the long-vacant designer position in the art department. He'd hired a guy who had just graduated from Pratt, the art school in Brooklyn that Ted had also attended, years earlier. The guy had been recommended by a professor they'd both had. "He's really good," the professor had told Ted. "And he's *really cute!*" Ted delivered this last bit of information with his usual perturbing aplomb. A six-foot-four crew-cut bottle-blond from Brisbane, Ted exhibited an unsettling, insightful sense of humor, effortlessly veering from manners to mannered in a single moment.

"Is he the guy I saw you with yesterday?" I inquired.

"Yeah, the guy with the goatee," confirmed Ted, noting that I'd noticed.

Jay Bishop started work two weeks later. Ted introduced him to the staff at the daily ten o'clock editorial meeting held in the art department and, afterward, I went over to say hello.

"We ran into each other the day you came for your interview," I reminded him, experiencing the same inexplicable affinity I'd felt that first time.

"Yeah," he said. "I remember."

That was pretty much the extent of our conversation his first week. Ted kept Jay busy and my regular responsibilities kept me busy. We didn't talk again till Friday, when Ted announced a spur-of-the-moment barbecue he and his other half, Tim, were throwing that evening at their Brooklyn brownstone apartment. Like everyone else I worked with, Ted had come to realize that parties were not on my list of things to do, but he nonetheless handed me an invitation, which I dutifully thanked him for and then absentmindedly shoved in my back pocket.

At the end of the day, I packed up as usual, but as I left my office, I ran right into Jay, who was also on his way out.

"Hey, long time no see," he joked. "Was it something I said?"

I felt an easy and unexpected smile crawl across my face. "No, I just had a lot to do this week," I replied, feeling for some strange reason that I owed him an explanation. "More than usual," I added, still trying to make it right.

He grinned. "No problem. We can make up for lost time tonight."

"Tonight?"

"At Ted's party."

"Oh, right," I said tentatively.

"You're going, aren't you?" he asked.

"Yeah," I heard myself say.

"Good, then it's a date. See you in a bit," he said, heading down Sixth Avenue.

I couldn't believe I'd told him I was going to Ted's; I already had other plans for that evening. When I arrived at my Upper West Side apartment, I fed my cat, Flannery, traded my office attire for jeans and a T-shirt, then returned to the subway, catching a south-bound No. 1 local at Seventy-Second and Broadway. I got off in Chelsea at Eighteenth, proceeded two blocks north on Seventh and hung a left, traversing four long and unfamiliar blocks before I finally reached my destination.

I had never been to 454 West Twentieth but it was exactly as I had pictured it, a four-story red-brick row house, indistinguish-able from every red-brick row house in Manhattan, except for the front yard—I was surprised to see that it had a front yard, a small patchwork of slightly uneven concrete slabs, surrounded by a knee-high, gated wrought-iron fence. I lifted the latch and let myself in, walking the ten or twelve paces to the stoop and then peering at the vestibule through the glass upper-halves of the double doors. The doors were ornate affairs, turn-of-the-century originals, no doubt, with details that had been dulled beneath too many coats of thick black enamel. The doorknob was another mat-ter, a beautiful, intricately etched brass orb polished to perfection by the palms of everyone who had ever passed through this place or called it home.

I turned to survey the yard, mindful for the first time of a twenty-foot tree growing in the far corner, so big and so out of place I hadn't noticed it earlier. Then, beneath the failing twilight, I took a seat on the stoop and closed my eyes, listening for what I had come to hear.

It was a few minutes before I did, emanating from an open window somewhere above me, the unmistakable sound of some-one typing on a manual typewriter, a mad, incessant staccato of sharp mechanical snaps, of frenzied fingers mashing a metal key-board with confident strokes. It was a cool April evening in 1951, and, inside, Jack Kerouac was manically pounding out his poetic masterpiece *On the Road* on a portable Royal, ecstatic, emphatic, joyfully baring his soul in a whir and blur of words that would define a generation as Beat and change the world in ways he could never imagine.

I had come in search of solace and communion. In my desolate resolve to live without living, Time had become my adversary. So much Time to fill, to pass. Every day a struggle to let a few numb seconds slip by, unnoticed. I had learned to beat Time at the gym, where weights and wires conspired to confound the clock, and in books, where words evoked worlds more benign and beautiful than the one I occupied. At the moment, I was lost in Kerouac's world, seeking stimulation in his spontaneous prose, a simulation of life as I would have liked to live it. In this place where he had breathed and dreamed, I hoped to hear the lone lively voice in the lonely void of my life whisper secret wisdoms that would deliver me from the desperation that filled my days.

And I did hear a voice as I sat there listening, faint at first and then more insistent, beneath the sound of the typewriter and then beyond it, inserting itself in my psyche and dragging me back to the present, a warm July night in 1995. I opened my eyes to see a tall thin brunette standing in front of me, attempting, I assumed, to enter the house, but I was blocking her way.

"Hello," she said. "Sorry to bother you."

"Not at all," I assured her, sliding to one side.

"Waiting for someone?" she asked.

"Uh, not really. Just..."

"Visiting?" She smiled knowingly.

"Yeah."

"He wrote it up there," she said, pointing to the window above the door. "In the second-floor front apartment."

"I guess you get a lot of people stopping by."

"Occasionally. You can always tell. They have a certain look about them."

"What look is that?"

"I don't know. Starry-eyed?"

"Sounds about right."

"Anyway," she said, "I hope you found what you were looking for. This place seems to evoke strong feelings in some people. The way certain strangers do. Kinda makes you wonder, you know?"

I nodded. I knew.

She disappeared inside, leaving me once again alone with my thoughts. Had I found what I was looking for? I wasn't sure. I stood and took another look, one last look, as I turned to go, heading east, back to the subway. Remembering that I had used my last token for the trip downtown, I reached for my wallet and pulled out a dollar, pulling out a folded piece of cardboard in the process. It took a second for me to realize what it was—the invitation to Ted's party that must have slipped into my wallet when I'd stuffed it in my pocket earlier. I purchased a token and pushed through the turnstile, pausing to stare at the invitation between the stairs to the uptown train, which would take me home, and the stairs to the downtown train, which would take me to Ted's. As I stood there, hesitating, I recalled what I had said to Jay and what the woman at 454 West Twentieth had said to me. Maybe I *had* found what I was looking for. I headed for the downtown train.

"WOW, EVEN HARRY CAME," said Ted when I arrived. "What's the occasion?"

I shrugged, not entirely sure what the occasion was myself.

"Food's in the kitchen," Ted told me. "And the kitchen is that way."

I headed that way, making small talk with a few fellow staffers. As I studied a table covered with homemade desserts, however, I felt a hand on my shoulder.

"Can I buy you a beer?"

It was Jay, grinning affably and holding a Heineken.

"Thanks, but..."

"No thanks? What's the matter? Not up for drinking?"

I debated what to say and decided that less was more. "Maybe later."

"That's okay. I've got other ways of making you talk. Come on. Let's get lost."

Waving for me to follow, he squeezed through the crowded kitchen and then through a door on the back wall that led outside to a nearly empty roof deck lit by a dozen or so votive candles placed along the perimeter.

"So, you like Chet Baker?" I asked.

"Who's he? One of the copy editors?"

"No. A jazz trumpet player from the fifties. He has a song called 'Let's Get Lost.'"

"Never heard of him," said Jay. "So, Harry, what are you into?"

"What am I into?"

"Yeah, besides not drinking and obscure musicians."

"Chet Baker isn't..."

"What's your *road*, man?"

I did a double take.

"Yeah," continued Jay. "'Holyboy road, madman road, rainbow road, guppy road, any road...' I finished the sentence for him. "'...It's an anywhere road for anybody anyhow.'"

It was his turn to be taken aback. "You're into Jack Kerouac?! Whoa! You've been holding out on me."

For the next hour, we were lost in an unlikely and lively exchange, attracting curious and questioning glances from our fellow partygoers each time one of us erupted with a wild affirmative "Yes! Yes! Yes!" at every indication and subsequent confirmation that we shared a similar sensibility and awe for a rebel romantic who had found truth in everyday experience and turned his life into his art. It was the first time in a year that I'd had such a conversation, the first time in a year that anyone had drawn me out, and it was as unsettling as it was exhilarating.

"You know what this means, of course," said Jay. "It means that you and I are going to be... *Zahra!*"

A soft and silent figure suddenly materialized from the shadows. She was petite and pretty, with dark hair and dark eyes and a shy, exotic smile. Jay gave her a hug and a quick kiss.

"Harry Charity, Zahra Kaviani."

"*Hel*-lo," said Zahra, in a silvery, lyrical whisper. "Sorry I'm late. Did I miss anything?"

"Harry and I were just getting to know each other better," said Jay, lighting a cigarette for Zahra and then one for himself.

Zahra took a deep drag on the Camel Light and slowly exhaled. "So, Harry," she said, "what are you into?"

I looked at Jay and laughed. "Funny you should ask…"

"Actually," said Jay, "Zahra's the one who got me interested in Kerouac."

"I like all the Beats," she said. "Allen Ginsberg, in particular."

He looked at her approvingly and then jumped right back into the conversation we were having before she arrived. While Jay and I talked, Zahra silently observed, staring from Jay to me and from me to Jay with a curious look in her eyes, as if she saw something the two of us had yet to see.

"You should come out with us to the Limelight sometime," she said excitedly when Jay and I paused to catch our breath. "Or the Roxy. We go there all the time to dance."

"Really?" I asked. The clubs she suggested were places where guys were more likely to dance with other guys than girls.

Jay looked at her affectionately. "Yeah, you should."

"Jay learned to dance in the Marines," said Zahra.

I laughed, assuming she was joking.

"No, really!"

I looked at Jay, noting the single silver hoop in his left ear. "You were in the Marines?"

He jabbed an index finger in my face and stifled a smile. "Don't ask!"

"Don't tell!" added Zahra.

They looked at each other and laughed, but I couldn't figure out whether it was the punch line to a well-rehearsed routine or merely a spur-of-the-moment comeback.

3

SHORTLY AFTER I ARRIVED at *Element*, following a one-year stint at a Philadelphia monthly called *Rittenhouse Square*, I discovered that it was standard practice for publicists to deluge national magazine editors with advance copies of whatever products they were pushing in the hope of landing an article or even a few lines in a magazine's pages. *Element* was at the top of every publicist's list.

A legendary large-format arts and entertainment weekly, *Element* had debuted on newsstands during the golden age of glossies, rivaling *Life, Look* and *Holliday* in sales and subscriptions. But *Element* had unfortunately followed the same trajectory as its contemporaries, slowly ceding readers to a score of trendy newcomers until it finally faded from public consciousness and ceased publication.

Recently purchased by a European media magnate with a portfolio of hot style, celebrity and fashion titles, *Element* had been reinvented for a new age as a flashy water-cooler read filled with provocative pictures and tantalizing articles that simultaneously celebrated and decimated pop culture. The overall effect was akin to a decadent dessert—tempting to behold and delicious going down but ultimately devoid of any redeeming qualities. Nonetheless, *Element* had quickly become the essential manual for separating the utterly indispensable from the completely disposable.

As a result of the magazine's popularity, my office, like the offices of my fellow editors, was overflowing with review copies of books, CDs and video releases, most of which, due to sheer volume and lack of any obvious appeal, went unread, unheard and unwatched. It seemed like such a wasted effort, so I decided to start asking publicists for items that actually interested me and thus stood at least a chance of getting mentioned in the magazine.

First thing Monday morning, I called the publicity department of Viking Press to request two new Kerouac-related volumes, an anthology called *The Portable Jack Kerouac* and *Jack Kerouac: Selected Letters, 1940-1956*. I had already received a set a few weeks earlier and I was hoping the publicist wouldn't remember she'd sent them to me. She didn't, or didn't care. "No problem," she said. "I'll have a courier bring them right over."

Two hours later, just after the books arrived, Jay happened by my office. I had thought about him all weekend. Such an unlikely coincidence, our Kerouac connection. I had always maintained that there was no such thing as coincidence. What might have seemed like a random occurrence at the time it happened, always seemed, in retrospect, like a link in a chain of inevitable events. Like karma, fate, destiny. I had attempted to take control of my own destiny. I walked a narrow, well-worn path. And I walked it alone. My strategy had been successful until I took one small step off the path by going to Ted's party. Why had I taken that step? Because of Jay, obviously. Because, even in our brief encounters at the office, I had felt some sort of instantaneous but unidentified intrigue, as invisible as gravity yet just as irrefutable. Did Jay feel it, too? Why else would he have urged me to join him? In truth, I liked Jay. Despite my determination to never again feel anything for anyone, I found that I liked him. And, following Jay's lead, I found myself adding the next link to the chain, choosing to disregard the verity that one link always led to another.

"Hey, Jay. I just got a package for you."

He squinted at the large brown envelope on my desk. "It's got *your* name on it," he said.

"Trust me," I assured him, "it's for you."

Still not entirely convinced, he smiled and attempted to remove the row of staples that held the envelope closed.

"Try the rip cord," I suggested, pointing to a red string protruding from the corner.

He gave it a yank and the envelope split open to reveal its contents. "Oh, wow!" he said, clearly taken aback. He stared at the books for a moment and then looked at me. "Harry, I don't know what to say. I saw these in a bookstore and really wanted to get them but I couldn't afford them."

"Jay, I just thought that if anyone should have them, *you* should."

He seemed a little uncomfortable and it suddenly struck me that I had foolishly not considered all the possible implications of my offer, that it might appear to have more strings attached than the one sticking out of the envelope.

"I didn't *buy* them, Jay. They're review copies. They were free."

"But what about you? Wouldn't you like them?"

"I have my own copies. Also free."

He picked up the volumes, one in each hand. "Okay, then. Thanks." For a moment, he stood awkwardly by my desk and then sat down. "You want to read the anthology together, Har?" he asked, flipping through the pages.

I paused. "Sure."

"We can talk about it over lunch. What are you doing for lunch?"

"I don't have any plans." I always ate at my desk.

"I *hope* you weren't planning on eating at your desk. Come on. Let's grab a bite."

Jay lit a cigarette as soon as we were outside. "Where to?"

"I usually just grab a sandwich," I replied, not really answering the question.

"So do I," he said. "There's a place I go that's good."

We walked to Forty-Sixth Street and hung a right, pausing in front of a deli halfway down the block. I looked up at the sign above the door. There was an image of a four-pointed star on it with the word "Burger" below it.

"Star Burger?"

"What's that?" asked Jay, tossing his cigarette butt on the sidewalk and crushing it under his boot.

"The name of this place."

"I never noticed."

We started eating lunch there a couple times a week, talking about Jack Kerouac over tuna fish sandwiches. Jay would appear in my office doorway around two o'clock. "Would you be lunching?" he'd ask, and we'd head out. Our conversation centered on whatever section of the Kerouac anthology we'd just finished. *The Portable Jack Kerouac* included excerpts from nearly all of Kerouac's books, which, according to Kerouac, were written to comprise "one vast book like Proust's *Remembrance of Things Past* except that my remembrances are written on the run instead of afterwards in a sick bed." Jay and I talked endlessly and obsessively about Kerouac's writing, the honesty, the intensity, the energy, the holy, unhampered exuberance that encapsulated the Beat ethos of preaching and practicing universal kindness because (as Buddha's First Noble Truth tells us) all life is suffering.

Over the next few weeks, as Jay and I continued reading *The Portable Jack Kerouac*, he made an interesting discovery in the introduction to *Lonesome Traveler*.

"Kerouac wrote that his mother had 'a Norman name, L'Evesque,'" he said over lunch. "That was *my* grandmother's maiden name. And she's French-Canadian—just like Kerouac's family. Maybe we're related. I've always felt a strange connection with him."

I, too, felt a strange connection between Jay and Jack. Both were athletic. Both had enlisted. And both had lost their fathers, a painful coincidence I discovered in the course of a conversation about astrology, of all things. Jay had noted that his and Kerouac's birthdays were only two weeks apart.

"Kerouac's is March twelfth," I said. "When's yours?"

"March twenty-fifth," he replied. "I'm an Aries. How about you?"

"A Taurus, April twenty-second. The day Kerouac finished writing *On the Road*."

"Pretty cool," said Jay. "So, a bull and a ram."

"Yes, Venus and Mars," I observed, unconsciously quoting from my passing knowledge of star signs. "Both are very passionate. One is more deliberate while the other is more adventurous. They have a lot to teach each other. They're a good match." I stopped short. "Astrologically," I added. "They're a good match, *astrologically*."

Jay smiled but then turned suddenly serious. "Just so you know, Har, I don't make a big deal out of my birthday. My father died three years ago, three days before I turned twenty-five, so I never feel much like celebrating. He died of a massive heart attack on a Sunday morning. He got out of bed and fell over. My mom's a nurse. She tried to save him with CPR, but there was nothing she could do. He was fifty-eight. Not a day goes by that I don't think of him."

Besides all the circumstantial similarities, I thought that Jay actually *looked* a little like Kerouac, the Kerouac who stared from the black-and-white photographs on the covers of his various books. Same dark hair. Same strong handsome face. Same sad soulful eyes. But there was something that went beyond the physical resemblance. Something that sprang from somewhere inside, something sensed but not seen. A *tenderness*.

4

EVEN AMID THE CLUTTER of press kits, newspapers and magazines on my desk, the envelope was impossible to miss. A large, square, lime-green affair embossed with a magenta MTV logo. Inside were two complimentary tickets to the MTV Video Music Awards at Radio City. Ted popped his head in my door even as I realized what I was holding.

"Yippee! I got a pair, too!" he said, waving his tickets at me. "Who are *you* going to take?

"Maybe Jay?" I said, as much to myself as to Ted.

"Sure, ask him!" said Ted. "And who knows? Get a few drinks in him and maybe you'll get lucky!"

Typical Ted, I thought as he disappeared. But I immediately began to wonder whether I really should ask Jay. Ted's party aside, neither of us had ever proposed doing anything beyond the boundaries of work or our daily lunch hour and I wasn't entirely sure how he would react. I also worried whether our co-workers would be quick to assign a disingenuous motive to my invitation, as Ted had done. After much thought, I decided that it would be better for Jay and me both if I didn't invite him, if I just gave my tickets away.

Come the day of the show, however, the tickets were still in my possession. I wanted to go. I wanted to go with Jay. And I was mad at myself for caring what Ted and others might have to say about it. As the day wore on, and I overheard half the office excitedly anticipating the show, I finally just said the hell with it and offered Jay the ticket.

Our seats were in the first mezzanine.

"Not bad," said Jay, checking our view of the stage.

"Yeah, not bad," I agreed, relieved to discover that we were sitting nowhere near any of our co-workers.

As we flipped through the funky pink-fur-covered program books we found on our seats, however, I became anxious that I wouldn't be able to rely on Jack Kerouac to fill the long silence of the night that stretched before us. Anxious that I had made a mistake in giving Jay the slightest indication that I wanted to take things further. Anxious that by doing so I had opened myself up to the unbearable pain of inevitable separation I'd willingly traded for the lesser pain of planned loneliness many years earlier.

Michael Jackson and Lisa Marie Presley interrupted my doubts. Confirming rumors of an unscheduled appearance only weeks after confirming rumors of their unlikely marriage, the self-proclaimed King of Pop and the only daughter of the undisputed King of Rock strolled on to the stage as the houselights dimmed, standing hand in hand in the spotlight and acknowledging the thunderous ovation with self-conscious yet strangely self-satisfied smiles. After a full minute, the two fell into an awkward embrace, Jackson planting an even more awkward kiss on Presley's lips and then addressing the audience. "Just think," he quipped in an eerie whisper, "nobody thought this would last."

Jay caught my eye and smiled. I relaxed, suddenly sure that everything was going to be all right.

At work the next day, right after the ten o'clock editorial meeting had broken up but before everyone had scattered from the art department, Ted asked Jay and me what we thought of the show.

"It was great," Jay enthused. "Wasn't it, Har?"

"Yeah, it was," I agreed. "Especially…"

"Wait a second," a voice behind us interrupted. "You two went to the VMAs?" The voice belonged to Mercedes Hamilton, a bright, young and ambitious assistant editor whose talents were often obscured by her notorious lack of tact.

"Yeah," Jay answered.

"*Together*?" she asked incredulously.

"Yeah, together," said Jay matter-of-factly.

"Harry never does anything with anyone," said Mercedes. She stared at me suspiciously. I could feel my face burning.

"We had a great time, didn't we, Harry?" said Jay, catching but not acknowledging her unsubtle insinuation.

"Yeah, we did," I said weakly.

Mercedes opened her mouth to speak, but Ted cut her off.

"Time for a cigarette," he announced loudly. "Would you care to join me outside, Jay?"

"Sounds good," said Jay, grabbing his Camel Lights. "Feel like taking a walk, Har?"

"What's up?" I asked.

He seemed unsure. "Oh, I was just wondering if you'd finished with the Dogs."

"The Dogs" was shorthand for the magazine's popular "Bomb-Sniffing Dogs" column, a dissection of the week's top trends that was equal parts validation and evisceration. I was the column's anonymous author.

"I wrote it yesterday," I said. "And it's already been fact-checked. I *told* you that at the meeting this morning."

"Oh, right," he said with a strange smile.

"Is that all?" I asked, annoyed that he'd forgotten we'd gone over this only a few minutes earlier.

He didn't answer me. "So, Ted told me that you asked Jay to the VMAs."

"You and Jay seem to, *uh*, get along very well," he continued.

Jay followed Ted out of the art department and I followed Jay, casting one last look at Mercedes, who eyed me skeptically. En route to the elevator, my name rang out as we passed the office of the managing editor, Donal Kelly. I told Jay and Ted to go ahead without me and stepped into Donal's office.

"First Mercedes, now Donal. "Yeah?" I said stonily.

"What's *that* supposed to mean?"

"Oh, nothing. It's just something Ted and I picked up on."

I shook my head and left his office without another word.

Back in my own office, I wondered whether it wouldn't be better for me *and* for Jay if we didn't become closer. Better for me because maybe I really wasn't ready to expose myself to the uncertainty of emotional entanglements. Better for Jay because he shouldn't have to deal with the gossip.

I was still mulling this over when Jay swung by for lunch, suggesting we eat, not at our usual place, but a cheap chicken teriyaki joint he'd discovered just off Times Square. As we headed out, however, Mercedes suddenly appeared, blocking our path.

"So, Jay, what's up with you and Zahra?" she asked, attempting but failing to sound casual.

Jay stared at her with a slight frown. "Nothing's up with me and Zahra."

"Really?" she persisted. "I heard that you two aren't living together anymore, that you moved out. Are you still...?"

"We are," said Jay.

Mercedes was about to start in again when Jay interrupted.

"We *are*," he said flatly. "Come on, Har."

I was somewhat surprised. On more than one occasion I had asked Jay how Zahra was doing and he had always answered that she was doing fine. I had no idea that anything had changed.

"I can't believe Mercedes," he said as we walked along Forty-Eighth.

"She's okay," I said. "But she does take some getting used to."

"It's just that she's already tried to ask me that same question several times," Jay explained, "and I don't really like to talk about my personal life. I like to keep it personal." He paused as we paid for our teriyaki—it *was* cheap—and found a table on the second floor. The moment we sat down, he began again. "The reason I moved out..."

"Jay," I interrupted, "you don't have to tell me."

"I want to tell *you*," he insisted. "The reason I moved out is because Zahra and I are just in two different places. She's still in school and I'm not, and our lives aren't meshing the way they did when we were both in school. Zahra is occupied with schoolwork day and night and even on weekends, while my work is done when I leave the office. We still love each other very much, and we're still together, but we needed to make a change. It's a shame, but love alone isn't always enough. I've moved back home with my mom on Long Island—I can't afford a place of my own because I have a lot of student loans to pay off—but I stay at Zahra's a few nights a week."

"I understand what you're going through," I said, startled by his unexpected frankness. "I loved someone very much once but it wasn't enough."

"Yeah?" asked Jay expectantly.

"Yeah," I replied, but didn't elaborate.

5

IN 1951, WHEN JACK KEROUAC sat down to write what would become his most famous book, he began by taping together several rolls of Teletype paper to create a one-hundred-twenty-foot scroll. Anxious to experiment with a new stream-of-conscious style of writing, he wanted to eliminate the breaks in concentration caused by having to constantly insert new sheets of paper into his type-writer. Working day and night, he finished the manuscript a mere three weeks later and couldn't wait to present the results to Rob-ert Giroux, his editor at Harcourt, Brace. Giroux had championed Kerouac's first book, *The Town and the City*, a lyrical, traditionally crafted novel heavily influenced by Kerouac's literary idol, Thom-as Wolfe, and described in a modest review by *The New York Times* as "a rough diamond."

When Kerouac called Giroux to say he was ready to deliver the manuscript of his second book, Giroux was expecting to see a follow-up to *The Town and the City*. Instead, Kerouac burst into his office and elatedly unrolled the scroll manuscript of *On the Road*, as unconventional in form as its author's new approach to prose. For a moment, Giroux was speechless, too astounded to say a word. When he finally did speak, all he could say was that the scroll would be impossible to edit. It wasn't what Kerouac wanted to hear. After enduring extensive editing of his first book, Kerouac swore that no one was going to lay a finger on his second book. He rewound the scroll and stormed out.

On the Road would not be published for another six years, under the aegis of another editor, Malcolm Cowley, at another imprint, Viking. In *The New York Times*, Gilbert Millstein would hail it as "an authentic work of art." For most of the six years prior to that review, Kerouac held the scroll close, carrying it with him in his rucksack wherever he went. After *On the Road* finally saw the light of day in 1957, however, the whereabouts of the scroll were unrecorded, raising doubts about its fate.

"Where do you think it could be?" mused Jay over lunch.

"It's probably buried beneath several inches of dust in some publisher's vault," I ventured. "Right here in Manhattan."

"Imagine if we got a chance to see it," said Jay. "Imagine being *that* close to someone's genius."

"I'll make a few calls," I said. "See if I can find out where it is. I love a challenge."

I started with Viking Press and asked the publicist who'd sent me the new Kerouac books if she knew the location of the *On the Road* scroll. She said she didn't, but added that Ann Charters might. Charters had edited the Kerouac books and, years earlier, written Kerouac's biography. "Give her a call," she suggested. "Ann likes to talk to Kerouac fans." She gave me Charters' number at the University of Connecticut, but when I tried it and got the drop-click of an answering machine, I hung up. I figured I'd have a better chance of getting a response to my question if I were able to speak to her directly rather than leave a message.

In the meantime, I decided to take another tack. It was Friday afternoon and my work for the week was finished. I headed to the magazine's research department and logged on to the Nexis terminal to access the database of articles from newspapers, magazines and journals. In the *search* field, I typed the words "Jack Kerouac and On the Road and manuscript." In a few seconds, the results appeared on the screen: One hundred seventeen articles.

One by one, I pulled them up. The first, a recent story from *The Ottawa Citizen* about the "lucrative world of rare texts," included a list of valuable first editions. A first of *On the Road*, it said, was worth two thousand dollars. The second article, from *The Calgary Herald*, was headlined "Back On the Road with Jack Kerouac" and detailed "the blossoming new interest in The King of the Beats." The third, published in London's *Sunday Telegraph* and titled "Bad Dharma," concerned the fight over his estate between John Sampas, nephew of Kerouac's third wife, Stella Sampas, and Kerouac's only daughter, Jan Kerouac. "At the time of his death," the article pointed out, "the value of Kerouac's estate was estimated at a modest ninety-one dollars, and nobody batted an eyelid when he left it all to his mother. It is now said to be worth around ten million, and the knives are out." The piece went on to suggest that the Kerouac archive was no longer intact, that "original manuscripts, books and letters have been offered privately to collectors, along with Kerouac's shoes, pork-pie hat and his raincoat, which was bought earlier this year by the actor Johnny Depp for ten thousand dollars."

Just as I was about to stop reading, I hit pay dirt. "There have even been rumors of the original Teletype-roll manuscript of *On the Road* being offered for around one million," the article continued. "That is in the vaults of the New York Public Library, not available for public inspection."

"I found it," I told Jay a few minutes later.

"Found what?" he asked.

"It," I repeated. "*It!*"

"The scroll manuscript?!"

"It's in the New York Public Library. Three blocks from here! It's supposedly not available for public inspection, but I'll get us in."

"Do you really think so?" he asked.

"You bet," I assured him. "Who do you think we are? The public?"

FIRST THING MONDAY morning, Jay stopped by my office brandishing a manila envelope. Without a word, he bent back the metal clasp, pulled out two four-by-six-inch pieces of white paper and handed them to me.

"I wrote these over the weekend," he said. "Let me know what you think."

He was gone before I realized what he had given me, two poems that had been typed on a typewriter—a very old typewriter, judging from the uneven lines and letters clogged with ink.

The first poem, "Brother," appeared to be an offer of consolation and a promise of support to a kindred spirit who had endured an agonizing loss but sealed himself off from any assistance. "From the blood comes the water to quench the thirst…" It certainly hit home with me.

The second poem, "Farewell Old Friend," was equally touching. "Soon, you will be a mere memory, / but I will always remember the times we've shared. / I've scraped pennies together / for you / when I had nothing. / I've stood in endless lines for you, / and never left without you. / I've wept with you clenched in my hands / You've never let me down / when I've stumbled to get home… drunk and broken / You've walked with me and have never judged my actions." A stirring elegy to a lost loved one, or so I thought, right up until the loved one in question was identified in the last line, "I'll miss you… my token friend." I smiled at the realization I was reading an ode to the old subway tokens that were being phased out and replaced by plastic Metrocards.

After I read the poems, I read them again, and then again, not sure whether I was more moved by the poems or that Jay had chosen to show them to me.

"So, what do you think?" he asked eagerly as we sat down to lunch later at our usual place.

"I think they're really good."

"You *do?*"

"The first one's about my younger brother Anthony and his reaction to our father's death," Jay explained. "He just refused to deal with it. In some ways, he never did."

I nodded. "And the other poem…"

"Yeah, well, I meant to save a token before they all disappeared and I had one set aside but I had to use it the other day to get home."

"I have a few left," I said. "I'll give you one."

"Would you? Thanks. So, when do I get to read something of yours? I assume you write more than 'Bomb-Sniffing Dogs.'"

"I don't know, Jay. I used to write a lot, but what I wrote didn't seem to matter."

"Then write something that *does* matter."

"I *do* have one idea," I said. "I'll show it to you if I do anything with it. I'm just not sure where it will go."

"You don't *have* to know that," said Jay. "The other day, I wrote this in my journal: 'Begin and end all stories with *dot dot dot*.' An ellipsis. To indicate things have come before and things will go on afterward. Nothing has an exact beginning or an end. Life isn't like that. Life goes on, you know?"

"Yeah," I agreed, thinking of my own.

"One day, Har, it's all just going to explode. You're going to sit down and start writing and it's all going to come out of you. Like diarrhea. Well," he added with a laugh, "maybe not *quite* like that..."

LATER THAT AFTERNOON, Zahra stopped by the office and invited me to join her and Jay for a going-away dinner after work—in a few days, she was taking advantage of a break in her studies to spend two weeks on the West Coast with her father. I declined for fear of feeling like the proverbial third wheel, but Zahra insisted.

"We're going to Zuni," she explained as the three of us headed south on Ninth Avenue. "Great margaritas."

"Harry doesn't drink," said Jay.

"Oh, I'm sorry," she said. "I didn't know."

"It's okay," I assured her. "I don't have a drinking problem. Not any more, at least."

She looked at me, trying to determine if I was serious.

"That was a joke," I said. "I *did* have a drinking problem, but we broke up."

At that, Zahra laughed.

"That *wasn't* a joke," I said.

She looked horrified.

"Just kidding."

She smiled and shook her head. "I give up. I don't know *where* you're coming from."

"I'm not always sure myself," I said with a shrug.

The three of us paused simultaneously to peruse a street vendor's table of used books. Buried in a pile near one end, Zahra found a title that intrigued her, *Patterns of Prophecy: How to Discover the Blueprint of Your Life.*

"How much?" she inquired, holding up the small leatherbound volume.

"Five dollars," the seller replied.

She considered it for a moment.

"Three dollars?" he asked almost immediately.

"Okay," said Zahra. She fished in her handbag for the money and we continued on our way.

At Zuni, a small, nearly inconspicuous eatery tucked between a diner and a bodega just north of Forty-Second Street on Ninth Avenue, we consumed an assortment of tasty burritos, fajitas and flautas. Zahra and Jay sipped margaritas. I considered ordering one but refrained. Some other time, perhaps. I was nearly ready to have a drink, but not quite. As the waitress cleared the table, Jay asked to see the book Zahra had bought earlier. His eyes widened as he flipped to the title page.

"This is a first edition!" he said. "And it's inscribed by the author! 'May your blueprint of life be fulfilled.' Way to go, Zahra."

I considered what the author had written. "Do you think lives have blueprints?"

"Do this," ordered Zahra in response, extending both of her hands, palms up. "Your left one first."

I did as instructed and she immediately began examining it.

"You're so old!" she exclaimed after only a split second.

I turned to Jay, incredulous.

"Your *soul*," he explained. "She means your *soul*." Zahra continued her inspection, turning my hands over and over, tracing the lines on my palms with her fingers and bending my own fingers this way and that.

"You're very perceptive," she said, "but you don't always follow your intuition."

That was dead-on. The situation that propelled me into isolation a year earlier had been plastered with warning signs and I had chosen to ignore them all.

She asked me to make two fists, studying the creases formed at the base of my little fingers and frowning after a few seconds.

"What?" I asked.

She shook her head. "Nothing."

"*What?*"

"You had a serious relationship," she replied, although I could tell that wasn't the answer to my question. "And you made more out of it than you should have. You will have another," she added. "One that will last. That person will be your soul mate."

"Pretty good, huh, Har?" asked Jay, standing to go to the men's room.

"*Now* do you know where I'm coming from?" I joked to Zahra when he'd gone.

"Jay really likes you," she responded eagerly, as if she had been waiting all night to tell me. "He talks about you all the time." I flushed in embarrassment, involuntarily revealing that the feeling was mutual. She smiled, as if I had just confirmed what she already suspected. Jay returned a few seconds later.

"I told Harry how much you like him," said Zahra immediately. "And how much you talk about him."

Again, she seemed to derive a certain amount of delight from the disclosure, certain that she was exposing a secret that shouldn't be a secret, certain that she was only fanning the flames of a fire that had already begun to burn.

It was Jay's turn to be embarrassed. "Yeah, well."

"You know," I said to both of them, "I haven't had a night like this in so long. Just having dinner with two friends."

They looked at each other and smiled.

"A new chapter," said Jay.

"We'll get together again," said Zahra. "Soon. Right after I get back from my trip out West. In the meantime, you two have fun."

"Sounds like a plan," I said.

"It *is*," Jay assured me. "She's seen the blueprint."

I wondered what she'd seen.

6

"LET'S GO TO BED."

My heart started pounding. Somehow, I really hadn't anticipated his staying the night, although now that the moment had arrived, I couldn't believe I hadn't considered it. He finished his beer, stood up and emptied the contents of his pockets on the table. Lots of change, a set of keys, a worn leather wallet.

"Lead the way," he said with a grin.

In the bedroom, he switched on a lamp and sat at the bottom edge of the mattress on the floor that served as my bed. He stripped off his T-shirt and slid out of his jeans. I sat next to him and did likewise. We sat there side by side in our boxers, saying nothing for several seconds, both of us staring at the floor. He was so close I could feel the warmth of his body. Finally, he crawled to the top of the bed and rested his head on a pillow.

The instant he did, I awoke, sitting bolt upright in a startled sweat and tossing off the dampened sheets. I was alone, except for Flannery, who stared at me but stayed put on the next pillow, intrigued but unruffled, a witness to my disquieting recurring dreams many times. I sat still for a few seconds and then hit the shower, standing under the falling water for a full fifteen minutes to clear my head. Moments later, as I scanned my closet for a clean shirt, my eyes drifted upward and came to rest on a beat-up box I had placed on a shelf a year earlier. A Budweiser logo was visible beneath multiple layers of packing tape, but no amount of tape

LARRY CLOSS

could contain the contents or keep it from invading my sleep. I grabbed a shirt and closed the door, shaking off a distant memory that wasn't distant enough as I headed to work.

At lunch, Jay started right in about something that had caught his attention in the latest section he'd read from *The Portable Jack Kerouac*, an essay about the origins of the Beat Generation.

"He writes about the wild picture of him that was used on the book jacket of *On the Road*. A friend told him not to comb his hair and he showed up at the photo shoot looking like he had just rolled out of bed. His description of that picture is so vivid I can almost see it. Which is good, because I'll probably never see a first edition of *On the Road*."

"You never know," I said. "But there *is* a book of photographs of the Beats I remember reading about in the *Times* review of *The Portable Jack Kerouac*. Maybe that photo's in there. I'll try to track it down."

Back at the office, I called my favorite bookshop in New York, the nearby Gotham Book Mart. If any place had the volume of photographs, Gotham would. "We're pretty well stocked with Beat books," said the woman who answered. "But I'm not sure about that one. I'll have to ask Lester." I listened as she described the book to a co-worker. A deep muffled voice responded. "Lester said that the book you're looking for is called *Scenes Along the Road* but it's out of print. He said if he knew where to get one, he'd go buy it himself."

Determined to locate a copy, I went through the Yellow Pages, calling every used-book store in Manhattan at random, including The Strand ("eight miles of books") and Skyline, which specialized in the Beats. No luck. The woman at Argosy, one of New York's largest used-book stores, said they didn't have a copy either and weren't likely to get one. She suggested that I might want to commission a book search. Argosy didn't do searches, she told me, but Yunga Vishneyda, The First Edition Finder, did. She gave me his number and I gave him a call.

"The First Edition Finder, Floyd speaking." said a male voice.

I told him about my unsuccessful efforts to find a copy of *Scenes Along the Road* and he said he would be happy to run an online search for it, contacting a network of seven-hundred-some book dealers from across the country. The results of the search, he told me, would take a day or two.

"Are you interested in the Beats in general?" he asked.

"Yeah, but mostly Jack Kerouac," I replied.

"Oh, we have a first edition of *On the Road*."

"Really?"

"Yeah, and it's in very good condition. The dust jacket is only slightly worn."

"What do you want for it?"

"Six hundred fifty dollars."

The price seemed impossibly low in light of the article I'd read on Nexis, which placed a value of two grand on the book.

"It's tempting," I sighed. "But I really can't justify it."

"We could get you first editions of most of Kerouac's other books for a lot less," he offered.

"I'll have to think about it."

"Well, it's here if you want it. I'll call you if I locate a copy of *Scenes Along the Road*."

Over lunch the next day, I asked Jay which was his favorite Kerouac book.

"I'd have to say *On the Road*," he replied, after some deliberation. "That was the one I read first, so it will always be special."

When we got back to the office, I called The First Edition Finder. This time, Yunga Vishneyda himself answered. I got straight to the point.

"I was wondering if I could stop by and take a look at that first edition of *On the Road*?"

"Sure," he said. "Whenever you like."

The First Edition Finder's business was housed in a decaying but still magnificent old apartment building near Tompkins Square on the Lower East Side. A guard in the lobby announced my arrival and a few minutes later I found myself on the third floor, standing in front of an unmarked door that was slightly ajar. I knocked once and stepped into a small windowless room. Books were everywhere—piled haphazardly high on tabletops, stacked in shaky three-foot towers on the floor and arranged in solid rows on shelves that covered every square inch of wall space and stretched all the way to the vaulted ceiling.

"Hi," said a voice. It took me a second to locate the source, a muscular man with short black hair and a Fu Manchu who was barely visible behind a mountain of hardcovers. Yunga Vishneyda, I presumed. "I was afraid I'd missed you," he said. "Didn't find that book you were looking for. Let me do another search for it right now."

He took a seat at a computer. "What was that title again?"

Scenes Along the Road.

"Oh, the Kerouac is right there," he said, pointing to a bookshelf.

I went over and began reading the titles of each volume, working my way from right to left. I didn't see the one I was looking for, however, and I stood there staring stupidly. Noticing the look on my face, The First Edition Finder reached over and plucked a book from the shelf above the shelf I'd been searching and handed it to me.

The dust jacket was covered in clear acetate and my first thought was that it must have come from a library. I checked the spine for a Dewey decimal number but there was none. Beneath the acetate, the dust jacket itself was black, a little frayed at the edges, with a very small illustration dead center—a red, blue and gray stylized city skyline. The title appeared beneath it, on an uneven horizontal line, rendered in all caps in a white sans-serif font. At the top left corner of the cover, in the same font but smaller, were the words "a novel by Jack Kerouac."

I turned the book over. On the back was an excerpt, one of the most famous and one that had only recently taken on a new resonance: "...the only people for me are the mad ones, the ones who are mad to live, mad to talk, mad to be saved, desirous of everything at the same time, the ones who never yawn or say a commonplace thing, but burn, burn, burn, burn like fabulous yellow roman candles exploding like spiders across the stars..."

"Sorry, but no one has responded to my search for *Scenes Along the Road*," said The First Edition Finder.

"That's okay," I told him, telling myself that I'd just found something a lot more desirable. Although I had convinced myself that I had only stopped by because I wanted to *see* the first edition of *On the Road*, I now told myself that there was no way I was leaving without it.

"How firm are you on the price of this?" I asked.

"You know," he said nervously, "I bet my assistant told you it was six hundred fifty dollars..."

"Yes, he did."

"That's actually the price for a *dealer*."

Money being money, I failed to see what difference it made who it came from.

"It really should go for about a thousand, you know," he continued. He dug around on his desk and produced a small white catalog from a rare book dealer in San Francisco listing a first edition of *On the Road* for, coincidentally, a thousand dollars. "And the description of *that* book's condition," he needlessly told me after I'd read the description, "is very similar to the one you're holding. So, there's really no way I can let it go for any less."

"Well, then, I guess that's that," I said. I wasn't in the mood to bargain.

The First Edition Finder looked alarmed. "How would you be paying for the book?"

"With a check. Unless you can take a credit card."

"Well, if I gave it to you for the dealer's price, there would also be sales tax."

I sat down again and thought for a moment, mentally transferring money from my savings account to my checking account, conjuring a picture of the large water-cooler bottle in my apartment that was nearly filled with loose change (lots of quarters) and reminding myself that the following Friday was payday and it was the second check of the month so I didn't have to pay rent or bills out of it because they came out of the first check. As I was making these calculations, I flipped to the inside back flap of the dust jacket and spotted the photograph of Kerouac that Jay had talked about so excitedly a few days earlier, the photograph he never thought he'd see.

"Sold," I told The First Edition Finder, who immediately looked relieved. "One thing, though," I added. "I'm not a hundred percent sure this *is* a first edition." As I had continued examining the book, I'd noticed that the words "first edition" did not appear on the page with all the publishing information.

"Not *all* books say that," he said. He picked up a paperback reference book to make his case. "See?" he said, handing it to me. "It says here that for Viking Press, if there's only one date listed, then it's a first edition."

I looked at the page in *On the Road* again. There was only one date listed, 1957, the year it was first published. Still, I wasn't completely convinced.

"Look, I'll write a receipt that says you can have a full refund if it's not a first edition."

"Sounds good," I said, and we were back in business.

"So, you collect Kerouac?" he asked.

"Sorta," I replied. "But this isn't for me."

"Must be for someone very special."

"Yeah," I replied. "It is."

7

F OLLOWING UP ON THE INFORMATION my Nexis search had revealed concerning the whereabouts of the original *On the Road* scroll, I called the New York Public Library and worked my way through several special collections before I finally found the one I was looking for, the Henry W. and Albert A. Berg Collection of English and American Literature, where the scroll was on loan from the Kerouac estate. I told the attendant there that I was researching a story on the revival of interest in Kerouac and the Beats for *Element* and would like to see the scroll, if possible.

"I don't know why you want to see it," he said skeptically. "The Dead Sea Scrolls are in better shape."

"Actually," I said, "that's one of the things I'm interested in finding out."

He explained that I needed to call Elena Harrington, the acting curator of the Berg Collection. Elena was very pleasant but said that the manuscript was "in conservancy"—whatever that meant—and she would have to get permission from the Registrar for us to see it.

"You don't want to photograph it, do you?" she asked.

Of *course* we do, I thought, but of course I said, "No, we don't."

"That's good," she said, "because if you did, you'd have to ask John Sampas, the executor of Kerouac's estate, and it would get very involved."

"No," I told her, "the less involved the better."

She laughed at that, and said she'd call back the next day.

Jay stopped by my office around one to tell me that he was having lunch with Gina Donatella. Gina was the managing editor of *Element Online*, a planned web-based version of the magazine with only one other staff member—Sil Kagen, the editor-in-chief. *Element Online* had been on the drawing board for months but had not developed beyond a wall of logo treatments and page mockups commissioned by Gina and Sil from several freelance designers. The two were hampered by a cautious parent corporation anxious to appear cutting-edge by embracing an exploding new medium but fearful of losing readers and revenue from the print edition. As a result, the financial commitment to the project was an on-again, off-again affair that frequently left *Element Online* more of a virtual enterprise than a real one, a situation exacerbated by a lack of support from the magazine staff that was in turn due to a lack of understanding of what all the fuss was about. Taped to Gina's door was the cover of a recent issue of *Time* hyping "The Strange New World of the Internet," and, to most of *Element*'s editors and writers, the Internet was beyond strange—it was a complete unknown. The office had no Internet connection and had only just been wired with an internal email system. I had gotten to know Gina because I was more curious than my colleagues and because her office was right next to mine. I wasn't sure how Jay had gotten to know her. In fact, until he told me they were having lunch, I wasn't even aware that they'd ever crossed paths.

THE CALL CAME the next day at eleven-thirty in the morning.

"Mr. Charity? This is Elena Harrington at the New York Public Library. You can come see the Kerouac."

"*Really? When?*" I asked, unable to conceal my excitement.

"Whenever you want," she replied.

"Tomorrow at two?" I suggested.

"Fine. Meet me in my office, room 316, and I'll take you down to the Conservancy."

I hung up, feeling like I was going to explode. At that exact moment, Jay appeared in my office door.

"Jay!" I yelled. "The Library called! We're going to see the manuscript! Tomorrow at two!"

Jay's eyes widened and his mouth opened but nothing came out. "You did it!" he said finally. "You really did it!"

By next morning, he was so excited that he could hardly sit at his computer, getting up to walk past my office every hour or so and whispering the words "scroll manuscript" under his breath but just loud enough for me to hear. After his third pass, I sent him an email, rewording the ruminations of Sal Paradise, the narrator of *On the Road*, to suit the occasion, from, "With the coming of Dean Moriarty there began the part of my life you could call my life on the road," to, "With the coming of Jay Bishop there began the part of my life you could call my life on the road to find the scroll manuscript."

Dean Moriarty and Sal Paradise were, of course, the legendary literary alter egos Kerouac created for his best friend Neal Cassady and himself. Cassady was a Midwestern mystic obsessed with girls and cars whom Kerouac idolized and believed to be his "blood-brother," a smooth-talking sex machine who apparently could convince anyone to sleep with him and skillfully juggled simultaneous affairs with several women, not to mention Allen Ginsberg at one point. In a frenetic thirteen-thousand-word letter describing his narrow escape, naked, through a tiny bathroom window when he was caught making love to a young girl named Cherry Mary, Cassady crystallized in one fell swoop the "wild form" of writing that Kerouac had strived for years to achieve, the "wild, undisciplined, pure" modern prose he employed when he sat down to write *On the Road*. Kerouac envisioned his two protagonists as Irish and Italian Americans, plucking the name of his narrator from a handwritten poem by Allen Ginsberg in which he misread the scribbled words "Sad paradise" for "Sal paradise."

At exactly one-forty-five, Jay was standing in my doorway.

"Ready?" he asked.

"Ready," I replied.

An hour later, in the basement of the New York Public Library, Jay and I were poring over the scroll, excitedly pointing to passages we knew by heart. "Look at this!" Jay would say, reading a sentence aloud. "And *this!*" I'd counter, reading another. We went on like that for several minutes, caught up in the thrill of seeing Kerouac's spontaneous mind in action, overwhelmed to think that we were witnessing, although many years removed, the actual moment of creation.

"What's that?" asked Jay suddenly, leaning in and squinting at something neither of us had noticed.

"It looks like… a copy editing mark," I said. "Made in pencil. It indicates where to insert a paragraph break. And that one," I added, pointing to another, "means, 'juxtapose these words.' "

As I continued to scan the scroll, something else jumped out at me. "Look at this sentence about Neal: 'Apparently he was fucking with her.' That's not in the book."

"But then it says 'banging her,' " said Jay, reading a barely visible correction.

"That's not in *On the Road*, either," I said. "And look here. He says he was living with his mother but he changed that to his aunt."

"Huh," said Jay.

"So, he really did edit it," I said, absorbing the truth just as Jay did.

We'd heard, of course, that the scroll had not actually been published verbatim, as many wanted to believe. Jay and I wanted to believe, blurring the line between what we hoped to be true and what we suspected to be true by filtering out the facts that didn't fit and focusing on those that did, choosing not to acknowledge the truth until we had no choice.

"Well, it's still incredible," said Jay.

"It's absolutely *fucking* incredible," I said.

Jay laughed. "Got that right! And look—he used *all* the real names, not just Neal!"

And *we* were off again for another twenty minutes.

Finally, Jay looked up at Elena Harrington and Russell Brooks, the Library officials who had arranged for us to see the scroll. "Do you want to take any notes, Harry?"

"Nah, I'm okay," I replied, not catching his hint that I might want to *pretend* to jot down a few observations for our supposed article about the Beats.

Jay sighed. "Well, then..."

We both stood and turned our attention to Elena and Russell.

"Is it possible to take a picture?" I asked.

"I'm afraid not," replied Elena. "We don't own it."

"I understand," I said. "Just wanted proof that we saw it."

"How long is the scroll going to be in the Library?" asked Jay.

"At this point, it's uncertain," said Elena. "From here it will go on exhibit at the Whitney in November. That's why we're futzing over it so much. Trying to build a proper exhibit mount. After that, it may come back here for safekeeping. Or it may go back to Kerouac's estate."

"What's the Whitney exhibit?" I asked.

"A celebration of Beat culture and influence. The *On the Road* manuscript will be on display. So will a lot of other original manuscripts."

Jay and I looked at each other. "Don't worry," I whispered. "I'll get us in."

Watching Russell place the re-rolled, re-wrapped manuscript back in its box, I was struck by an inspiration. "Is it okay if we take a picture of the *box*?" I asked Elena.

"As long as the box is closed and you can't see the scroll," she replied.

"Okay," said Jay. "So, how much of the scroll is going to be displayed at the exhibit?"

"Nine inches," said Russell. "Less than what you saw. It's too fragile."

"I guess it didn't help matters that it spent years stored in the safe of Kerouac's literary agent, Sterling Lord," said Elena. "A safe was a terrible place to store it."

"So that's where it was," I said.

She pointed to the box that once again contained the scroll, safely shielded from the lens of my camera. "You can take a picture of that if you like."

"Thanks," I said. "*We* know what's in there."

Jay and I took turns posing next to the box on the table. When we were through, I asked Elena if she could take one of both of us. "Take a few, actually," I said, handing her the camera. She did, but for some reason the flash didn't go off until the fifth and final frame on the roll of film.

"I hope we showed you guys enough," said Russell, uttering the understatement of the day as we exited the Conservancy.

"It's really… never seen anything…" said Jay, at a loss for words.

"This was a personal as well as a professional quest," I said to Elena as she escorted us out.

"I picked up on that," she said knowingly.

At the end of the hall, she pointed in the direction of the side entrance on Forty-Second Street. "Just straight up there."

We walked toward the heavy revolving door. Jay could hardly contain himself and stepped in first, laughing and yelling and howling uncontrollably into his recorder. "Whew! Whoa! Whoa! *Ahhh*! I cannot *explain* what I feel like right now. Whoa! Whoa! *Whoa*! I feel like right now," he shouted outside. "Oh, God! Oh, my *God*! That was *so insane*! It was just, just…"

I jumped in where he left off. "…one of those things you hear so much about for so long and then you finally see it and you realize that everything everyone's ever said doesn't even *begin* to describe it."

"*Yes*!" agreed Jay. "It's so different from the book. It's, it's… *pure*."

"I *do* need a cigarette," I said.

Jay laughed, pulled out his pack of Camel Lights, took two out, lit them both and handed one to me. We both inhaled deeply and then slowly exhaled, looking at each other as we stood on the steps of the Library.

"We did it, man, *we did it!*" said Jay.

He hit the *rewind* button on his recorder, played back his howl and howled again. As we started down Forty-Second, he rewound the whole tape and pushed *play,* holding the recorder up between us as we walked along, arms flung over each other's shoulder, sparks flying off us in all directions, oblivious, delirious, insepa-rable, as we listened to the instant replay of our life-altering ad-venture, both knowing that we would never be the same again, bound by this moment in time, changed forever, changed together, spiritually, mystically and even physically in the presence of Jack Kerouac's scroll manuscript of *On the Road* in the basement of the New York Public Library on a Friday afternoon in August of 1995.

8

WE HEADED TO OUR usual place for lunch, listening to the entire tape along the way.

"I'm going to take the film to Pro Print," I said. "We'll have the pictures this afternoon."

At Star Burger, we ordered sandwiches to go and took them back to the office, where I decided to hazard a question I'd been turning over in my head.

"Hey, Jay, would you like to grab a beer after work? To celebrate?"

"I really would, but I'm supposed to get together with my friends Marilyn and Zeus. I haven't seen them since they got engaged a few weeks ago."

"Did you say *Zeus?*"

"Yeah, his real name is Jesus. We always used to say, 'Hey, Zeus!', and it just sort of stuck."

"Ah. Well, some other time then."

"Yeah, sure," he said, a little sorry, it seemed, that tonight was not the night.

After lunch, I headed to Pro Print and dropped off the roll of film, ordering two sets of prints. An hour later, I picked them up and was relieved to see that every picture had come out. I called Jay from my office and told him I had the photos. He was standing next to me in a few seconds.

"Let's see!"

I handed him a set of pictures. "These are for you. I got doubles."

We stood next to each other, shoulder to shoulder, looking at each print, flipping through all the individual shots of Jay and me, which were good, before we got to the ones of us together, which were not so good. All of them were a little dark and slightly out of focus, except for the very last one, the one where the flash had finally gone off.

"That's the shot!" said Jay. "That's the one!"

It *was* a good shot. Of both of us. Jay, hands folded, leaning on the table next to the box that contained the scroll manuscript. Me, hands on hips, standing next to him. The two of us staring straight-faced into the camera lens.

"Hey, Har, look," said Jay, examining the picture more closely. "There's a sort of halo around us. Elena must have moved a little, just as she pushed the button. The only things that are really in focus are you and me and the box."

I studied the picture. "Pretty cool."

"You know what it reminds me of?" asked Jay. "The picture of Jack Kerouac and Neal Cassady on the cover of the paperback of *On the Road*."

I retrieved my copy of the book from my backpack. The picture on the cover was probably the most famous of Jack and Neal, a black-and-white snapshot of the two best friends, Kerouac in sweatshirt and khakis, Cassady in jeans and rumpled shirt, leaning on each other as they leaned on the stark white plaster side of Cassady's San Francisco home, smiling for Cassady's second wife, Carolyn, the woman wielding the camera. Jay was right. It wasn't just the way we were standing, what we were wearing or the expressions on our faces. There was something else. Something the strange halo that surrounded us hinted at but didn't disclose.

"Jay, we *do* look like Kerouac and Cassady—maybe we were channeling them," I joked.

I gave him an envelope for his pictures and we both went back to work. At the end of the day, I wandered back to the art department to say goodnight just as Ted was telling Jay it was time to go home.

"You ready, Har?" he asked unexpectedly as he shut down his computer.

"Ready?"

"My friends bailed on me," he explained. "You still want to grab a beer?"

"Sure."

He shouldered his backpack and walked with me to my office where I packed up before the two of us headed outside.

"Do you feel like going someplace crazy?" he asked.

"Yeah, Jay, take me someplace crazy."

He smiled. "It's a bar called Rudy's, in Hell's Kitchen," he said as we walked over to Ninth. "It's got the best jazz jukebox in the city and every time I go there, something outrageous happens. Last time, my friends and I ended up jitterbugging. Time before that, this old woman—she had to be ninety—fell off her barstool right onto my lap. I didn't know what to do but somebody came along and just propped her up again. It was wild."

At Rudy's, the buzz of the big red neon sign outside segued almost seamlessly into the buzz of the animated after-work crowd inside. Jay pointed to the only empty booth in a long row of red vinyl booths, all the way in the back, and we made our way to it, squeezing past a few patrons who were singing along to "Let's Get Lost" by Chet Baker, which just happened to be blasting from the jukebox.

"What would you like from the bar?" asked Jay as I sat down. I hesitated. "Jay, I haven't had any alcohol in more than a year."

"Come on. You can't ask me out for a beer and expect me to drink alone. It'll be all right. You're in good hands. *Mine.*"

"Okay," I relented. "Surprise me."

He returned a few minutes later with two overflowing frosty mugs and set one in front of me.

"A toast," he said, raising his in the air. "To Jack Kerouac. To *On the Road.* To the scroll manuscript. To you and me. To *us.*"

I tentatively lifted my mug and tilted it in his direction. He slammed his into mine and took a long draft. I drew a deep breath and followed suit, bracing myself for a flood of unwanted memories I would always associate with the taste of beer. I closed my eyes, expecting to be transported back in time, to discover myself in another place, with another companion, one I had desperately loved, but when I opened my eyes I was in Rudy's, with Jay. And Jay was looking at me with a hopeful half-smile.

"Well?" he asked anxiously.

"All good," I told him. No remembrance of things past.

"Har, do you have a typewriter?"

I shook my head. "Why…?"

"Can you get one?"

"You mean buy one? Sure."

"I want us to write something together," he said. "I want to get my typewriter overhauled, but as soon as I do, and as soon as you can get your hands on one, we'll get started. We'll get a roll of paper. And trade it back and forth. I'll write something, then you'll write something. Just like Kerouac and Burroughs."

William S. Burroughs, grandson and namesake of the man who invented the adding machine, was one-third of the Beat Generation literary troika that included Jack Kerouac and poet Allen Ginsberg. An astoundingly resilient one-time addict whose firsthand familiarity with an abundance of pharmaceuticals formed the basis of his best-known books, *Naked Lunch* and *Junkie*—alternately hailed as gibberish and genius—Burroughs originated the "cut-up" method of writing and influenced a generation of rock stars (Steely Dan was named for a super-powered sex toy in *Naked Lunch*). Although for a time he dearly loved Ginsberg, he nonetheless married (and had a son with) Joan Vollmer, whom he accidentally shot in the head during a game of William Tell while living in Mexico. Writing, he confessed in the preface to *Queer*, offered the only absolution from the horror of his wife's death that haunted him for the rest of his days, and he went on to become a media icon famed for his deadpan delivery and slightly sinister presence, a strangely sentimental devil in a fedora and gray flannel suit.

In 1945, Burroughs and Kerouac decided to write a mystery novel together, trading off every other chapter. The subject of the novel was a notorious incident concerning Lucien Carr, the Columbia University student who kickstarted the Beat scene when he introduced Ginsberg, Kerouac and Burroughs. Nineteen-year-old Lucien Carr had arrived in New York from St. Louis, Missouri, pursued by David Kammerer, his thirty-three-year-old former Scoutmaster. Carr and Kammerer were friends, united by common intellectual interests, but Kammerer was also romantically obsessed with Carr, despite the fact that the object of his affection made it clear that he loved women, not men.

Obsession turned to tragedy the night of August thirteenth, 1944, when Kammerer followed Carr out of the West End Bar to Riverside Park. The details about what happened next were disputed, but, according to Carr, who was the only witness, Kammerer jumped him, threatening to kill him and then commit suicide if Carr did not respond to his advances. Carr defended himself with the only weapon available, his Boy Scout pocketknife, of all things, stabbing Kammerer to death and then, in a panic, dumping his body in the Hudson River. Overwhelmed by remorse, Carr turned to Kerouac and Burroughs, who advised him to surrender to the police. Carr pleaded guilty to manslaughter and served two years of a twenty-year sentence. Upon his release, he landed a position as reporter with United Press International, and it was from UPI that he obtained a certain roll of Teletype paper that he gave to Kerouac, the same roll of Teletype paper that Jay and I had seen only a few hours earlier.

The novel that resulted from the literary tag-team of Kerouac and Burroughs, *And the Hippos Were Boiled in Their Tanks*, took its unlikely title from a newscast. At a bar one night, the two were watching a live report about a fire that swept through the St. Louis Zoo when the newscaster, faced with only a few seconds to wrap up, cut to the chase by blurting out, "And the hippos were boiled in their tanks!" Burroughs was so struck by the line that he suggested to Kerouac they borrow it for the name of their collaborative effort.

"Come on, Harry, let's do it," said Jay. "Let's write a book together."

"As long as it has a happier ending than *Hippos*," I said. Jay laughed. "Of course! And when we're done, we'll send it out. Get it published." He pulled a thick pad of coarse brown paper from his backpack, thought for a moment and then scribbled something on a blank page. "And this is what it will say on it." He pushed the notebook toward me so I could see what he'd written.

"By Harry Jay Charity Bishop," I read aloud.

Caught up in the moment, I suddenly felt free to say to Jay what till then I had said only to myself. Still, the words did not come easy.

"Jay, there's something I really want to say to you..."

"What's that?" he asked eagerly, not expecting a change of subject.

I gazed at my mug for a second but just as I was about to answer, three young women—two blondes and a brunette—slid into the opposite side of our booth.

"Do you mind if we sit here?" inquired one of the blondes. She had a British accent.

"No, no, go right ahead," I replied, taking their arrival as a sign that maybe some things were better left unsaid.

"Where are you from?" asked Jay.

"The U.K.," replied the second blonde.

"Are you two twins?" Jay asked.

They looked at each other and laughed, answering in unison. "No."

"Sisters, then?" I asked.

"No, not even," said the first blonde.

"Hi, I'm Jay and this is Harry," said Jay.

"I'm Caitlin," said the dark-haired one. "And this is Kathleen and Emily."

"You're the smiley one," said Jay to Emily, who did seem to

have a smile cemented on her face but didn't seem to appreciate Jay pointing it out.

We talked with the threesome for the next few hours, Jay kidding Emily the entire time. Over and over she would call her "the smiley one" and over and over she would respond by groaning and rolling her eyes. Each time, Jay would turn to Kathleen and Caitlin and say very sadly, "Emily doesn't like me," which, of course, would cause Kathleen and Caitlin to insist that Emily *did* like him. *And* to insist that Emily tell him so. "I don't know where you get the idea I don't like you," she'd say to him in exasperation. "I *do* like you." "You *do*?" Jay would say hopefully.

As the empty mugs began to multiply and the effects of the beer escalated, my contributions to the conversation grew fewer and farther between. Caitlin noticed.

"Why are you so quiet?" she asked.

"Oh, he *is* quiet," said Jay. "He's the quiet half. Right, Har?"

She looked at me with a mixture of concern and fascination, inching closer and pressing her thigh against mine. "I've always been attracted to broody types," she said suggestively.

I glanced at Jay and rolled my eyes. He stifled a laugh and shook his head.

At quarter to four, when the bartender gave last call, Emily, Kathleen and Caitlin decided to call it a night. Jay and I followed them out, saying goodbye on the sidewalk as they hailed a cab. I gave Kathleen and Emily each a quick kiss on the cheek and went to do the same with Caitlin but she turned her face at the last second and planted a kiss on my lips. I was still recovering as I watched Jay offer each a hug, first Kathleen, then Caitlin and finally Emily, who unexpectedly hurled herself at Jay at the last second and then climbed into the cab behind her two friends.

"Aww!" Jay yelled as she slammed the door and disappeared into the night. "She bit me!" He rubbed his neck and looked at his hand. "She *bit* me!" he said again, still in shock.

"Let me see," I said. He tilted his head so I could examine his neck. "You're okay," I assured him. "She didn't draw blood."

He continued rubbing his neck ruefully. "Ah, I'll get over it. You feel like getting something to eat, Har?"

I suddenly realized we hadn't eaten since lunch. "Sure. Where?"

"There," he said, pointing across the street.

The Westway Diner was nearly empty, save for the usual night-hawks who roosted at odd hours in twenty-four-hour eateries and dreamed of better lives over blue-plate specials and bottomless cups of questionable coffee.

"What are you getting?" I asked as we perused the menu.

"There's only one thing to get at four in the morning when you've been out drinking all night," said Jay. "A cheeseburger and fries!"

Our food arrived in just a few minutes, the speed at which all diners somehow seemed to operate.

"Jay, there's something I started to tell you earlier," I said as we began to eat.

"What's that?" he asked.

"Before we met, I was in love with a guy who wasn't in love with me. He really liked me, but he didn't love me. He couldn't. And I couldn't accept that. Until it was too late."

"Yeah, but now you know what you should have done," said Jay. "And it didn't end in murder, like Lucien Carr and David Kammerer. Unless," he added with a laugh, "there's something you're not telling me."

"No, it didn't end in murder," I said, forcing a smile. But there was something I wasn't telling him. "Jay, I really wish everyone were wired the same way. I really wish that anyone could just love anyone else."

"They can," said Jay. "But not everyone can love them the same way back."

I was quiet for a moment, trying to find words I wasn't even sure I wanted to say. "Jay, ever since we met, I've had this feel-ing... I've had these feelings.... And I allowed myself to hope...." I paused, wishing I could take it all back. Jay looked at me expectantly. "Ah, forget it. I've said too much already."

"You can't just stop like that!" yelled Jay. "You *have* to tell me."

I tried to begin again but my voice cracked and my eyes welled up. "I allowed myself to hope... I allowed myself to hope that we're going to be in each other's lives for a long, long time. I know how that must sound, especially in light of what we were just talking about, but I think I finally got it right. I finally… got it right."

I stared at the table, afraid that I'd said something I shouldn't have, afraid of what might happen as a result.

Jay reached over, put his hand on top of mine and looked into my eyes. "Harry," he said, "we *are*, we *were*, we *will* be."

I managed an uncertain smile, reassured by what he said but not exactly sure what he meant, and acutely aware of his touch.

"Besides," he added, "I've always been attracted to broody types."

9

IN THE SUMMER OF 1948, Allen Ginsberg, then twenty-two, had a vision. At the time, his life was at loose ends. His friends Jack Kerouac and William Burroughs were away, on the road. His lover Neal Cassady had just sent a letter saying he had moved on, to women. His mother, Naomi, was in a state mental hospital undergoing electroshock therapy for chronic paranoid delusions. And his poetry, traditional in style and substance, failed to live up to his own expectations. As Ginsberg sat on his bed watching the sun set over the tenement rooftops from the window of his East Harlem sublet, he read a poem from *Songs of Experience* by William Blake: "Ah! Sunflower, weary of time / Who countest the steps of the sun / Seeking after that sweet golden clime / Where the traveller's journey is done..."

Out of nowhere, he heard a voice, beautiful, tender, ancient. A voice he instinctively knew to be Blake's. And in that moment, Ginsberg had an epiphany, suddenly aware of his true calling—to write poetry that would resonate like no other.

After years of experimenting, Ginsberg finally found his form with the publication of *Howl and Other Poems* in 1956 with its signature opener: "I saw the best minds of my generation destroyed by madness...." Ginsberg unveiled "Howl" during a now-legendary poetry reading at San Francisco's Six Gallery, urged on by a drunken Kerouac, who sat by the side of the stage thumping a jug of wine and shouting "*Go!*" at the end of every line. In the audience was Lawrence Ferlinghetti, owner of San Francisco's City Lights bookstore. He'd never heard anything like "Howl" before and sent Ginsberg a telegram the next day asking for the manuscript.

A year and a half later, *Howl and Other Poems* became Number Four in the City Lights Pocket Poets Series, although the only ones who connected with the poem's dazzling juxtaposition of the profound and the perverse were the inhabitants of the Bay area's burgeoning bohemian community. It was not until the second edition, en route to Ferlinghetti's bookstore from the British printer, landed on the desk of a U.S. Customs agent that Ginsberg's poem truly resonated, though not as intended. "The words and the sense of the writing is obscene," declared the customs agent. "You wouldn't want your children to come across it."

Ironically, though Ginsberg's poem was full of four-letter epithets and jaw-dropping images, in the trial that ensued, Exhibit A, the second edition, was actually an expurgated version in which Ferlinghetti had replaced some of the most potentially problematic words and phrases with an appropriate number of dots to represent the missing letters. In Ferlinghetti's hands, one of the poem's most scandalous lines, "Who let themselves be fucked in the ass by saintly motorcyclists, and screamed with joy," became, "Who let themselves be . . . . in the . . . by saintly motorcyclists, and screamed with joy." When Assistant D. A. Ralph McIntosh called the first witness for the defense, Berkeley English professor Mark Schorer, their exchange was nothing short of surreal.

"Do you understand some of these pages where there are just little dots there?" asked McIntosh.

"I think I know the words that were intended," replied Schorer.

"Let's take page one-thirty-five," suggested McIntosh.

"Yes," Schorer responded.

McIntosh read from the slim stapled volume. "Fifth line up. 'Who let themselves be'—*one, two, three, four, five, six* dots—'in the'—*three* dots—'by saintly motorcyclists, and screamed with joy.' What does that mean?"

Though the judge, the Honorable Clayton W. Horn, was a

Sunday-school teacher who had once sentenced five shoplifters to a screening of *The Ten Commandments*, he nonetheless ruled that "Howl," described by the prosecution as "lewd and indecent," had "redeeming social importance" and concluded his opinion by pointing a finger at the prosecution. "In considering material claimed to be obscene," he wrote, "it is well to remember the motto: 'Honi soit qui mal y pense.'" Translation: "Evil to him who thinks evil." Or, as Jack Kerouac would later say, "Woe unto those who spit on the Beat Generation, the wind'll blow it back."

Ginsberg himself had not been on trial for writing "Howl." Ferlinghetti had been, for publishing it. And throughout the summer of 1957, as the courtroom proceedings made headlines across the country (including a picture spread in *Life*), Ginsberg was actually abroad, holed up in Paris and Tangiers helping William Burroughs put the finishing touches on *Naked Lunch*. But when Ginsberg returned to America, he discovered that his days of obscurity were behind him. *Howl and Other Poems* had cinched his status as an icon of the avant-garde.

He soon found a new and life-long companion in Peter Orlovsky, an artist's model and poet, with whom he traveled the world and discovered Buddhism and enlightenment in India. Back home, he finally came to terms with his mother's suffering and death in the elegiac lament "Kaddish," funneled his energies into the sixties counterculture—hanging out at be-ins, coining the term "flower power," assisting in an exorcism on the Pentagon—and poignantly survived Kerouac and Cassady, both of whom he had madly and sadly held so close. By 1995, he and Orlovsky had settled somewhere in New York City.

"Somewhere on the Lower East Side," said Jay over lunch. "Zahra has a friend, Bobby, who used to live in the same building. In the apartment right above him."

Now that Jay and I had seen the scroll, we were discussing what to do next. Jay had suggested we locate Allen Ginsberg.

"Maybe you could call him," Jay continued. "Hello, Allen, this is Harry.'"

"I'll ask him if we can buy him a drink."

"Many drinks!"

"Imagine the book collection he must have," I said. "All the first editions."

Jay nodded. "If I had a first edition of *On the Road*, Har, that would be my most prized possession. I think I'd frame it and hang it on the wall. Imagine—a framed book."

I smiled to myself, thinking about the copy I had in my apartment. Though Christmas was still a few months away, that's when I was going to give it to him. I wondered if he really would frame it.

Back at work, I tracked down Ginsberg's Manhattan office, where a young man answered. He listened politely to my proposition, which sounded incredibly farfetched, even to me ("My friend and I would like to take Allen out…"), said that Ginsberg might actually consider it, and asked me to put it in a fax, which I did, immediately.

I put both our names at the bottom and showed it to Jay.

He read it and smiled. "Well, it's *honest*. Naïve, but honest."

"'Naïve but honest,'" I repeated. "That pretty much sums us up, doesn't it?"

"For better or for worse," joked Jay.

I WAS IN MY OFFICE, in the middle of packing up for the day, when Jay appeared.

"Do you have any plans tonight?" he asked.

I could tell by the look in his eye that I did. "Not till just now."

"That's right," he said, grinning. "I'm taking you to see my favorite singer in New York, the most soulful singer you're ever going to hear."

He reached for his back pocket, whipped out a Day-Glo yellow postcard and flipped it over for me to see. On it was a picture of a dark-haired woman with enormous eyes that seemed to have seen all the sadness in this world.

"Her name's Deanna Kirk," he said. "She's got the most incredible voice I've ever heard and she sings the most incredible songs. I'm on her mailing list. She carries her mailing list around in her backpack. You're going to love her." He turned the card over. "She's performing songs from her new CD, *Mariana Trench*, at the Bitter End."

"*Mariana Trench*—that sounds vaguely familiar," I said, trying to recall where I'd come across the reference.

He read from the back of the card. "Located at the bottom of the Pacific Ocean near Guam, the Mariana Trench contains the deepest point on the Earth's surface, a depression known as the Challenger Deep that was sounded at a depth of 35,814 feet by the bathyscaphe *Trieste* in 1960."

"Oh, *that* Mariana Trench," I said.

Jay stopped reading and looked at me. "She's *so* deep." He was so serious that I didn't have the heart to point out the obvious.

We took the subway to West Fourth, walked a few blocks to Bleecker and arrived at the Bitter End at seven-thirty. The doorman told us the place didn't open till eight.

"Let's get a cup of coffee at Dante's," suggested Jay, leading the way to a nearby Old World-style café on MacDougal Street. "Zahra and I come here a lot," he said as we sat down. "They have the best tiramisu."

The waitress came by and took our orders. Jay asked for an iced cappuccino with Kahlua and, of course, tiramisu, and I asked for the same. While we waited, we both studied the wall beside us, which was covered with a huge aerial photograph of a European city.

"Florence," observed Jay.

"Ever been?" I asked.

"Yeah, when I was at Pratt," he said. "Zahra and I visited there while we were in Venice for six weeks to study."

My thoughts slipped out before I could stop them. "I wish you and I could go there, Jay. Or anywhere. Just the two of us, like Jack and Neal, seeing the world and sharing experiences." I flushed in embarrassment. For the longest time I had believed that I was good at keeping inside whatever I felt should stay inside. I'd been forced to admit that I wasn't very good at it at all.

"Harry," said Jay, "we're sharing experiences right now. You only have to be in the moment to realize it."

I nodded. I was so rarely in the moment.

Back at the Bitter End, open for business, we made ourselves comfortable at a small table by the side of the stage. Jay ordered a Johnnie Walker Red on the rocks while I studied the beer list. "A Heineken," I told the waitress.

When she returned with our drinks a few minutes later, Jay lifted his glass and tilted it in my direction. "Cheers!"

We sat in silence for a few seconds, taking in the scene. I knew that the Bitter End was a New York City landmark, the launchpad for an amazing array of luminaries. As I looked the place over, however, I couldn't help but think how extraordinarily ordinary the club seemed on the surface. Did the regulars realize just what they were witnessing when they crowded into the West Village watering hole to hear Bob Dylan or Joni Mitchell or George Carlin perform in front of the now-famous red-brick wall that backed the club's small stage? Two hours ago, I'd never heard of Deanna Kirk. Ten years down the road, would I recall the night I caught a legend-in-the-making at the Bitter End?

"Close your eyes, Har," said Jay as the place slowly filled. "Listen to everything that's going on around us."

I closed my eyes and concentrated, gradually becoming aware of the background music playing over the sound system, people talking at nearby tables, the clink of glasses, the creak of a door, laughter, footsteps, the hum of the air conditioner, the buzz of a light bulb, the strike of a match, Jay exhaling the smoke from his cigarette.

"Do you see what I mean?" he asked. "Life. It's all around us. Waiting to happen."

His words were still reverberating when the house lights dimmed and Deanna stepped on stage, accompanied by two musicians—one on upright bass, the other on piano. She leaned back on a barstool positioned between them and began to sing as a white spotlight singled her out of the darkness.

"Yooouuuuu..." she began, softly, slightly, sadly caressing the simple elegance of the jazz standard "You Go to My Head" and somehow managing to simultaneously express the pleasure and the pain of being so much in love you can't even think straight. Deanna had my undivided attention.

For the next hour, she sat there singing songs of love and longing, so barely propped up on that barstool I thought she might slip down and drown in the invisible pool of tears gathering at her feet. But she never did. Somehow, she kept standing, somehow she kept singing and somehow she kept hitting me right where it hurt most, dredging up feelings I'd buried so deep I thought I'd never feel them again. And it was not only her voice, it was her hands, hands that flew and fluttered and fell all around her as she sang, hands that seemed to have a mind of their own, attached but only barely attached, performers in their own right with whom she'd agreed to share the stage. With every song she sang she touched another tender spot.

"This is a love song," she said, her mouth breaking into a crooked smile. A love song. As if all the songs she'd sung before that one weren't.

As she sighed into the microphone and began to sing, I was hit with a pang of recognition. I leaned over to Jay. "This is one of my favorites," I whispered. He smiled and I turned back to listen. Deanna was singing "Let It Be Me," turning an Everly Brothers pop song into a hymn, a cry to heaven. Not only pleading with her new love but with God as well.

My eyes began to mist over. Why this song? Why now? There really were no coincidences. I gritted my teeth and tightened my jaw, determined not to let the moment get the best of me. This is why I stopped drinking, I told myself, so I would never lose control. But I *was* losing control. Deanna turned into a watery blur and the spotlight above her began to flicker. I closed my eyes in an effort to conceal their condition, hoping that Jay wouldn't notice.

There was nothing I could do but sit there and wait for her to finish.

Finally, she did, and after a reverent pause, applause broke the spell she'd cast on me and, obviously, many others. I took a deep breath and let it out all at once. *"Wow."*

"What'd I tell you, Har?" asked Jay.

Deanna interrupted. "We're almost at the end," she announced, as she and her sidemen began their final number. It was a song Deanna had co-written, about a girl named Mariana who once lived on the island of Sarigan in the South Pacific. She slipped into the Challenger Deep one day while making sandcastles, but her spirit roamed the waves, bringing solace to the sad and lonely. "Sail on my sea, sail on sail on," sang Deanna. "All my life will be your history, sail *onnnn...* Mariana's here and the truth will set you free..."

Jay leaned over and whispered in my ear. "Remember that, Har."

"Sail on..."

The crowd around us began clapping wildly even as the final notes were still sounding. Deanna bowed and left the stage, passing by our table and disappearing down the hallway behind us.

The waitress came by and we ordered another round, our third. I was beginning to feel the effect of the alcohol and I presumed Jay was, too. He got up to use the men's room and I scribbled some notes to myself on a napkin about the night's proceedings. Jay returned, saw me writing and sat down without asking what I was doing. I folded the paper in half and put it in my shirt pocket.

"One of these days, Har," he said, "it's going to come, it's going to come. One day, you're just going to explode. Like I told you before, it's going to come out of you like diarrhea."

I started laughing. "You know, Jay, that's in my journal."

"*I hope* that's not what I'm remembered for in your writing," he said, wide-eyed at the thought.

I told him the sloppy sentimental truth, but the truth nonetheless, courtesy of my three Heinekens. "No, Jay," I said, placing my hand on his heart. "I'll remember you in my writing because of what's in *here*. And, " I added, placing my hand on my own heart, "because of what's in *here*."

Outside, a few minutes later, Jay asked me how I was getting home.

"Cab. How 'bout you?"

"I have to take the subway to Penn Station and then catch a train to Long Island."

"You know, Jay," I said, "it's really late. The trains can't be running very often. You can crash at my place if you want."

He considered my offer for a moment. "Maybe... nah, I'm too wound up to fall asleep but I really appreciate the invite. Next time."

He waved to the driver of a passing Checker cab and opened the back door for me.

I held out my hand to wish him goodbye but he brushed it aside, wrapping his arms around me and pulling me close. Taken aback, I stood there for a second before I reciprocated, feeling slightly self-conscious until he let me go a few long moments later. I watched as he walked to the subway entrance across the street. On the sidewalk by the top of the stairs, an old black man was dancing by himself to a tune that nobody else could hear. Jay danced along with him for just a second, then shook his hand and disappeared underground.

I climbed into the cab and sighed. Last night, my first beer in more than a year. Tonight, my first hug. I thought about both all the way home, and, later, as I drifted off to sleep with Flannery curled up in my arms, I told her all about it. I didn't realize what was happening. But Flannery did. She was a wise old soul. And she'd heard it all before.

10

He SHOWED UP AT MY DOOR at midnight carrying all his belongings in a single large duffel bag slung over his shoulder. I emptied a few drawers in my dresser for him and after he unpacked we hit the sack. In bed, we were affectionate but not intimate. He smiled and said he had too much on his mind. I said I understood.

When we awoke the next morning, however, he lit a cigarette and stared at the ceiling for several minutes, deep in thought.

"Harry," he said finally, "I have feelings for you, but I'm not sure they're the same feelings you have for me."

A million things went through my head, but only a single word came out. "No?"

He looked at me. "No."

My face fell. "What about *this*?" I asked, indicating the obvious.

"*This* is good," he said slowly. "I like you. A lot. But it's not what you're thinking. You're a great guy but you're not my type. I wish you were. But you're not."

"No?"

"No."

My alarm clock went off as I was about to respond and he vanished as I opened my eyes. I got up, went to my bedroom closet and pushed the Budweiser box on the shelf as far back as it would go.

Thirty minutes later, as I finished getting ready for work, my eyes fell upon a small black-velvet ring box that had been sitting on my bureau for several days. Thinking back on everything that Jay and I had recently shared, I picked it up, flipped it open and smiled. The time had come, I decided, to show Jay just how I felt about him. I snapped the box shut and slipped it into the pocket of my leather jacket.

There was big news at the morning staff meeting. After Donal had dispatched with his managing editor duties, Vivien Verdurin, the editor-in-chief, stepped forward to announce that she was leaving her post at *Element* to become publisher at a newly created corporate Internet division. Not only would she speed the development of *Element Online*, she would initiate digital versions of the company's eleven other magazines. Vivien didn't believe in long goodbyes. She was out the door by mid-afternoon. The only thing she left behind was a press release that proclaimed her new appointment and listed her many accomplishments, the most impressive of which was the fact that she had aged only two years in her five years at the helm of *Element*.

A few hours after Vivien dropped her bombshell, I received a large Federal Express parcel from Rhino Records that contained two elaborate CD box sets, *The Jack Kerouac Collection* and *The Beat Generation*.

"I actually feel a little guilty," I said to Jay at Star Burger. "I got the sets using the same story I concocted to see the scroll manuscript."

"Why do you feel guilty?" he asked.

"Because there *is* no article on the renewed interest in the Beat Generation."

"You *could* write one," he suggested. "If not for *Element*, then for some other magazine. I'm sure you could sell it somewhere."

"Maybe," I allowed. "But I *am* going to write something else. I made you a promise when you showed me your poems that I would show you something of mine and I'm finally going to deliver. I'm going to write a story this weekend about one of our nights out. I'll have it for you on Monday."

"Great, I'll look forward to it," said Jay. "Well, I guess we should head back to the office."

He started to get up but I stopped him.

"Jay, wait."

He looked at me and dropped back into his seat.

"I have something for you," I said, reaching into the pocket of my coat and pulling out the ring box. "It's something I've wanted to give you for a while now."

I could feel him staring at me with a mixture of confusion and apprehension, but I deliberately avoided eye contact.

"You've come to mean a lot to me in a very short time," I continued. "And, well, I just wanted to let you know how I feel." I held out the box. He hesitated for a second and then accepted it, nervously glancing from the box to me and then back to the box again, not sure what to do next.

"Open it," I suggested.

He smiled uneasily. "Harry, I'm not sure…"

I nodded. "I know. But I am."

He ran his fingers over the outside of the box, rubbing the velvet surface for a moment before finally, tentatively, snapping it open. I watched as his eyes grew twice their size at the sight of the subway token inside.

"Oh, *man*!" he yelled. "You had me going! *You really had me going!*"

We both exploded, laughing until tears streamed down our faces, laughing until we ached, laughing until we couldn't laugh any more and then starting all over again.

"*Whew!*" Jay finally sighed, grinning ear to ear. "I can't believe you did that!"

"Actually," I admitted, both to Jay and to myself, "I can't believe I did it, either."

"I'm going to keep it just like this," he said, smiling and shaking his head as he snapped the box shut. "And don't worry. I'll get you back."

"It was a gift," I said innocently. "No reason to get me back."

He just smiled and shook his head again. "We'll see."

I GOT UP EARLY on Saturday and wrote for eight hours, straight through from morning to evening, tapping away on my laptop and detailing everything that was going on in my head and in my heart the night Jay took me to see Deanna Kirk. I put in another eight hours on Sunday, and when I was finished, I hit *print* and collapsed on the couch, exhausted. When I opened my eyes a few minutes later, I spotted the two CD box sets from Rhino Records leaning on my stereo, right where I had left them on Friday night. In my obsession to write, I had forgotten all about them. I listened to a track from *The Jack Kerouac Collection*, Kerouac reading from *On the Road* and *Visions of Cody.*

"Well, a lot of people have asked me why I wrote *that* book, or *any* book," said Kerouac. Finally, I thought, a *voice* to put with those remarkable words, a voice leaping across the decades, rendering time irrelevant, a voice immediate, touching and heartfelt. "All the stories I wrote were *true*, 'cause I believed in what I saw."

On the subway to work in the morning, I read the story I'd written over the weekend for the first time and realized as I did that I'd actually written two stories—one describing my unabashed awe for Deanna; the other, my unabashed fondness for Jay. I wondered whether it was too personal, too honest. I wondered what Jay would think, whether I should show it to him at all. But then I remembered the poems Jay had shown me, how personal they were, and how honest. The poems Jay wrote were true because he believed in what he saw. I did, too. How could I *not* give him my story?

"Jay, I've got something for you," I told him as we passed each other in the hall late-morning.

"Another ring box?"

"Do you want another ring box?"

He followed me to my office. "You and I are like *this*, right?" I asked, holding up my right hand and crossing my fingers. He smiled and nodded. "And nothing's ever going to change that, right?" He nodded again. "Then here," I said, handing him the story. "It's about the night we went to see Deanna."

His eyes lit up when he saw the title. "Dot dot dot." I like it already! Let's take an early lunch."

"You're not going to read that *now*, are you?" I asked.

"Yeah, while we eat," he answered. "I can't wait."

I frowned, not sure I wanted to be around when he read it. He sensed my hesitation. "I can read it tonight, if you like."

"Maybe that would be better," I said, but even as I uttered the words I wondered what difference it ultimately made. "Nah, go ahead."

At our usual place, he started reading right away, turning pages in between bites of his sandwich. He laughed out loud after only a few seconds.

"She's so deep,'" he quoted from the story. "I didn't realize I made such a bad pun."

"Just *read*," I said, anxious for him to finish now that he'd started.

I studied his face, trying to figure out what he was thinking as I recalled the line from one of Deanna's songs that Jay had whispered to me. "The truth will set you free." Would it? Was such an absurdly simple sentiment really the answer? Or would the truth screw everything up? I couldn't tell one way or the other from Jay's expression, which alternated between extreme concentration and an occasional smile. I kept looking at the clock on the wall behind him. He'd started reading at two-twenty-five. At two-forty-five, he was done.

"I like it," he said finally.

"You *do*?" I asked. "You weren't surprised by what I wrote, were you?"

"No, I wasn't surprised," he said. "Because different people perceive things differently. You *think* too much. So does Zahra. You remind me of each other so much sometimes." He smiled. "Broody types."

"I *do* think too much," I said, not quite sure what to make of the

Zahra comparison. "Jay, it's just that... when I'm getting to know someone, and they're getting to know me, I'm always afraid I'm going to fuck things up."

"Har," said Jay, "maybe the *other* person will fuck things up."

11

I SPENT THE NEXT MORNING calling businesses listed under Typewriters in the Yellow Pages, looking for a store that not only sold vintage models but repaired them, so I could buy one and Jay could have his refurbished and we could start our joint writing project. I had called about ten places and was beginning to get discouraged when I noticed a listing that looked promising. "Tytell Typwrtr Co.," it said. "Special Purpose Typewriters. 145 Languages In Stock. 2 Million Pieces Of Type. On Premises Machine Shop. Antique Restorations. 65 Years Exper./Parts Accumulation. Huge Stock Of Manual, Electric Typewriters. Repairs. Rentals. Sales. 116 Fulton Street, Manhattan."

I punched in the number but the elderly man who answered didn't even give me a chance to state the reason for my call.

"Hello? Hello?" he asked.

"Do you sell…"

"Hello?"

I paused, waiting for him to run out of steam. "Do you sell…"

"Hello?"

I forged ahead, finally managing to get out a complete sentence. "Do you sell vintage typewriters?"

"Martin Tytell, eighty-one, been in business sixty-six years," he said. "I've been queer for typewriters since I was fifteen. A typewriter saved my life. I was in the army in World War II and my unit got shipped out to a place occupied by Japanese forces. The Japanese put out white flags as if they were surrendering, but when my unit went in, they were massacred. I wasn't there because the day before I was supposed to ship out, I was ordered to the Pentagon to fix some general's typewriter."

There was no stopping him.

"People leave me their typewriters in their wills because they know I'll make sure they'll be around for another fifty years. My shop is an old-age home for typewriters. One guy left me a gold-plated typewriter on condition that I not sell it. So now I have it. Some people leave me typewriters and tell me to use them for parts so that other typewriters can stay in service."

"It's like organ donors," I observed as he took a breath.

"Yeah, like organ donors," he agreed.

I asked him if he had working vintage models for sale and he told me he had a large selection, each one priced to go at around three hundred fifty dollars. After we hung up, I wandered to the art department and related all this to Jay, who had come in late after picking Zahra up at the airport the previous evening.

"Maybe I'll bring my typewriter in tomorrow and we can go there after work," he said. "I'll ask Zahra if she wants to come. My typewriter needs a tune-up and I'd love to have it appraised. Zahra gave it to me for my birthday last year and I think it's worth a lot more than she paid for it."

I called Martin back and asked if he was open late on weeknights.

"Harry, what do you want? I'm eighty-one years old!" he yelled. "I'm open from ten to three, including Saturdays. Come on Saturday. You can try a few typewriters out and see how they feel. You won't know what kind you want until you try them out. Everybody prefers a different touch."

I repeated Martin's schedule to Jay over lunch.

"Yeah, Saturday sounds good," he said. "Oh, I forgot to tell you—on Saturday night, a bunch of us are going to see Bo Diddley at Chicago Blues. Like to join us?"

"Sure, who's all going?"

"Marilyn and Zeus, maybe my brother Anthony."

"Zahra?"

"Yeah, of course, Zahra will be there. You know, last night, when we got back to her apartment from the airport, I played one of the CDs you loaned me from the *Beat Generation* box set and Zahra said, 'Did Harry give you that? I was going to get that for you.' I told her, 'No, it's Harry's. He only lent it to me, so you can still get it for me.'"

He laughed, but the implications made me uncomfortable. I hoped Zahra wasn't planning on getting him a first edition of *On the Road*.

The following day was a typical Friday. Since the magazine was put to bed on Thursday each week, Fridays tended to be rather slow, with no one rushing to begin work on the next issue. That particular Friday was slower than most, so much so that Jay stopped by my office around eleven and said he was going out for a walk to look for a copy of *The Jack Kerouac Collection*. I told him I'd go with him and we headed to Coconuts, where Jay ordered a copy because there were none in stock. A few minutes after we returned to the office, we both realized that neither of us had anything pressing to do so we turned around and headed back out for a long lunch.

Our first stop was the Gotham Book Mart. At 41 West Forty-Seventh Street, right in the middle of Diamond Row, it was the only store on the block that didn't sell jewelry. I had discovered Gotham when I began collecting books by Edward Gorey, the eccentric writer-illustrator famous for such amusingly twisted tales as *The Beastly Baby*, *The Loathsome Couple* and *The Deranged Cousins*. In the space of one visit, I learned that Gotham was not only the center of the Gorey universe but one of the best bookstores in the world.

Beneath the store's famous cast-iron sign ("Wise Men Fish Here"), Jay and I paused to study a display of rare James Joyce volumes in the window. A moment later, we proceeded down the three steps to the entrance and went inside, where we were welcomed by the wonderful musty smell of old books and the comforting creak of the polished wood floor. In a section devoted to the Beats, Jay immediately spotted two signed and numbered limited editions of Ginsberg's just-published *Journals Mid-Fifties, 1954-1958.*

"Harry! Look at these!"

The books were in green-leather slipcases with the numbers 28 and 94 on small squares of white paper that wrapped around the spines. Jay plucked number 28 from the shelf and flipped it over to reveal the price.

"Seventy-five dollars!"

"Jay, the book is never going to go *down* in value. A year from now it'll be selling for two hundred dollars. Think of it as an investment. Besides, there are only two copies. They obviously have our names on them."

Jay contemplated my justification for a moment, turning the book over several times before reaching a decision. "You're right," he said finally. "Let's do it!"

As we finished at the cash register, Jay paused at a bulletin board near the front of the store.

"Hey, check this out," he said, pointing to a pamphlet announcing a "Three-Day Novel-Writing Contest" over Labor Day weekend. He studied it for a minute. "You should do it, Har."

"Write a novel in three days?! Even Kerouac took three *weeks* to write *On the Road.*"

Jay pulled the pamphlet from the bulletin board. "Come on, Har, I *know* you can do it," he said, tucking it into my shirt pocket. I smiled and shook my head.

Later that afternoon two videos I'd read about in the booklet inside *The Jack Kerouac Collection* arrived—*Pull My Daisy,* a half-hour black-and-white film inspired by a Kerouac play, and *Kerouac, The Movie,* a documentary that featured footage of JK himself. I'd tracked down the company that owned the rights to both, Mystic Fire, and called to request review copies. I couldn't wait to watch them and, after work, I hurried home, popped *Kerouac* into the VCR and settled on the sofa with Flannery. A few seconds after I pushed *play*, fifties and sixties TV fixture Steve Allen appeared in a vintage clip, circa 1959, wearing his trademark black-rimmed specs and sitting at a white baby grand.

"In the early nineteen-fifties, the nation recognized in its midst the social movement called, *uh*, Beat Generation," he said, picking up a jet-black-jacketed book sitting on top of the piano. I recognized it right away—*On the Road*, hot off the press, the studio lights reflecting off its still-shiny cover. The camera zoomed in for a close-up. "The novel titled *On the Road* became a bestseller and its author Jack Kerouac became a celebrity," Allen continued, "partly because he'd written a powerful and successful book, partly because he, *eh*, seemed to be the embodiment of this new generation. So here he is, Jack Kerouac."

A dimly lit figure sitting in the background stood and walked forward. It was Kerouac, who emerged from the shadows and sat at the back of the piano. He was dressed casually, in a gray sport coat and white shirt, collar open, no tie.

"Jack told me a little earlier he was nervous. Are you nervous now?" asked Allen.

"No," replied Kerouac, shaking his head, sullen and sad-eyed.

"No? Good," said Allen. "Jack, *uh*, got a couple a square questions but I think the answers will be interesting. How long did it take you to write *On the Road*?"

"Three weeks," said Kerouac.

"How many?"

"Three weeks," repeated Kerouac.

"Three weeks? Geez, that's amazing. How long were you on the road itself?"

"Seven years."

"Seven years." Allen mulled this information over for a moment. "I was on the road once for three weeks and it took me seven years to write about it," he said. Scattered laughter erupted from the audience. "The other way around. I've heard that you write so fast that you don't like to use regular typing paper but instead you prefer to use one big long roll of paper. Is that true?"

"Yeah, when I write narrative novels and I don't want to change my narrative thought, I keep going," explained Kerouac.

"You don't want to change the pages at the end, you mean?" asked Allen.

"A hundred-foot-long Teletype paper," said Kerouac.

"Oh, Teletype rolls. Where do you buy them?" asked Allen.

"Huh?" asked Kerouac, looking slightly confused.

"Where do you get the paper?" asked Allen again.

"Eh, *Teletype paper*," said Kerouac with a shrug. "For narratives it's good. Keep going."

"I got the most hard question of all but everybody always puts it to you, I'm sure," said Allen, "uh, *because* everybody always puts it to you. How would you define the word *beat*?"

Kerouac laughed. "Heh heh. Welllll... *sympathetic.*"

Yes, I thought. Exactly.

12

I ARRIVED AT WORK the next morning to discover my office door open. I stopped short when I saw Jay inside, sitting at my desk and writing. For a moment, I just stood and watched him, noticing how the early morning sunlight that filtered through the window traced his silhouette, catching a stray strand of hair that fell across his forehead, outlining the small bump in his otherwise strong straight nose and exaggerating the five o'clock shadow he already had at nine o'clock in the morning. He glanced up unexpectedly and I did a double take, suddenly aware that the few seconds I'd been standing there seemed like an eternity.

"Hey! I was just leaving you a note—this is my baby," he said, gesturing toward a red canvas bag on my desk. He fumbled with the zipper and then yanked the bag open, exposing what looked like a small, battered old suitcase. A silver lock snapped open with a touch of his finger and he lifted the top to reveal his vintage Royal.

"Jay, it's beautiful," I said, admiring the smooth black metal casing and ebony keys.

"I thought I might take it to that place you found tomorrow, to get it cleaned up a bit. Needs a new ribbon. And a new handle for the case."

"I can look for one to buy while we're there," I said. "And then we can start writing our book together."

He closed the case and patted the top. "Would you like to try it out?"

"Sure."

I opened the case as soon as he'd gone and ran my fingers over the typewriter's smooth metal surface. A moment later I went to the art department and asked Jay if he had his journal with him, the pad of coarse paper he'd written in at Rudy's.

"Yeah, I do," he said, looking in his backpack.

"Can I have a page from it?"

Without asking why I wanted it, he ripped one out and handed it to me.

"Thanks." I returned to my office, placed it in the typewriter and wrote Jay a short poem off the top of my head titled "28&94."

"Little did we know when / we got to the / Gotham Book Mart / there were 2 copies of / Ginsberg's new journal, / slipcased, numbered and / signed, patiently waiting for / us to take them home."

I left it in the roller, closed the case and put it back in the red bag. Jay came by later and picked it up. I didn't tell him about the poem.

THE NEXT DAY, SATURDAY, I hopped a subway to Penn Station at one-thirty to meet Jay and Zahra. He was coming from Long Island, she was coming from Brooklyn and the three of us were going to see Martin Tytell. A moment after I arrived at Thirty-Fourth Street, I spotted Zahra just ahead of me in the tunnel to the station, awkwardly trying to balance a large brown leather bag on one shoulder and the red canvas bag that contained Jay's typewriter on the other. I called her name and she turned, squinting in surprise.

"Welcome back!" I said, swooping up and relieving her of the red bag.

"Harry!" She smiled and then turned serious. "I can carry that."

"You carry *that*," I said, pointing to the leather shoulder bag.

"No, really," she persisted.

"No, *really*," I countered.

Reluctantly, she acquiesced.

"So, how was the West Coast?" I asked as we walked.

"I had a good time with my dad but I missed Jay. I'm glad to be home."

Jay's train was just pulling in. While we waited for him to appear at the top of the stairs from the platform, I set the red bag down. As soon as I did, Zahra picked it up and held it tightly.

"Hey!" yelled Jay when he spotted us. He gave Zahra a kiss and a hug and slapped me on the back. "Are we ready?"

We headed to the subway but just as we were about to go through the turnstile for the downtown A/C line, a loudspeaker sputtered with the news that the trains were experiencing significant delays.

Jay looked at his watch. "How late is Martin open, Har?"

"Three o'clock. And it's already two-fifteen. Maybe we should just take a cab."

Jay flagged a taxi on Eighth. I held the door open for Zahra to go in and then waited for Jay to get in beside her.

"I'm not sitting in the middle," he said, laughing.

I didn't want to sit in the middle either but I gave in. Jay climbed in behind me.

"Fulton Street," Jay told the driver. "And hurry, there's a fire." Inexplicably, the cabbie turned onto Thirty-Fourth Street, right into the Saturday afternoon traffic jam that always surrounded Macy's and Madison Square Garden. Jay, Zahra and I looked at each other in disbelief.

"Go around, go around," urged Jay as we came to a stop behind another cab.

"The fastest way is the FDR Drive," said the cabbie.

"Fine, then take it," said Jay.

The driver made a left and headed east. Ten minutes later, we were only two blocks from Macy's.

"Did you pick the *slowest* street?" asked Zahra.

We got to Fulton Street at three-fifteen, tumbled out of the taxi and practically ran up the block to number 116. The door was locked. Zahra pushed a buzzer next to it. No response. Then she noticed a frayed wire protruding from the wall just below the buzzer. Clearly it had been disconnected.

"*Ohhh,*" she sighed.

The three of us stared at the door, each thinking the same thing. We were so close.

"Are you looking for Martin?" asked a voice behind us.

Standing on the sidewalk was a woman in a dark blue suit, with a knot of gray hair on the top of her head crisscrossed by tight braids.

"Yes," I replied. "We're looking for Martin. But we're a little late."

"I'll let you in," said the woman, taking out a key and unlocking the door. "I'm his wife, Pearl."

Jay and Zahra stepped inside. I watched as Pearl walked to a car parked across the street. There was an elderly man in the passenger's seat whom I assumed was Martin Tytell. I called to Jay that Martin was on his way, noticing as I did that he and Zahra were standing in the back of the small foyer, arms wrapped around each other, kissing passionately. Embarrassed, I turned around just as Martin came through the door.

"Martin, my name's Harry, I had called you about…"

"Yes, yes, I remember," he said, pointing to a worn marble staircase. "Come on. I've already turned the elevator off."

He led us up to the second floor, through a wooden door with a pane of frosted glass, like the door of a detective's office in a classic film noir. Inside, it was cramped and chaotic, with shelf upon shelf of typewriters in various states of repair. Martin called a name I didn't catch and an Indian guy in a white lab coat appeared out of nowhere.

"Show this man some typewriters," Martin instructed him, pointing to me. Then, to Jay, "And what can I do for you?"

"I'd like you to take a look at my typewriter," said Jay. "It needs a little work."

He placed his red bag on a table, took out the typewriter case

84

and opened it. For a second, he stared at the sheet of brown paper in the roller, the paper that contained the poem I'd typed. I'd thought he would discover it the previous night but I realized he was seeing it for the first time. Without a word, he pulled the paper out of the roller, folded it in half and slipped it into his back pocket.

"What was that?" asked Zahra. "Something you wrote?"

"No," said Jay. "Something Harry wrote."

Zahra's face clouded in confusion for a moment. She looked from Jay to me and then back to Jay as Martin immediately started examining the typewriter.

"I haven't seen one *this* old in a long time," he said.

The Man in the White Coat, meanwhile, was busy showing me a succession of models he pulled from seemingly random locations around the room.

"Anything older?" I asked when he unveiled a typewriter that looked to be from the early sixties.

He stepped back to survey a bank of shelves that stretched from the floor to the twenty-foot ceiling.

"I need a ladder," he said, heading off for parts unknown.

"Come with me," said Martin to Jay and Zahra, and the three of them headed off in another direction.

I tapped at the keyboard of an old Underwood sitting atop a filing cabinet for a few minutes, then followed the sound of Martin's voice to a worn wooden workbench where he was demonstrating to Jay and Zahra the benefits a thorough cleaning would have on a typewriter.

"Give it a bath and it's good for another fifty years," he said, holding up a shiny steel gear.

I wandered back to the area just inside the door, where Martin's assistant was stepping off the bottom rung of an old wooden ladder holding a black case. He set it on a table and opened it, revealing a sleek black Royal inside, just as Martin returned, with Jay and Zahra in tow.

"Wonderful machine," said Martin, eyeing the Royal. "Fifty-one years old. They don't make 'em like that anymore."

I slipped a piece of paper into the roller and tried it out while Martin explained to Jay what his typewriter needed.

"So, that comes to five hundred eighty-five dollars," I heard Martin say to Jay. "Just write out a check while I make out a receipt."

"Do you want it *now*?" asked Jay.

"Yep," replied Martin matter-of-factly as he walked over to a desk in a small office. "Can't afford to put the money out in advance myself."

Jay and Zahra looked at each other, unprepared for this turn of events.

"Jay," I offered, "if you want, I could..."

"No, Har, it's all right," Jay assured me before I could finish. "We'll just have to come back."

"If you read me the model number on the back of the machine, I'll tell you how old it is," called Martin. Jay did as asked and Martin returned a few minutes later, fairly glowing. "That machine is from 1933," he said. "Fifty years old is an antique, which means that one's a double antique."

"Martin," said Jay, "I'm really sorry, but I can't pay you right now."

"Then come back when you can," said Martin with a shrug.

"Could I leave my typewriter here so I don't have to carry it back and forth?" asked Jay.

"I suppose," said Martin. Jay closed his typewriter case, removed it from the red canvas bag and hoisted the empty bag over his shoulder. "Here's your receipt," Martin continued. "Hold on to it." He looked at me. "What have you decided?"

"I've decided I like this one," I said, indicating the Royal. "How much is it?"

"Six hundred and fifty dollars."

The same price as a first edition of *On the Road*. "I need to think about it."

"Fine," he said. "Come back when we have more time."

Outside, Pearl was waiting patiently behind the wheel of the car at the curb. Martin slid in beside her and the two took off up Fulton as Jay, Zahra and I headed in the opposite direction.

"What did he say your typewriter is worth?" I asked Jay.

"Around two thousand, after it's completely overhauled."

"Way to go, Jay," I said.

"Way to go, *Zahra*," he countered. "Best birthday present I ever got." He took her hand in his as she smiled. "Har, are you going to get one?"

"I think so," I said. "I wasn't prepared to spend six-fifty, though."

"Har, it's never going to go *down* in value. Think of it as an investment."

I smiled, recognizing the words I'd said to him about the Ginsberg journal the day before.

We decided to get something to eat, so we walked to the South Street Seaport and stopped in a café, where we had a mediocre meal of dry sandwiches. When we finished, Jay got up to make a few calls from a pay phone to confirm plans for the Bo Diddley concert later.

"So, who's all going?" asked Zahra when he returned. "Your brother?"

"No, Anthony's sick," said Jay.

"Marilyn and Zeus?"

"Zeus, yes, but not Marilyn."

"Nestor?"

"Yes, Nestor. It's not quite as big a crowd as we thought."

"Who's Nestor?" I asked.

"A friend of mine from Pratt," replied Jay.

"Speaking of which," said Zahra, "did you tell Harry about my show?"

Jay shook his head. "I forgot."

"I have an exhibit opening in two weeks," she explained. "In the main gallery at Pratt. You have to come."

"I'd love to," I told her.

Jay asked if we were ready to go. Zahra wondered aloud

whether she should get a cappuccino.

"Based on the quality of our lunch, I doubt this place makes the kind of cappuccino they serve at Dante's," I said.

"Oh, have you been to Dante's?" she asked.

"Yeah, Jay took me," I replied.

She looked at him, an unspoken question on her face.

"The night we went to see Deanna," he explained.

She turned to me. "Dante's is *our* place," she said, beaming at Jay.

We all fell silent for a few seconds and then Zahra suggested we get ice cream.

Jay perked up. "We used to have ice cream every night when we lived together," he told me, smiling at Zahra. She smiled back at him. "We'd just sit there and eat a whole pint each," he continued. "My favorite was Häagen-Dazs mint chocolate chip."

"I have a weakness for Ben and Jerry's chocolate chip cookie dough," I confessed.

"What are we waiting for?" asked Zahra.

We stood up and headed for the door. Glancing back at our table, I noticed Jay had forgotten his now-empty red bag, which he'd placed on the vacant chair next to mine. I grabbed it and followed Jay and Zahra outside.

"Let's look for a Häagen-Dazs place," said Jay, who stopped suddenly after we'd taken only a few steps. "I forgot my bag!" he yelled, whirling around.

"It's all right, Jay, I've got it," I said, holding it up for him to see.

"Oh, thanks, Har," he said, quickly reaching for it.

"I can carry it," I offered.

"Nah," he said, taking it from me. "Really. That's all right."

We found a Häagen-Dazs shop on the pier and bought cones—butter pecan for Zahra, butterscotch vanilla for Jay and cookie dough for me (it was good but not as good as Ben and Jerry's). As we meandered back through the Seaport up to Fulton, Zahra said that she was going to her apartment in Brooklyn to get ready for the concert. She asked Jay if he was going out to Long Island to do the same.

"No, it's too late," he said. "It's nearly four o'clock and we're supposed to meet everyone at the Art Bar at seven before we head to Chicago Blues."

They wandered several steps ahead, talking quietly, and I purposely lagged behind to give them some privacy. When they turned around after a few minutes and waited for me to catch up, however, I sensed their moods had shifted. It was nothing I could put my finger on, but I knew that something had changed. As we continued up Fulton, Zahra stopped to have her palm read by a sidewalk fortune-teller. Jay watched from several feet away, deep in thought.

"Any good news?" he asked Zahra when her consultation had concluded. I didn't catch her reply, only her tone, which was somber.

A moment later, we arrived at the subway entrance, where Jay and Zahra stopped.

"What are we doing?" I asked.

"We're going to Brooklyn to take showers and get changed," said Jay. "Aren't you taking the subway, too?" For a second I thought he was asking me to go with them. He sensed my confusion. "Uptown, I mean."

"Yeah, I guess I am," I said. "So, should I call you?"

"I'll call *you*," said Jay. "After we figure out what's going on." We headed down the stairs to the A/C line. The uptown and downtown trains left from opposite sides of the same platform so we said our goodbyes there.

"See you soon," said Jay, shaking my hand.

Zahra gave me a hug. My train arrived first. I got on and waved to Jay through the door. He waved back. As the train pulled away I noticed that he and Zahra were standing several feet apart.

At home, I took a quick shower and had just finished toweling off when the phone rang. It was Jay.

"I'm not going tonight, Har," he said over the sound of the

subway in the background. "I'm on my way out to Long Island. I don't know if you still want to go, but I'm not."

"What's wrong?" I asked, startled by the sudden turn of events.

"I'm just going through some stuff. It's... I don't want to talk about it."

"I had a feeling something wasn't right earlier," I said. "Are you sure you don't want to talk about it?"

"Yeah. I'll talk to you on Monday."

I hung up, stunned and not sure what to do. I figured that something must have happened between him and Zahra and I felt bad, for both of them. I wanted to help but I wanted to respect Jay's wishes. Best to wait until Monday.

I called Chicago Blues, thinking that I might go to see Bo by myself. More bad news. "Bo Diddley won't be performing tonight," said the woman who answered. "He's having back trouble."

13

COME MONDAY, I WAS ANXIOUS to talk with Jay and find out what had happened on Saturday. When he didn't stop by my office first thing, I figured he was running late, so I was surprised to see him sitting at his desk, already working, when I went to the art department for the ten o'clock editorial meeting. He looked up and smiled but he didn't say anything. After the meeting, I went over to talk with Jay's fellow designer Mitch about a layout he was doing for a story of mine, and when we were through, I walked over to Jay, who was thumbing through the new issue of the magazine.

"Everything all right?" I asked quietly.

"Yeah," he replied without looking up.

I left, sensing that everything wasn't all right, but I figured I would find out what was up over lunch, when we would be alone, when we could talk.

I headed to the art department at one-thirty but Jay wasn't at his computer. Ted said that he'd already left for lunch, a few minutes earlier. I didn't know what to think. Jay and I ate lunch together nearly every day, and if for some reason one of us couldn't make it, we always let the other know.

I walked over to our usual place but he wasn't there. I bought a sandwich and brought it back to my office where I sat at my desk and ate it but didn't really taste it. Afterward, I wandered to the art department, carrying a copy of the Ann Charters Kerouac biography I'd promised to lend Jay. I figured I would just leave it on his desk while he was out. When I got to the art department, however, there was Jay, sitting at his desk with his checkbook in front of him, paying his bills.

"I brought this in for you," I said, setting the book next to his keyboard.

He looked at it without looking at me. "Oh, thanks," he said just as his phone rang, cutting off any further conversation. I wandered away, still unsure of what was going on.

Later that afternoon, I glanced up from my computer as Jay was passing my office. He looked at me without saying anything and continued walking. Before I could stop myself, I called out his name. He came back and stood in the doorway, expressionless.

"Jay, is everything okay?" I asked, surprised by the tenuous tone of my voice.

He smiled slightly. "Yeah, I just need a little space."

"I sensed that you did. I was just worried…" I trailed off, unable to continue.

"Everything's fine," he insisted. "I'll explain it to you when the time is right."

"Okay," I said. "I just needed to hear you say that."

He smiled weakly again and then disappeared.

I felt relieved, but the effect was temporary. When I went to the art department with another question for Mitch, I saw Jay and Ted joking with one of the magazine's researchers, a young woman named Marthé who had recently moved to New York from Belgium. Marthé ping-ponged between boyfriends so often that Ted had affectionately dubbed her "the Belgian Waffler" and teased her about it incessantly. On this occasion, Jay had joined in, and he was laughing as though nothing was bothering him. I didn't know what to make of it. Was it just another example of Jay keeping his personal life personal, or was there something wrong between Jay and me that I was unaware of? My doubts began to get the better of me. I tried not to listen, but when Jay left at the end of the day without saying goodbye, I caved. He was consciously avoiding me.

That evening, I sat on my bed thinking back over everything we'd ever said to each other and everything we'd ever done together, trying to convince myself that the Jay I thought I knew was the Jay I really knew. "You think too much," he'd told me. And I did. It was a curse. He'd assured me that everything was fine, that he'd tell me what was going on when the time was right, that he just needed some space. That should have been enough to allay any doubts. Shouldn't it?

My confusion deepened the next day. Mitch was alone in the art department when I arrived for the morning meeting. Ted had the day off, he told me, and Jay had called and left a message on Mitch's voicemail saying that he had "a family emergency." I wondered if there was more going on than I had imagined and I debated whether to call him but decided against it. Give him some space.

First thing the following morning, I was at my desk, staring out the door of my office, deep in thought, when Jay walked by. For a second, I didn't even see him.

"What's up, Har?" he asked as he passed, just as he usually did, though I thought I saw a sadness in his eyes I'd never seen in them before.

A few minutes later, I headed to the art department for the morning meeting, arriving before any of the other editors. Jay and Mitch were the only two there. No sign of Ted.

"Just you and Mitch today?" I asked Jay, in a tentative attempt to generate small talk that might indicate where things stood.

"Yeah," he replied. "Ted's buying a new house and has a few details to take care of."

He looked at me and smiled and it seemed as though whatever had been bothering him wasn't bothering him any longer. An hour later, he walked by my office again, slowing down to proudly point out the Coconuts bag he was carrying. I waited a minute for him to get to his desk and then gave him a call.

"Is that *The Jack Kerouac Collection*?" I asked, trying to sound matter-of-fact.

"Yeah," he answered. "Just came in."

I sensed that we were back on track and I was hoping that we would be able to talk about what had been going on over lunch. On my way past the art department around one, I noticed Jay at his desk reading the booklet that came with *The Jack Kerouac Collection*. Half-hour later, I called to see if he was ready to eat. Mitch answered Jay's line, however, and said that Jay wasn't there. He'd already gone to lunch.

Once again, I didn't know what to think. I wandered over to our usual place, got a sandwich to go and sat on the wall in front of our building, where I forced myself to eat the first half and then threw the rest away. Not ready to return to work, I retrieved the copy of *Jack's Book* Jay had loaned me from my office and resumed my position on the wall. Forty minutes later, when I realized I could barely remember a word of what I'd read, I headed back to my office, decidedly unsettled.

I was at my desk for only a moment when Mercedes stormed in and collapsed in a chair.

"Help me," she pleaded. "Donal is torturing me. I asked him if I could do a story on Rusty from *Shining Time Station*. He said yes, but he's told me to redo it five times already. I can't take it!"

As a fellow target of Donal's petulance, I sympathized with her. Donal could see as well as I that Mercedes had the makings of a good writer, but whereas I tried to nurture her talent—Mercedes was one of the few staffers from whom I accepted contributions to my "Bomb-Sniffing Dogs" column—Donal unwittingly often discouraged it, validating her story ideas and then forcing her to do so many rewrites that she questioned whether she was capable of constructing even a simple sentence. At that point, she usually turned to me, and I would patiently assist in pulling together all the loose threads and advise her how to weave them into an actual article.

"Haven't you learned how to handle Donal yet?" I asked. "The only time he gets a chip on his shoulder is when you get a chip on yours. I don't know why—that's just the way he is. But if you ask him for help, he'll be the first to give it to you. He enjoys being a mentor."

"I don't always *feel* like being mentored," Mercedes sniped.

"Well, then, you get what you deserve," I said. "You know what he's like. Use it to your advantage. Now let's see what you've got."

As Mercedes spread several sheets of false starts on my desk, I was thankful to have something so cut-and-dry to occupy my mind.

"So, who's Rusty?" I asked.

"Thomas the Tank Engine's new friend on *Shining Time Station*," Mercedes explained.

"And what makes him so special that you want to write an article about him?"

"Well, that's just it. Rusty isn't a him."

"Then what makes *her* so special?"

"Rusty isn't a her, either. The show's producers say that Rusty is neither a him nor a her."

"That's pretty special all right," I allowed. "Progressive, even."

"The thing is," said Mercedes, "kids love Rusty. Rusty's video, *Rusty to the Rescue*, is outselling all the other *Shining Time Station* videos."

"And the reason is...?"

"That's what I'm trying to figure out for my story. There is some disagreement."

"I can imagine."

"The producers say that a character who is 'gender neutral' allows both boys and girls to identify with Rusty's personality."

"And what *is* Rusty's personality?"

Mercedes shrugged. "'Spunky,' according to the producers."

"And what does Rusty look like?"

"Androgynous. But kind of creepy, if you ask me."

"*All* of those trains on *Shining Time Station* are creepy. Why don't their faces move, anyway? They look like something Edvard Munch dreamed up. Haven't the producers ever heard of special effects? It's enough to give a kid nightmares. It's enough to give *me* nightmares. You should do a story on *that*."

Mercedes sighed and rolled her eyes.

"Okay, okay. Let's stick to Rusty. You know, this scenario begs a bigger question: Why assign trains a gender to begin with? What makes one train a *him* and another train a *her*? Isn't that confusing? Aren't all trains inherently a Rusty, free to be and love whomever they like? Maybe that's why kids like Rusty. Feeling confused about male and female trains? Rusty to the rescue!"

"Um," said Mercedes, "the producers didn't say anything about love."

"Right. So, have you talked with anyone else?"

"I wasn't sure who to ask for an opinion."

"Try RuPaul."

"RuPaul?"

"Yeah, I'm sure he'll be happy to weigh in—and he gives good sound bites."

Mercedes frowned for a moment and then brightened. "Ah, right."

As she headed to her cubicle, I looked up to see Jay going by my office on his way back from lunch. I'd been gone a long time; he'd been gone even longer. He walked past without stopping, without pausing, without even glancing in my direction. Instead, he stared straight ahead, seemingly lost in thought.

Half-hour later, I realized I needed to talk with him about a layout he was designing for an article I was editing. I headed to the art department but he was on the phone when I arrived, loudly joking and laughing with whomever was on the other end of the line. I left without him seeing me, wondering if I was the only one he wasn't talking to.

Back in my office, I felt so frazzled that I debated whether to leave for the day but decided that I needed to know what was going on. I waited a while and then returned to the art department, where I found Jay at his computer, working on the layout for my story.

Sensing someone standing behind him, he turned around.

"You're editing this, right?" he asked.

"Yeah," I answered weakly, taking a seat next to him on the edge of his desk.

He studied me for a moment and from the concern in his eyes I realized how awful I must have looked. I dictated a headline for him to replace the working title and made a few suggestions about the layout, but mostly I just sat there, quietly watching him work.

Forty minutes later, he hit *save*. "To be continued tomorrow," he announced. "Time to go home."

"Mind if I walk out with you?" I asked as he shouldered his backpack.

He nodded tentatively. "Sure."

I went back to my office and grabbed my own backpack. Jay swung by a moment later. Neither of us said a word on the way to the elevator or during the ride to the lobby. It was not till we were about to enter the revolving door and head outside that I finally broke the silence.

"Jay, is everything the same between us?" I managed to ask. My mouth was so dry my tongue stuck to my teeth. "Is everything okay?"

In his eyes I saw the same sadness I'd seen in them that morning. "We'll talk about it. All right, Har?"

My heart sank as I pushed through the door. "It sounds like everything *isn't* the same."

He said nothing as we both walked toward the entrance of his subway at Forty-Seventh, pausing at the top of the steps.

"Tell me what's going on, Jay," I said, my voice quavering.

He searched my eyes, for what I wasn't sure. "I wanted to talk with you, Har, but before I did, I really wanted to make sure I used the right words. I didn't want to just blurt something out."

"It's okay, Jay, just say it."

"Har, remember how I said I like to keep my personal life separate from work? Well, this is why: Last Saturday I felt like I was in a really weird situation." I thought he was referring to a weird situation between him and Zahra. "Har, I felt like I was in the middle of two people vying for my attention. Zahra felt... in the restaurant, you picked up my bag for me."

"What?" I didn't see his point.

"You picked up my bag without telling me and then you carried it for me until I noticed I'd left it behind."

"Yeah, but it was no big deal."

"And then you ordered the same ice cream as me."

"No I didn't."

"Har, they were things that wouldn't have made a difference if you and I were alone."

Suddenly, I realized the awful truth of the matter and every hesitation I'd ever had about letting Jay into my life materialized before me. I thought I had been so careful. I thought I had allowed myself to feel for Jay only what Jay felt for me. But, no. I had made the same mistake I had made once before, a mistake I swore I would never make again. I had allowed myself to think of Jay as something he wasn't, something he could never be. Lost in the giddy, dizzy discovery of someone who seemed to care for me as much as I cared for him, I had lowered my defenses and ignored the warning signs that I was indulging a tendency to believe what I wanted to believe, to see what wasn't there. And, to make matters worse, I had come between Jay and Zahra. I had thoughtlessly and carelessly stumbled into a space that was theirs and theirs alone, a space that could ever only hold two, not three.

But had I really misinterpreted everything? Jay had said that what had happened wouldn't have mattered if he and I were alone, which suggested that he was comfortable with the level of intimacy we shared. It also suggested that Zahra was not, despite her allusions to the contrary. If that were true, however, shouldn't Jay have foreseen the inevitable? No, this had nothing to do with Jay, nothing to do with Zahra and everything to do with me. *I* was responsible for what had happened. *I* was the reason he'd canceled on Saturday. It was all too much to take.

"Har, I felt like you were clinging to me," said Jay quietly, still struggling to find the right words. "And I know why. And I understand. But Zahra's the most important person in my life. She's the one I'll always turn to. I have a commitment there." He paused. "Har, this is really hard because I know you're really vulnerable right now."

"Yeah, I *am*," I replied. "But I don't want you to feel that you can't say what you want to say because of that. I want you to want me in your life because you like me, because you enjoy my companionship. Not because I'm vulnerable. I've really enjoyed all the time we've spent together, just you and me, but I knew it couldn't last. I know that you have other important people in your life."

"I had lunch with Marilyn and Zeus today," he said. "I haven't seen them in a few weeks."

"I *know* you haven't, Jay, don't misinterpret this—it's the only way I can think to describe it—but it's like we were going through our honeymoon period."

Jay smiled at my choice of words and attempted to elicit a smile from me but I was beyond smiling.

"Come on, Har, lighten up. You're too sensitive."

"I know I am."

We were both quiet for a moment.

"So, are things still the same between us?" I asked.

"Har, we're still friends," Jay replied. "Nothing's changed. We'll still do all the things we said we were going to do. Over time."

Despite his assurance to the contrary, his final qualifier seemed to suggest that things *had* changed, however slightly, and I said the only thing I could think to say.

"You mean a lot to me, Jay." But even as I uttered those words, I realized that they only served to illustrate exactly why we were standing there at that moment.

He gazed at me affectionately. "I'm not going anywhere, Har. Trust me. Are you all right?"

"Yeah, I'm all right," I said, trying to sound convincing.

"Are you *sure*?" he asked, putting his hand on my shoulder.

"Yeah," I insisted, but I could tell he still didn't believe me.

"Har, I've got to run. I'll see you tomorrow."

He smiled and extended his hand. I placed mine in his and he held it tightly for a moment and then let go and hurried down the stairs to the subway below. I opened my mouth just as he was about to disappear from view. "Jay, I really am all right," I wanted to yell. But I didn't. Because he probably wouldn't have heard me. And because I really wasn't.

14

I WALKED THE WHOLE way home. All thirty blocks. Crashing next to Flannery on my bed when I arrived at my apartment, I lay there for a full hour, rethinking, retracing, reexamining every last detail of the past several months, sifting for evidence I should have seen the first time around, clues that indicated I was repeating a pattern I thought I had finally broken.

Looking back, it was all so obvious. Looking back, I could clearly discern every moment of self-delusion, every instance when I had disregarded everything I thought I had learned, all leading up to the incident of the red bag. I had told Jay that it was no big deal. I had told myself the same thing. But, in reality, it *was* a big deal. The fact that I enjoyed carrying Jay's bag for him, even for a minute, that I was happy to surprise him with it and that I offered to continue carrying it all indicated what was going on below the surface, even if I chose to think otherwise. It wasn't just the tip of the iceberg. It *was* the iceberg.

A part of me wanted to believe that Jay and I shared a passionate and heartfelt friendship. And we did. It was a friendship unlike any other I'd ever had. That much I knew. But another part of me had plumbed the depths of that friendship in hope of finding something else. That much I now knew. Or, more accurately, that much I now admitted to myself.

I was in love. That was the simple truth of the matter. I was in love with someone who was unavailable, in every sense of the word. I had put Jay in an awful position, and I had only to think of how awkward I felt when that dark-haired girl at Rudy's pressed her leg against mine to realize how awkward Jay must have felt. Even worse, because I was so vulnerable, as Jay had noted, because Jay knew my story, even if he didn't know all the details, because I had no one else to turn to, he must have felt responsible for me. He must have felt trapped. What had I done?

I picked myself up off my bed and attempted to resume some semblance of normalcy. I tried reading more of *Jack's Book* but I couldn't see the words on the page. I tried eating but I couldn't swallow. What I really wanted to do was to talk with Jay. Despite everything we'd said, there was still so much more to say. I hesitated for hours, fearing that any further conversation would only make matters worse, but I finally convinced myself of the contrary and called him at his mother's house on Long Island at nine-forty-five. His mom answered.

"Hello, Mrs. Bishop?" I began. I'd never spoken with her before. "My name's Harry. I'm a friend of Jay's. Is he in?"

"No," she replied. "He's over his brother's. He said he'd be in around ten."

"Could you ask him to call me?"

I returned to *Jack's Book* but I still couldn't concentrate, watching the numbers on a digital clock slowly advance—10, 10:17, 10:31, 10:53. I never should have called, I concluded. He got my message and he's not going to call back. I *had* made matters worse. Emotionally exhausted, I drifted off to sleep on my couch, waking with a start at eleven-twenty and deciding to turn in. The phone rang just as I did.

"Har, it's Jay. What's up?" A familiar voice, a familiar tone.

I cleared my throat, buying time as I tried to clear my mind. "Jay, I just wanted to say... I don't *know* what I wanted to say..." I paused. "Jay, I'm scared. I'm scared I'm going to screw this up. I'm scared I already screwed this up."

"Har, calm down. Everything's going to be all right."

"Remember how I told you that I'm always afraid I'm going to fuck things up?"

"Yes, and remember what I said in response? Believe me, Har, it wasn't you. It was the situation."

"Jay," I said slowly, preparing to get to the heart of what had happened, "I hope you know how I feel about you. I'm really fond of you, fonder than I ever admitted to myself, even though my feelings must have been obvious. I tried to be straight with you, but I'm not sure I always was."

"I know how you feel," said Jay. "And you've always been straight with me. In a manner of speaking." He laughed a little at that, trying to get me to laugh along with him. I managed to, for a moment.

"Jay, I hesitated to bring it up, but I had to, just in case you weren't sure. I wanted to be honest with you."

"I think you're more honest with me than you are with yourself, sometimes," said Jay. "You're not that hard to read, you know. Really. But, believe me, none of this was about you, Harry. It was the *situation*."

It was the second time he'd used that word and it seemed an odd selection, albeit one that he'd arrived at after much careful consideration, specific but not too specific, intended to incriminate no one.

"Har, listen. There are a few things going on I can't really talk about but the reason this happened is because Zahra really needs me right now. She's going through a lot—she's moving, she's trying to finish her thesis, she's thinking about graduation. I can't tell you everything, but I can tell you that we're at a point in our relationship where it's just the two of us. Nobody else."

Reading between the lines, it seemed that Zahra had definitely been unsettled by the easy, elusive affinity into which Jay and I had fallen while she was not around. But what was she afraid of? That our friendship would evolve into something else? That it even could? Or, was there some other aspect to all this that I hadn't fathomed?

"Jay, I understand what you're saying but I wish you felt that you could have talked with me without waiting so long. Silence is the worst. I know now that you were searching for the right words, but I had no way of knowing that till you told me. From my perspective, it just seemed like you were avoiding me and I didn't know why. I hope nothing like this ever happens again, but if it does, if we have a misunderstanding of some sort, please, just talk with me."

"I will, Har," he promised. "I'm sorry I put you through that."

"Jay, the worst thing for me was that all the ghosts from my past appeared. People I loved who are no longer in my life. I thought I was beyond all that, but there they were, once again, and I started to doubt things that are true."

"I'm not anyone you've ever known, Har," said Jay simply.

A single unstoppable tear burned down my face. "No, Jay, you're not."

"Har, listen. The longer we're in each other's lives, you'll see sides of me you've never seen. And vice versa. We'll get past this. We're *already* past this. There'll be other things like this and we'll get past them, too."

"Jay, today at lunch I was reading *Jack's Book* and it struck me how the Beats stuck together no matter what. Whether they had a misunderstanding, whether they moved far away from one another, whether one of them said, 'Go ahead, you can sleep with my girlfriend,' or, 'Go ahead, you can sleep with my boyfriend....' Jay laughed. "...they remained friends. Whatever brought them together to begin with kept them together. That was all that ultimately mattered."

Jay was quiet for a moment, thinking. "So, what are you saying?" he asked finally. "You want to sleep with my girlfriend?"

"No," I replied. "Not even."

"'GOOFING AT THE TABLE,'" Jay began, as we took a seat at our usual place for lunch the next day.

"Been listening to *The Jack Kerouac Collection?*" I asked, recognizing both the poem and Jay's Kerouac-inspired recitation of it right away.

"Yeah, it's great. So, I gave my signed and numbered first edition of Ginsberg's *Journals* to Zahra."

"Really?" I knew how much it meant to him.

"Yeah, it only seemed right, because she's the one who got me into the Beats and she's more into Ginsberg than I am."

I wondered if it also only seemed right because of what had happened a few days earlier. Though we were already past those events, just as Jay had said we would be, and things had returned to the way they'd been, I knew that things had to change. I knew that *I* had to change. Or I would only bring us back to where we'd just been. I'd been given another chance to get it right. And if I were ever to alter the shape of things to come, I *had* to get it right.

It had occurred to me that one way to deal with the situation would be to leave, to tell Jay that I could no longer be his friend because I was incapable of changing how I felt about him as long as we remained a part of each other's lives. My feelings for him would always be in the way, something that would make both of us uncomfortable, something that would bring both of us pain. Best to make a clean break.

But to leave would be to deny that Jay and I *were* friends, before anything else, and to deny that I *could* change my feelings. No, the right thing to do, I'd decided, was to stay. To stay and fall *out of* love, to stay and be the friend to Jay that Jay was to me.

But how to fall out of love? There was little point in turning to the Beats for insight. Their lives were full of long-standing one-sided loves, further complicated by open relationships and occasional flings that offered momentary hope but guaranteed long-term frustration. The Beats may have achieved a certain enlightenment in their artistic endeavors, but when it came to their romantic affairs, they were no more enlightened than anyone else. After much thought, I decided to follow the common wisdom: Change your behavior, change your feelings. It made sense. It was a plan. And I needed a plan.

"So, are you going to write a novel this weekend?" asked Jay.

He caught me by surprise. "You *would* remember."

"This *is* the weekend of that contest, right?"

"Yeah, it is. Labor Day. The pamphlet with the entry form is hanging on the bulletin board in my office."

"I was thinking about giving it a try," said Jay. "I'm really busy this weekend—I'm helping Zahra move on Saturday, and there's a big family barbecue on Monday. But I *do* have Sunday."

"You're going to write a novel in one day?"

"If I could write a novel in three days, I could write a novel in one. Well, maybe a novella."

"But your typewriter's in the shop," I reminded him.

"I've got another typewriter, an electric one, that belonged to my dad."

"I'd like to try it," I said. "But I don't know what to write about."

"I'm sure you'll think of something."

Back at the office, I made him a photocopy of the entry form, noting that it had to be postmarked no later than that day. We each filled one out, sending them on their way in white legal-size envelopes bearing thirty-two-cent Elvis stamps.

"Good luck," said Jay. "To both of us."

Saturday morning I got up early and started right in. I'd decided that I wasn't going to write about the adventures of Jay and Harry. I would want to share whatever I wrote with Jay, and sharing something I'd written, I'd found, evoked a certain level of intimacy. If what I wrote was about the two of us, it would evoke a deeper level of intimacy, and that was the last thing I wanted to do. So, I decided I would try to write about my last year in Philadelphia, the year I went for a wild joyride with a wild co-pilot named Matteo. I had done everything in my power to put that year behind me, but the days before the fateful finale were filled with moments that I would never forget, no matter how hard I tried. It was a situation not unlike the one in which I found myself with Jay, and I thought that by revisiting it, by going back, I might finally be able to go forward. Change my behavior, change my feelings.

I sat at my keyboard and began to write, slowly at first, as I motored cautiously down a dimly remembered dirt road, and then gradually picking up speed as I hit the highway, flying by familiar landmarks with increasing comfort until I suddenly came to a complete stop. The memories were simply too much. Still.

I went to the gym to clear my mind. I always did my best thinking when I hit the weights. When I returned home a few hours later, my best thinking took me straight to my bedroom closet, where I reached for the Budweiser box I'd put on the shelf when I first moved to New York. Inside, under many layers of packing tape, were all the mementos I'd saved from the year I'd spent with Matteo. Letters, pictures, refrigerator notes, restaurant receipts, bar coasters, matchbooks, an empty Marlboro box, a one-dollar chip from the Taj Mahal in Atlantic City, a Valentine's Day card and a one-inch-thick pile of pink telephone messages from my days at *Rittenhouse Square* magazine with the words "Matteo called" written on every one.

Finally, at the very bottom of the box, I found something I'd forgotten I'd saved, a thick packet of letters held together by a rubber band. As I was about to close the lid, the packet shifted and the brittle band snapped, stinging my fingers as the letters fanned out. I hesitated, then picked one up, unfolded it and began to read. It was a letter I'd written to Matteo, an attempt to put into words what I felt but couldn't say. I had forgotten how much I'd cared for him, how much I'd loved him. In spite of everything.

15

ONE NIGHT, TWO YEARS EARLIER, I went to the Car Bar because I'd never been there. Actually, I hadn't been to many bars in Philly. I didn't particularly like bars. I was never much of a drinker and the degree to which one had a good time in a bar seemed directly proportional to the amount of alcohol one consumed. But on that particular night, I wanted a new experience, the kind of experience that only someplace unfamiliar would provide.

I made my way through the maze of dimly lit cobblestone alleys west of Broad, pressing through clouds of white steam that hissed at random from iron grates and broken pipes before I finally arrived at the nondescript wooden garage door of a nineteenth-century carriage house, the last in a row of three. The only indication that I was at the right garage door was an old Pennsylvania license plate—a vintage vanity plate—affixed to the bricks and illuminated by the light of a single low-watt bulb. On it were the words *Car Bar*, navy blue on an orange background.

I took a deep breath and pulled the handle of the door within the garage door. The door was heavier than I expected and when it finally gave, I was instantly hit with the smell of smoke and stale beer and the sounds of conversation and laughter over a hard rock soundtrack. I stepped inside, the door slammed behind me, and before I could take in anything else, I saw that everyone standing within ten feet of the entrance was staring at me. Glancing to my left I spotted the bar and quickly made my way over to it, taking a

LARRY CLOSS

seat on an empty stool at the very end.

A bartender appeared almost immediately. "What'll you have?"

I noticed he was missing a lower incisor. "Whatever's on draft," I replied, leaning back to check out my surroundings.

As my eyes adjusted to the dim light, I could see that the place was essentially still a garage—a long and narrow industrial space with a concrete floor, exposed brick walls and timber rafters. A single wooden bar ran the entire length from front to back. Behind the bar, above a shelf lined with various brands of whiskey, gin and vodka was another shelf lined with trophies—auto racing trophies, all won by the Car Bar's owner, a minor league stock car circuit runner who had hung up his helmet after a short but successful career and created the Car Bar with his winnings.

I had always heard the Car Bar attracted a rough crowd, but, to me, the patrons seemed pretty normal. Most of the guys sported nothing more daring than jeans and T-shirts. A few wore leather vests. The only serious road warrior—in black leather chaps, jacket, boots and cap—was a woman. And all the guys seemed to be ignoring her. All in all, the Car Bar just seemed like a hole in the wall, a comfortable hole in the wall, but a hole in the wall nonetheless.

The bartender returned with my beer.

"Thanks," I said as he set it in front of me and I took a swig.

He stared at me for a second. "That's one dollar."

"Oh, right." I dug my wallet out of my back pocket and handed him a buck. He took it and walked away.

Curious about the back of the bar, which I couldn't see from where I was sitting, I picked up my mug and maneuvered my way through the crowd, stopping midway to lean on the wall of the DJ booth. I suddenly felt conspicuously alone. Everyone but me seemed to be talking and laughing and having a good time with old friends or new acquaintances. In an effort to appear as though I were looking for someone I was supposed to meet, I squinted and slowly ran my eyes over the crowd. That bought me about a minute.

Nervously contemplating my next move, I took a few more steps toward the back and ran right into the inspiration for the bar's name—a bright orange 1970 Dodge Challenger with the number 22 painted on the hood and doors. In awe of the sheer incongruity, I stood and stared for a moment before realizing the car had headlights—the owner had restored the headlights removed from every stock car—and they were on. The smoke and darkness traced the trajectory of the beams. I casually turned my head to follow them and then froze. Outlined in the overlapping circles of light against the back wall was a pool table. But it wasn't the pool table that caught my eye. It was a pool player. He was slightly taller than me, tight and defined in a ribbed white tank top that accentuated his olive skin, with three days of dark stubble on his face and black hair buzzed to the same length. He had a square jaw and a thick neck circled by a silver chain and he exuded a toughness betrayed by vulnerable brown eyes that somehow sparkled even through the white haze that hovered over the pool table.

He was drinking beer from the biggest mug I'd ever seen—it must have held a quart—and he had a cigarette tucked behind his right ear, another dangling from his lips and a crushed pack of Marlboros protruding from the back right pocket of his jeans. He stood almost at attention, silent and straight-faced as he watched his opponent line up a shot, but when the ball whirled around a corner pocket and came back out again, he burst into laughter, gloating and effortlessly spinning his cue in one hand and strutting around the table.

"Come on, Matteo, just take your turn," said the guy who'd shot and missed, clearly annoyed.

Matteo leaned over the table, leveling one eye over the green felt as he carefully calculated angles and trajectories. He stood and shot in one quick decisive motion, pulling his stick back and slamming it into the cue ball with a single sharp thrust. The cue ball shot across the table and cracked into another ball that hit the cup of a side pocket with a loud dull thud and sank out of sight.

"Score!" yelled Matteo.

He had a slight Spanish accent and a deep scratchy voice, the kind caused by too few hours of sleep and too many cigarettes. After a long gulp of beer, he considered his next move, gleefully taking his good old time and grinning as his opponent stood by helplessly rolling his eyes. A few minutes passed before he was ready. Finally, he set his cigarette in an ashtray on a ledge behind the pool table, took his best shot and missed. It was the other guy's turn to gloat.

"¿Ah, y qué?" said Matteo, laughing like he couldn't have cared less.

With a half-smirk, he watched as the other guy carefully planned and executed his next shot, sinking the eight ball with just a gentle tap.

"Good game," said Matteo, walking over to the winner and extending his right hand. The other guy smiled and put his hand out but just as they were about to shake Matteo yanked his hand away. "Psych!" he yelled with a wicked laugh.

His rival shook his head and frowned. Matteo stepped over to a small blackboard with a list of names on it that was hanging on the wall near the pool table. He picked up a tiny stub of chalk and crossed out the name at the bottom, *Matteo Ortiz.*

"That's it for me," he said, grabbing his beer and a red and yellow jacket with the word "España" sewn across the back.

I stared at the blackboard. Matteo Ortiz, I said to myself. Matteo Ortiz.

"I've never seen you here before."

It took me a second to realize Matteo was talking to me. He'd taken a seat on an empty stool right behind me.

"I've never been here before," I stammered.

"Like a cigarette?" He pulled the pack of Marlboros from his back pocket and tilted it in my direction.

"No thanks," I replied.

"Well, you'd definitely like a beer," he said, nodding at my nearly empty mug. He polished off his own in one long gulp. "Sandy, can we get a couple of beers down here?" he yelled. The bartender with the missing incisor grabbed our mugs. "And get this guy a *real beer*," Matteo instructed, tapping his empty monster-size mug. He turned to me and winked. "We're going to be a while."

Over the next few hours, we told each other our life stories with the ease that only two strangers ever can. Eager to hear his history, I quickly rattled off details of my own—about growing up in a Philadelphia suburb, about my job as a magazine writer and, when Matteo inquired, about being newly single after a three-year relationship.

"So you are good boyfriend material," he said with a smile as he filled me in on his own background. Born and raised in a small town near Marbella on Spain's Costa del Sol, he had moved to America a year earlier to spare his mother and sister from the escalating tensions between him and his father. "My father does not approve of me," Matteo explained. "He said, 'Were you born with a dick between your legs or a pussy?' I came here to start a new life."

As the night wore on, Matteo downed three quart-size mugs of beer while I was still working on my first. I hadn't had any alcohol in months and one was enough for me. When he finished the third beer, he asked the bartender, a new bartender, for a glass of water. The bartender obliged, but begrudgingly. Half-hour later, Matteo asked for a refill. The bartender glared as he set the glass in front of him.

"The water's free, *Matteo*," he said brusquely, "but the service isn't."

Matteo jumped to his feet and leaned across the bar. "You have no right to tell me to tip you!" he yelled in the bartender's face. "I drink here all the time and I *always* tip good—if the *service* is good!"

The bartender took a step back, raised his hand in the air and snapped his fingers. In a split second, an enormous leather-vested, booted and buzz-cut bouncer appeared, scooped Matteo up, carried him to the door and tossed him outside. I was momentarily stunned, trying to figure out what had just happened. I noticed Matteo's España jacket still draped across the back of his empty stool, grabbed it and headed for the door, exiting the bar just in time to see Matteo disappear around a corner. I ran to catch up. He was more than a little surprised to see me.

"What the hell was that all about?" I asked.

"Ah, that bartender hates me," he said. "He looks for any excuse to throw me out."

We both stared at the sidewalk for a moment.

"Why'd you come after me?" he asked as he took one last drag on his cigarette and flicked the butt into the street.

I hesitated, realizing as I did that I was still holding his jacket. "Well, you forgot this," I said slowly as I handed it to him. "And, well, you just seemed like you needed someone to come after you."

He laughed. "You got that right."

Matteo and I started hanging out together after that. We never met by arrangement, only by coincidence—he was at the Car Bar nearly every night and, by coincidence, so was I. Once there, however, we were inseparable, buying each other giant mugs of beer and playing pool till last call. Still, at the end of every night, Matteo inevitably left with any friend who could give him a lift home. I couldn't offer him a ride because I never drove to the Car Bar—it was always tough to find a parking space and I lived a lot closer than Matteo—so I reluctantly walked home by myself, thinking the kinds of things you think about when you think you've met someone you really like.

Everything changed the night there was no one to drive Matteo home. The bar was relatively empty when I arrived. I spotted Matteo right away, shooting pool by himself. I made for the back of the bar, oblivious to the few patrons I passed who were lurking in the shadows along the way.

He lit up when I joined him. "I am so glad to see you."

"What's the matter?" I asked. "No one wants to play a game with you?"

"Nah, the other way around," he said. "No one I want to play a game with."

He tilted his head toward the darkness beyond the pool table and I looked in the direction he indicated. In a second, I realized why he was shooting solo. It was Monday night at the Car Bar. Jockstrap Night. The other ten or twelve guys who were there were sporting the suggested attire. And *only* the suggested attire. Unfortunately, it was not a particularly flattering look on any of them.

"I've had three beers and the view isn't getting any better," joked Matteo. "What do you say we get out of here?"

"Where to?" I asked when we were outside.

"Somewhere with beer," said Matteo. "Cheap beer. I'm broke."

"There are a couple of six-packs in my fridge," I offered.

He laughed. "Works for me."

As we walked up South toward Twenty-Ninth, I immediately had second thoughts about having him over. I was only halfway finished renovating my small, two-story row house and the inside resembled a construction site.

"I have to warn you that my place isn't much to look at," I said as I opened the door.

"I'm sure it's fine," he said.

I led the way to the living room, which was more presentable than some of the others.

Matteo crashed on the sofa and looked around. "What are you talking about, Har? You have a nice place."

"Well, it's not the place I'd like it to be," I said, walking to the kitchen to get two beers.

"So, whose is?" he countered with a smile.

"You're right," I agreed, feeling more relaxed as I handed him a bottle.

He pointed to the stereo. "How 'bout some music?"

I put on a tape I'd made. As the music started, Matteo slipped off his boots.

"You don't mind if I make myself comfortable, do you?" he asked.

"Of course not," I said. "I'm glad you feel comfortable enough to make yourself comfortable."

We sat on the couch for nearly two hours, making small talk at first. Three beers in, however, Matteo turned suddenly thoughtful, telling me that the new life he had come to start in America was currently on hold. He had arranged to work at an import-export business owned by his mother's brother, an American citizen. But ten months after he arrived, the business experienced a downturn and his uncle asked him to take an indefinite unpaid furlough. His uncle believed it was temporary, that business would bounce back and Matteo would return to work. Two months had already passed, though, and he was still waiting. Meanwhile, he was having a hard time concentrating on his studies for his citizenship test and he worried how he would pay the back rent in the group home he shared with a dozen fellow expats in Fairmount.

"Someday," he said, "I want to have my own import-export business."

"And you will," I assured him, touched that he had been so open.

He looked serious for a moment but lit up as the last song on the tape began to play. "Elvis! 'Can't Help Falling in Love.' This is one of my favorites."

"Mine, too," I said.

We listened in silence until the final verse, when Matteo began to sing along. He looked at me as he finished. "Let's go to bed."

My heart started pounding. Somehow, I really hadn't anticipated his staying the night, although now that the moment had arrived, I couldn't believe I hadn't considered it. He finished his beer, stood up and emptied the contents of his pockets on the table. Lots of change, a set of keys, a worn leather wallet.

"Lead the way," he said with a grin.

I pointed to the stairs as I turned off the lights. In the bedroom, he switched on a lamp and sat at the bottom edge of the mattress on the floor that served as my bed. He stripped off his T-shirt and slid out of his jeans. I sat next to him and did likewise. We sat there side by side in our boxers, saying nothing for several seconds, both of us staring at the floor. He was so close I could feel the warmth of his body. Finally, he crawled to the top of the bed and rested his head on a pillow.

"Buenas noches. Dios te bendiga," he said. "That's what we always say in my family."

I crawled up next to him. "I guess we should get some sleep, huh?"

"No," he replied as he put his arm around me. "We shouldn't."

16

I RESISTED THE TEMPTATION to call Jay over the three-day weekend, even though we always called each other on weekends. I wanted to give him some space and, more importantly, give myself some, too. I hadn't realized that I thought about him all the time until I tried to stop thinking about him all the time. That our friendship depended upon my success increased both my determination to master my emotions and my apprehension that I might not.

Conversely, I was concerned about what would happen if I did succeed. Change my behavior, change my feelings—change our friendship? How much of how close we were hinged on how I felt about Jay? Would we lose what we had if I no longer felt the same? Or was I just trying to confuse the issue, trying to justify not changing, trying to justify living in a familiar but love-starved limbo—Ginsberg's sad paradise—that Jay would surely rather I didn't occupy even if I were willing to do so?

No, I argued with myself, it wasn't a matter of what we would lose, but what we would gain. As good as I thought things were they would only get better. That was the truth, the truth that would ultimately set me free, even if, in the meantime, the truth hurt like hell.

I tried to dull the pain by putting in extra-hard workouts and by keeping a journal on my laptop. Writing about Matteo reminded me that things had started out great with him, too. Everything was perfect, in fact, until everything *wasn't*. And though my relationship with Matteo was of a very different nature than my relationship with Jay, the two shared a common thread. And a common threat. I didn't want what had ultimately happened with Matteo to happen with Jay. Jay could have run, turned his back on me, but he didn't. He stayed. He was there for me. Just as he'd always been. And first thing Tuesday morning, he was standing in the doorway of my office, just as he always was.

"Well?" he asked.

"Well what?" I replied, pretending not to know what he was referring to.

"You know as well as I do," he continued, refusing to give up.

So *I* did. "Well, I didn't write a novel."

"Neither did I," he confessed.

"But I do have *something* to show you," I said, handing him a manila envelope that contained the Matteo and Harry story. "It's a first chapter from a novel, maybe."

"All *right!*" He peeked inside and headed to the art department.

Around two, he was back, envelope in hand. A few minutes later, we were at our usual place, pondering the contents of the deli case when the guy behind it interrupted our deliberations.

"Do you two eat lunch together *every* day?"

"Huh?" asked Jay.

"You two are always together," continued the deli man in a tone that suggested some clandestine design he couldn't quite discern. "I never see one of you without the other. And you always order the same thing."

I felt self-conscious, as if the deli guy was a Greek chorus pointing out that something was wrong with this picture. There *was* something wrong with this picture, but I was trying to fix it.

"We're friends," said Jay simply, much to my relief. "We work together. And we don't *always* order the same thing."

A light bulb clicked on in the deli man's brain. "Oh," he said, seemingly surprised that so simple an explanation had eluded him. "So, what would you like? We got excellent meatloaf today. Just out of the oven."

"Sounds good," I said. "With gravy. On a kaiser roll."

The deli man looked at Jay. "Two the same?"

Jay looked at me and sighed. "Yeah," he answered. "Two the same."

We found an empty table in the back. "Jay," I began as we sat down, "before you read that story, there are a few things I have to explain..."

"I already read it," said Jay. "I couldn't wait."

"You did?!"

Everything I'd disclosed in the story flashed before my eyes. I'd never told Jay anything specific about Matteo. Not even his name.

"You must have a million questions."

"Not a million, but I do have *one*. Something I really need to know."

I braced myself. "Shoot."

"When can I read the next chapter?"

On the way back to the office, Jay said that he wouldn't be able to have lunch with me the next day. My first thought was that the deli guy's observation had hit home after all, but that wasn't the case.

"I'm having lunch with Gina and Sil from *Element Online*. It's about a job."

"What job?" I remembered the day Jay and Gina had gone to lunch a few weeks earlier.

"Art director."

"Whoa! That's great! Does Ted know?"

"No. You're the only one I've told."

The following afternoon, after lunch, Jay asked me to join him outside on a cigarette break, where he related the gist of his conversation with Gina and Sil.

"So, here's the deal," he said excitedly. "They definitely want me. And the salary would be a substantial increase over what I'm making now. I gave Sil my portfolio and he said I should know in a week whether it's a go. They just have to clear it with the new head of digital publishing—our former editor-in-chief, Vivien. She's calling the shots on all the Internet hires now."

"This is awesome, kid." I was so happy for him.

"You're telling me. I'm already thinking that I might be able to pay off my school loans *and* finally get my own apartment. Har, maybe *you* should think about giving Vivien a call. She's a fan of yours."

"It's something to consider," I allowed.

We continued our conversation in the art department, where Jay motioned for me to sit on his desk so no one else could hear what we were discussing. When Zahra suddenly strolled in, however, I flushed with self-consciousness for being too close to Jay—literally, this time—and I kicked myself for letting my guard down. Change your behavior, I reminded myself. Prepared for an unpleasant reaction, because I wasn't sure how Zahra felt about me after what had happened a few weeks earlier, I was pleasantly surprised when she only smiled, kissing Jay and then kissing me on the cheek. Still feeling slightly awkward, I stood to leave, but I was stopped in my tracks when Zahra produced a small white rice-paper envelope from her leather shoulder bag and handed it to me.

"Here's your invitation to my show," she said sweetly.

"Thanks," I replied, taken aback by her tone.

Inside the envelope was a three-by-five piece of graph paper printed with the location, date and time for the opening of Zahra's "Exhibition of Drawing and Sculpture."

"Nice invite," I remarked.

"Jay designed it," said Zahra, beaming proudly as she glanced in his direction. "Oh, look at that!"

She pointed to the screen saver that had just appeared on Jay's computer. It was a short looping video clip of Jay making silly faces that he'd shot earlier in the day with a digital camera the magazine had just acquired.

"You should see Harry's screen saver," said Jay. "It's his cat, Flannery."

"Flannery?"

"After one of my favorite writers, Flannery O'Connor. You know, 'A Good Man Is Hard to Find.'"

"Oh, I read that story in an American literature course."

"Zahra has two cats," Jay explained.

"Yes," said Zahra. "Frida and Georgia, after two of my favorite artists, Frida Kahlo and Georgia O'Keeffe. Can I see your screen saver?"

Thinking I could use the time alone together to apologize and smooth over any remaining rough spots in our relationship, I led Zahra to my office where she admired the life-size image of Flannery on my monitor and then studied the items tacked to a bulletin board above my desk. Among them was a Gap ad I'd ripped from an issue of *Rolling Stone* that featured a black-and-white photo of Jack Kerouac with the tag line "Kerouac wore khakis."

"Zahra," I began as she returned her attention to my computer, "there's something I'd like to say to you."

She looked at me expectantly. "What is it?"

"I just wanted to tell you..."

"Cigarette?" Jay was standing in my doorway.

Zahra and I looked at each other and smiled.

"I'll be back," she assured me.

A few minutes later, however, Jay returned without her. "Zahra had to run to get to a class," he said. "She didn't realize the time. She asked me to say goodbye for her and said she hopes you'll come to her exhibit."

I looked at the invitation Zahra had handed me.

"I'm helping her install it on Sunday," Jay continued. "The opening is Monday night. Wait till you see her stuff, Har. It's all about found objects and words and it's all arranged on grids. That's why I printed the invitations on graph paper."

"What do the grids represent?" I asked.

"That nothing is random. That there's an unseen scheme. That, despite evidence to the contrary sometimes, all things are connected. That, ultimately, there's a reason for everything."

17

ON SATURDAY, I SET aside some time to shop for a present for Zahra to celebrate her exhibit opening. After giving it some thought, I had decided that a book by Allen Ginsberg would be ideal, a rare or signed edition even better. I called the Gotham Book Mart, explained to the woman who answered what I was looking for and she connected me to Gotham's manager, Mr. Finnegan.

"What price range did you have in mind?" he inquired.

I told him and he said that he would put together a selection I would find very interesting, including first *and* signed editions.

"So, you have a lot of rare Ginsberg?" I asked.

"Yes, we specialize in poetry, and Mr. Ginsberg is a customer of ours," he answered.

I couldn't get to Gotham before it closed, so he told me to stop by on Monday.

"What time?" I asked.

"Any time," he replied.

At *Element* on Monday, Jay and I spent most of the day working on a nine-page spread about *Star Trek: Deep Space Nine.* I was responsible for all of the magazine's *Star Trek* stories, elaborate affairs that had begun appearing several times a year ever since someone in the sales department noticed that putting *Star Trek* on the cover accompanied by the words "Collectors' Edition" boosted newsstand sales by a quarter million copies. Although I liked *Trek* and had enjoyed the original series as a kid, I wasn't a rabid Trekkie (all Trekkies are, by definition, rabid), or even a Trekker (the term preferred by true believers). I was handed the *Trek* beat simply because I happened to know more about it than anyone else on the staff. That said, coming up with a fresh angle on *Trek* every few months that was newsworthy and noteworthy enough to merit the cover of *Element* was a challenge. For the story at hand, I had zeroed in on *Deep Space Nine*, the dark star in the *Trek* continuum. Michael Dorn, who had played the contentious Klingon Worf in the recently canceled *Next Generation*, was joining the cast. Stop the presses!

When Jay was finally satisfied with the layout, I slipped out and headed to the Gotham Book Mart to pick out Zahra's present. I asked the woman at the cash register where I could find Mr. Finnegan.

"Mr. Finnegan is in his office," she said.

She led me to the back of the store where she paused before pushing open a half-closed door.

"A man's here to see you about some Ginsberg books you set aside?" she said hesitantly.

Over her shoulder I could see a man with dark brown hair and a thick mustache seated at a large wooden desk.

"I have to change!" he said.

"I could come back later," I offered, not really sure what he meant but assuming this wasn't a good time.

"No, no, it's all right," he assured me. "It's just that there's a reception for Paul Bowles on the second floor in eight minutes and I still have to change." He reached for a pile of books on a shelf above his desk and set them on his lap. "Let's see what they pulled."

The volume on top was a first edition of *Howl: Original Draft Facsimile*, featuring an annotated reproduction of the poem's manuscript. It was signed by Ginsberg but inscribed to a friend of his and I wasn't sure whether I liked it more or less because of that. At sixty-five dollars, though, it wasn't all that expensive.

Mr. Finnegan flipped dismissively through the next book and

tossed it aside. "I *told* them only to pull *signed* editions," he sighed.

Next were hardcover editions of *Mind Breaths* and *Plutonian Ode* from the City Lights Pocket Poets series. "They're both signed," Mr. Finnegan pointed out. "And only three hundred hardcovers of these were published." They were fifty dollars each—a bargain, I thought.

"If you would excuse me," said Mr. Finnegan, "I really must go get changed for the reception."

"No problem," I replied.

As he left me to sort through the stack on my own, however, it suddenly occurred to me that I might be making a mistake by giving Zahra a rare Ginsberg book. Ginsberg was, after all, something she shared with Jay, and here I was, once again, unwittingly about to insert myself between them. I breathed a sigh of relief—a mind breath of my own—at having avoided such a close call but tensed at the return of Mr. Finnegan, who, I assumed, would be less than thrilled by my decision to leave the store without buying any books.

"Well?" he asked.

I noticed he was wearing a fresh shirt and tie. "Thanks for showing these to me," I began, bracing for another outburst, "but I need to think about it."

"Take your time," he answered, calm and collected at last. "And *next* time, call me before you come in."

I laughed to myself and headed for the door. Halfway there, I ran into a familiar face.

"Hey," said Lester. "You like Kerouac, right?"

"Yes, very much," I assured him.

"I have a few rare titles I'm looking to sell. Would you be interested in a first-edition paperback of *On the Road?*"

"A first edition?! Definitely."

"It's not in the best condition, I'm afraid."

"That doesn't matter. Really."

"Okay. Then I'll bring it in."

I couldn't believe my luck. *Another* first edition of *On the Road?*

I seemed to be attracting them. On my way back to work, I made two stops. The first was a wine shop, where I bought a bottle of Mumm's. The second was an art supply store, where I bought a beautiful buckskin-bound sketchbook. Both were for Zahra. They were less personal than any of the Ginsberg items, but that was the point.

At five-thirty, Jay stopped by my office sporting a vintage tan leather coat I'd never seen before. It looked like something from Sears, circa 1968.

"Nice jacket," I observed.

"Yeah, Domsie's," he replied cryptically as he handed me a page torn from his notebook. "I'm leaving a little early to help Zahra with some last-minute preparations. Here are the directions to Pratt. If you get lost when you get off the G train, just follow the art students. You won't have any problem recognizing them. I'll see you there. I gotta run. I still have to buy flowers!"

I spent the next half-hour wrapping the champagne and the sketchbook in several sheets of graph paper I serendipitously discovered in the office supply room. After stuffing the gifts in my backpack, I finally headed out a little after six, making good connections and arriving in Brooklyn in less than thirty minutes. I found the Pratt campus easily enough and then the building with Zahra's exhibit, taking a set of marble steps to the second floor where I found Jay standing just outside the gallery talking with two friends.

"Harry, I'd like you to meet Marilyn and Zeus," said Jay.

Marilyn was attractive, thin, with short stylish blond hair and friendly blue eyes. Zeus was strapping and solid, with a buzzed head and a big grin.

"Jay's told us *so* much about you!" effused Marilyn, but in a sincere sort of way.

"He's *really* hoping you're the one!" effused Zeus, mimicking Marilyn in an insincere sort of way.

"What about Zahra?" I asked him, playing along.

"Oh, right," said Zeus, thinking hard. "Make that the *other* one."

I looked at Jay, who only smiled.

"So," I said to Marilyn and Zeus, "I hear congratulations are in order."

"They are?" asked Zeus.

Marilyn slugged him playfully on the shoulder.

"Oh, yeah, that's right," he said, smiling mischievously. "We're getting *married.*"

"Jay and Zahra are next," joked Marilyn.

"Nah," said Jay. "We're not the marrying kind."

"What kind are you?" asked Zeus.

"Ah, I never kiss and tell," said Jay.

"I do," said Zeus. He leaned over, slid a big arm around my shoulder and smiled suggestively.

Jay yanked me away. "Well," he said, "I think you now know everything you need to know about Zeus."

"Not everything," said Zeus. "But enough for the first five minutes. It's the next five you have to worry about. Just ask Marilyn." She shook her head. "I don't kiss and tell, either."

"Who said anything about kissing?" asked Zeus.

"So, Jay," I interjected, "how do you guys know each other?"

"We met in the Marines," he explained.

"They were looking for a few good men," added Zeus with a shrug. "So was I. It all worked out. Hey, Harry, would you like a beer?"

"Not just yet," I replied. "Maybe later."

"Well, I'd like one *now,*" he said, "but this being an *art exhibit,* there isn't any beer. Only wine and cheese."

Jay and Marilyn looked at each other and rolled their eyes.

"Zahra's showing some folks around," Jay told me, pointing to a small group across the gallery.

"I'll be back," I said, taking off in Zahra's direction. She turned around just as I approached.

"Harry!" she cried, giving me a hug. "I'm so glad you came."

"Congratulations," I said, presenting her with the two gifts I'd brought.

"Oh, you didn't have to do this. And look at the wrapping! I'm going to open them *right now*!"

She immediately set the bottle on the floor and began ripping the paper away from the sketchbook, gleefully letting the various pieces fall where they might.

"Oh, this is *perfect*!" she exclaimed. "This is perfect for when I go on pigment hunts!"

I wasn't quite sure what "pigment hunts" were but I was glad the book was perfect for them. "You know, Zahra, I've been wanting to talk with you for a while now. There's something I want to tell you. I tried once before, when we were in my office, but we were interrupted by..."

I paused and we both laughed. "Yes, I know," she said.

"Anyway," I continued, "something happened a month ago. And, and... well, I've given it a lot of thought and what it really comes down to is this—I'm sorry for what happened a few weeks ago. I just want us to be friends."

She suddenly grew serious. "You didn't have to say that, you know."

"Maybe I didn't have to say it for you, but I did have to say it for me. There are some things I'm trying to work through, to get right, but I don't want anything to ever come between us again."

"Oh, Harry," she said, clutching the sketchbook close to her chest. "You are *so* sweet."

"Don't open that one now," I said, pointing to the still-wrapped bottle of Mumm's at her feet. "It's champagne, for you and Jay to share later."

Jay appeared at that moment, attracted, no doubt, by all the fuss.

"Jay, look what Harry gave me," said Zahra. "And look—graph paper!" I felt slightly embarrassed but he only smiled serenely, wrapping his arms around her waist and resting his head on her shoulder. "Oh!" said Zahra suddenly, looking toward the gallery door. "There's Nikki!"

"Come on, Har," said Jay after she excused herself. "Let's get some wine and I'll show you around."

We returned to the hallway where Zeus and Marilyn were sharing a stool next to a linen-covered table spread with several vases of exotic flowers, a dozen bottles of wine and a huge silver platter filled with Brie, bread, grapes and strawberries. Tom Waits growled from a boombox on a second stool off to the right; I recognized the song "Cold, Cold Ground" from his *Frank's Wild Years* CD.

"We're guarding the food," said Zeus. "Or should I say *I'm* guarding the food. Marilyn is eating it."

Marilyn made no attempt to deny the accusation. "I can't help it, I'm hungry," she admitted.

"Eat," said Jay. "That's what it's there for." He selected a bottle, poured two glasses and handed one to me. "Ready for the grand tour?"

We started with a collection of four drawings hanging just inside. Three of the four were executed on pages torn from a notebook. The first was covered with hundreds of short, animated vertical lines, the second with blocks of script in Spanish, French and Italian as well as languages I didn't recognize and the third with sewing needles affixed with tape. The fourth page, from a yellow legal pad, appeared to be a letter written in English that had been entirely obscured by thick black bars, like a censored government document in which every word had been deemed too sensitive. I felt a simpatico with what Zahra had so brilliantly shorthanded—the intoxicating amalgam of elation and trepidation that accompanies every new intimacy, from scattered first thoughts to full disclosure, from conflicted second thoughts to full reversal.

"That's actually a letter Zahra wrote to me," Jay explained, pointing to the last page. "She wrote it with a quill I found in the street when I was in Venice. And the quill is..." He looked around the gallery. "...over there."

I followed him to a chest-high dais where the quill, a feather and an antique key were arranged on a flowered handkerchief.

"Now *this*," continued Jay, leading me to an enormous ten-by-twenty-foot black grid painted on the gallery's rear wall, "this is Zahra's masterwork."

Each ten-inch-square compartment of the grid contained a different object—keys, buttons, pins, bundles of letters, foreign currency, tiny plastic bags of dirt and colored powders, a rusty bottle opener.

"It tells a story, from right to left," Jay explained. "It starts out in New York, then goes to Venice, then New York again, then Los Angeles. Every object has a special significance. These small bags contain pigments she makes. Here's a bundle of lira from Italy. This is a piece of rubble from the Colosseum in Rome. Packets of salt and pepper, representing good and evil. And, this, of course," he added, pointing to the compartment in the lower right-hand corner that contained three small black circles, "is the essence of the whole show."

"Dot dot dot," I said.

"Dot dot dot," repeated Jay, steering me toward a battered old suitcase that was lying open on the floor and filled with a checkerboard of bottles as well as several neatly folded men's dress shirts. "Now this is an homage to another artist. Again, the bottles are arranged in a grid and filled with the pigments she makes."

I pointed to two bottles that contained a granular white substance. "What's in those?"

"Sugar," he replied. "Of course, you know what *that* symbolizes. *Bobby!*"

I was startled by the appearance of a slim, tattooed spike-haired guy to my right.

"I'm sorry, Jay," he said. "I didn't mean to interrupt you."

"You're not interrupting," Jay assured him, hugging him tightly. "Harry, this is Bobby. He's the guy who used to live in the same building as Allen Ginsberg."

Bobby shook my hand and blushed, looking me in the eye and then immediately staring at his feet.

"I lived right above him," said Bobby. "On the fifth floor."

"Now, where exactly was this?" I asked.

"Four-thirty-seven East Twelfth," he replied.

"Remember that address," I said to Jay.

"I never talked to him much," Bobby continued. "He was kind of standoffish for a long time, although he did warm up a little the last few months I lived there and he started saying hello."

"So you never went to his apartment?" asked Jay.

"No."

"We were wondering what he must have in that apartment," I said. "The books, the photographs, the manuscripts."

"He's got two mailboxes," Bobby offered. "I think he's got two apartments, side by side, that he made into one. He's lived in the building for like twenty years. I've still got a set of keys."

"Maybe you could distract him while Jay and I run in," I joked. He laughed, a little nervously, it seemed, looking from Jay to me and then back to Jay.

"I should say hello to Zahra," he said finally.

"Okay," said Jay. "Good to see you."

"You, too," Bobby replied. "Harry, it was nice to meet you."

"Ditto," I said as he headed off.

"Now where were we?" asked Jay. "Ah! Over here." We walked over to a final set of four drawings, similar in style to the other four but much larger, and rendered on thick white paper. Marilyn and Zeus joined us as Jay offered his insights.

"The first, you can see, is a field at night," he explained proudly. "The second, a field in the day. The third is a beach. And the fourth..."

"What did you say this is?" interrupted Zeus, pointing to drawing number three.

"A beach," Jay repeated.

"If you ask me," said Zeus, "it looks like a giant piece of matzoh."

18

ELEMENT'S NEW EDITOR-IN-CHIEF, Cliff Palmer, appeared without fanfare, arriving at the office before anyone else on a Monday morning and making himself at home in the spacious corner quarters formerly occupied by Vivien Verdurin. Cliff was one of Vivien's protégés, recruited from another national entertainment magazine, and he and I hit it off. After only a couple of conversations, we quickly realized that we were both insatiable pop-culture aficionados who loved everything from the trashy to the transcendent. A shared appreciation for the somewhat obscure but seminal skit comedy series *SCTV* solidified our relationship, and in story-idea meetings with the senior staff, Cliff frequently injected cryptic references to the show's most infamous characters and sketches. He'd begin meetings by asking if anyone had a "topic, eh?" (à la Bob and Doug McKenzie, the eternally topic-starved beer-swilling brothers of *The Great White North* talk show), weigh in on story proposals he considered lame with an "Ooooo, scary!" (à la Count Floyd, the has-been host of the decidedly unscary *Monster Chiller Horror Theatre*) and wonder aloud if a certain overly affected actor would "blow up real good" (as they always did on Big Jim McBob and Billy Sol Hurok's *Farm Film Report*). On cue, Cliff would inevitably turn to me for a nod of recognition and approval while my fellow editors, unacquainted with his source material, could only shake their heads or shrug their shoulders.

Following one such story meeting on the Friday after Zahra's exhibit opening, I swung by the art department to grab Jay for lunch. Since it was pouring outside, we decided to stay inside, exploring the tunnels beneath Rockefeller Center in search of a place to eat and eventually stopping at a tourist-filled diner called Huxley's for burgers.

"Have you heard anything from Sil about your portfolio?" I asked as we ate.

"No, I haven't," said Jay. "Which could be bad, because he doesn't like it, or it could be good, because he's showing it to other people. I didn't see it in his office when I walked by."

"Try not to read too much into it," I advised. "These things take time, kid, they really do."

I paused, replaying what I'd just said in my head. That was the second time I'd heard myself call Jay *kid*, a term of endearment that had somehow spontaneously generated in my subconscious. It was a troubling reminder that I had made little progress in my effort to reverse-engineer *love* to *like*, an effort made all the more challenging by the fact that things between Jay and me were pretty much the same as they'd always been, despite my true feelings coming to light. Though we didn't talk about it, I doubted Jay assumed that my affection for him had diminished or had just dissipated altogether when I was forced to confront the reality of the situation. If only the rules of attraction worked like that, I thought, if only someone could only be attracted to someone who was attracted to him or her, life—and love—would be so much simpler.

I supposed that Jay never asked about the obvious because he had faith in me, because he believed that I could fall out of love with him on my own. I so wanted to justify that faith, so I never brought it up either. That was a new approach for me—I almost always wanted to talk about such things—but I considered it part of the "change my behavior, change my feelings" approach. Based on my *kid* comment, which had obviously sprung from somewhere deep inside, the change was only an external one, but the underlying premise of a change in behavior effecting a change in feelings seemed to be that external changes would, sooner or later, induce internal ones. I hoped that was the case, because even though, on the surface, our days passed much as they always had, just below the surface, just beneath the elation I felt being with Jay, I wrestled with a subliminal ache every minute we were together, a subliminal ache accompanied by shards of guilt that I ever thought of him as anything other than a friend.

"Well, I don't intend to *ask* Sil what he thought of my portfolio," said Jay. "I don't want to seem like I'm begging for the job. If he offers it to me, I want to be able to say, 'These are my terms.' "

"Then you're playing your cards exactly as you should be playing them," I assured him.

Back at the office, I spent that afternoon on the assignment I'd received at the story-idea meeting earlier—trying to land a TV star for the cover of the Halloween issue. "Think witches, vampires, ghosts, monsters," Cliff had told me, but there were very few TV stars, it seemed, who wanted to pose in a silly costume on the cover of *Element*. Roseanne, who made a big deal out of Halloween every year on her sitcom, had agreed to dress up as a witch but canceled when a personal problem took priority. Somehow, the publicist for Fran Drescher's show, *The Nanny*, got wind of my predicament and actually called *me*.

"Fran would *love* to be on the cover," he said, and for a second, my problem was solved. "But only as Mary Poppins," he continued.

"Why Mary Poppins?" I asked.

"She's a nanny," he replied. "Don't you get it?"

I didn't, but I didn't say so. I thanked him and explained that I needed something a lot scarier than a nanny, unless, of course, Fran was up to channeling the psychotic au pair once portrayed by Bette Davis. She wasn't.

Cliff stopped by just as I hung up, dropping into a chair as he always did and asking the question he always asked. "What's happening?"

I proceeded to relate my Halloween horror stories and then proposed a possible solution. "What about *The Simpsons*?" I suggested. *The Simpsons* made a lot of sense, because the show's annual "Treehouse of Horror" episode was the most popular of the year.

"Nah, *The Simpsons* has been on for seven seasons now. It's run out of steam," opined Cliff, rising to go. "Ask for an original illustration but we'll only use it as a last resort."

Reluctantly, I called the show's publicist, whom I had worked with on many prior occasions, and made my pitch. She was thrilled, since *The Simpsons* hadn't appeared on the cover of *Element* in quite some time, and promised to have an illustration in my hands in a few days, even though it wouldn't be easy. Knowing that it was probably all for naught, I felt like a heel.

As was his wont, Cliff stopped by once again a little later. "I've got it," he announced. "*Brotherly Love.*"

I blanched. *Brotherly Love* was a struggling new NBC series starring Joey Lawrence of *Blossom* fame ("*Woh!*") and his two younger brothers, Matthew and Andy.

"We need to do an NBC cover, anyway," Cliff continued. "We haven't done one in a while."

Such was the science, sometimes, of deciding who or what appeared on the cover of *Element.* "Woh" was me.

That weekend, I spent most of Saturday afternoon writing in my journal—trying to work out on my laptop what I couldn't seem to work out in real life—and most of Saturday night reading *The City and the Pillar* by Gore Vidal. I had called for a review copy after reading a piece in *The New York Times* that recounted the controversy surrounding the book's publication in 1948. *The City and the Pillar* told the tragic tale of one man's lifelong love for his best friend after a single night of intimacy as adolescents. In the 1940s, Vidal was a revered young war novelist, and when he handed in the manuscript for *City*, editors and publishers told him that he would be blacklisted for writing such a book. Vidal had forged ahead anyway, and, despite the fact that the *Times* refused to run ads for it, and virtually every major newspaper in the country refused to review it, the book became an immediate bestseller.

Since the book was only two hundred pages, I thought I would be able to finish it in one sitting. That night, I only made it halfway, but I was intrigued by Vidal's purposely unsentimental prose, particularly the passage in which he described the physical bonding of his two male protagonists, Jim Willard and Bob Ford. It was an event that Jim would remember forever and Bob would quickly forget, and though the situation was not exactly parallel, I couldn't help but think of my own relationship with Matteo. And my feelings for Jay.

Brotherly love, indeed.

EARLY NEXT MORNING, I wandered over to a flea market held every Sunday in a school parking lot at Seventy-Sixth and Columbus. Time was when I stopped at the flea market every week, if only for a quick walk through, but I hadn't done so for months because I had spent the last dozen or so Sundays writing about how Jay and I had spent the previous Saturday nights. There was nothing to report that day, however, since Jay and I hadn't spent the last few Saturday nights together, and I decided that I needed to get out of my apartment. I needed to do something on my own. And I needed to do something that didn't remind me of Jay.

I had always enjoyed the element of the unexpected at the flea market. Every Sunday a new batch of merchants showed up, hopefully displaying the accumulated flotsam and jetsam of their ancestors on tables from the school's cafeteria. Part of the fun was stumbling upon something I didn't even know I was looking for but suddenly had to have. On this particular Sunday, an object buried beneath a battered aluminum table caught my eye. There, nearly hidden under a dented cookie tin, was an old black manual typewriter case. Inside was a gunmetal gray Underwood with a perfectly functioning keyboard. A small white tag tied to the handle revealed the price: Thirty-five dollars. Cheap.

"Do you know how old this typewriter is?" I asked the man standing behind the table. He had white hair and a matching mustache.

"Thirty-five dollars," he answered.

"Yes, but how *old* is it?"

"Oh, forty, fifty years, I guess."

"How flexible is that price?"

"Oh, this is a flea market," he said with a smile. "I'll knock five dollars off."

"Sold," I told him, taking out my wallet and counting out the cash.

As I started to walk away, he called after me. "Hemingway wrote on that typewriter!" I grinned at him. Yes, he did, I thought. And now I will write on it. Now Jay and I can begin the book we said we'd write together. So much for not thinking about Jay.

Pausing at another table on my way out, I couldn't believe what I saw—a black Art Deco Remington Rand. Again, all the keys were in working order.

"How much do you want for this?" I asked the guy at the table.

He looked to be about my age, late twenties, maybe a little younger, tall, well built, good-looking, with jet-black hair and aquamarine eyes. He tapped a guy standing behind him on the shoulder. "How much is the typewriter?"

"Twenty-five dollars," replied the second guy.

The first guy turned back to me. "Twenty dollars."

"That's a good price," I said, more to myself than him, thinking of Martin Tytell's six-hundred-and-fifty-dollar Royal. "You know, I've been looking for a typewriter like this for a while now, and I just bought one five minutes ago right over there."

"When it rains, it pours," he said with a smile.

"You know what? I'm going to buy this one, too," I said, handing him a twenty.

"Do you collect typewriters?" he asked.

"I think I just started."

Spurred by my Sunday morning success stories, I decided to head downtown to Skyline Books on Eighteenth Street. I had called Skyline when I was searching for a copy of *Scenes Along the Road*, the book of photographs of Kerouac and company. The store's listing in the Yellow Pages said it specialized in the Beats and I had been meaning to visit the store for weeks. Inside, I quickly discovered a whole section devoted to the Beat Generation, where, in turn, I quickly discovered a copy of *Scenes Along the Road*. Flipping through its pages, I realized that I had seen most of the pictures before, but I decided it was definitely worth getting for those few I hadn't, especially since it was only twelve bucks.

As I scanned the other books, I spotted a mint-condition first-edition paperback of *The Dharma Bums* with a sticker price of only eight dollars. On the cover was a lurid illustration of a despondent and introspective woman clinging to the leg of a man who stared aloofly into the distance. The drawing was accompanied by even more lurid prose. "The sensational bestseller about two reckless wanderers out to scale the heights of life... and love." I wondered, "Is this the book I read?" I carried the two volumes to the cash register and headed home.

That evening, after I'd put myself through a particularly heavy-duty workout, I updated my journal and then polished off *The City and the Pillar*. I couldn't believe how it ended. Many years after Jim and Bob's bout of boyhood abandon, and their subsequent separation as life made different demands on each of them, they finally met again and renewed their friendship. Jim had done nothing but think of that one moment and convinced himself that he could reignite an affair with the now-married Bob. I recognized the pathology of self-delusion in Jim's belief that Bob's preference for women could only add to the significance of their relationship.

It was all downhill until the inevitable but unpredictable climax. Once more, I felt as though I were reading a variation on either the Matteo and Harry story or the adventures of Jay and Harry. Could anything but disaster ever come from a lopsided love?

Not according to Gore Vidal. The final few pages were so overwhelming I had to read them twice.

"YOU'LL NEVER GUESS what I got this weekend," I said to Jay in my office on Monday morning, pulling the books I'd bought at Skyline out of my backpack.

"Wow, pretty cool," he observed as he looked them over.

"I also got something else," I said. "But I'll tell you about it at lunch."

He looked around my office. "I have to wait?"

"Yep."

"All right," he sighed. "Hey, you'll never guess who I saw on TV!" He didn't give me a chance to try. "Martin Tytell!"

Speaking of typewriters, I said to myself.

"He was being interviewed on a show about hard-to-solve crimes. He helped detectives figure out who wrote a ransom note by tracing it to a certain…"

"Typewriter!"

He laughed. "Yeah, so afterward I gave him a call about my typewriter. He said that if I couldn't afford to pay for the overhaul now, I should come pick it up because he's had a few break-ins. A couple of typewriters were stolen and he doesn't want the responsibility of having my typewriter in his shop. He also asked about you."

"Me?"

"Yeah, he said, 'Does your friend still want to buy a typewriter?' I told him yeah. You do, right?"

"Uh, *yeah*," I said, trying my best to sound convincing.

"So, what's the big secret?" he asked on the way to our usual place a little later.

"It's nothing that big," I replied. "There's this flea market every Sunday near my apartment…"

"You got a typewriter?" said Jay. I looked at him in disbelief.

"Is that the end of the story, you got a typewriter?"

"Yes, I got a typewriter," I answered, exasperated.

"So, you're going to tell me just like that?" he continued with a completely straight face. "With no lead-in? No buildup?"

I stared at him for a second and then slugged him on the arm, allowing him to think I had finished my story until after we'd ordered sandwiches and taken a seat.

"There's more, Jay," I continued as we began to eat. "Right after I bought that typewriter, I wandered over to another vendor and, there, right in front of me, was…"

"Another typewriter!"

He listened without interrupting as I told him the tale of type-writer Number Two, the Remington Rand.

"I'm sure you could always take them to Martin and put them toward that Royal you really liked," he said when I finished.

"Yeah, I could probably get at least a hundred bucks for the pair of them."

"Unless," said Jay, "you take them to Martin and he says, 'I recognize these typewriters—they're the two that were stolen from me!'"

I laughed. "So, anyway, Jay," I said hopefully, "now that I have not one but *two* typewriters, we can finally get started on our book."

He nodded slowly. "Sure. One of these days. Over time."

It wasn't the reaction I was expecting. Jay had used that phrase once before, when my feelings for him became obvious, when he had struggled to assure me that we were still friends and that we would still do everything we'd ever planned, "over time." Hear-ing him use it again, so matter-of-factly, brought me back to earth. I needed to be brought back to earth.

"What about *your* book?" asked Jay.

"My book? I haven't started writing a book yet."

"Why not?"

"I'm waiting for something to happen."

"Like what?"

"I'm not sure. *Something.*"

Back at work, I discovered a small package on my desk from a publicist I'd known for many years. Inside were two advance videotapes for a new PBS series called *The United States of Poetry* as well as an invitation to a preview party at the Coffee Shop on Union Square. A quick scan of the press release revealed that Allen Ginsberg was one of the poets featured in the series. I considered the unlikely intersection of television, poetry and Howlin' Allen.

Sometimes, I concluded, the world worked in ways that were more mysterious than I could ever imagine.

I showed the tapes and the invitation to Jay a few minutes later. "Ginsberg's in the show," I pointed out. "Maybe he'll be at the party."

"October fifth," said Jay, studying the invitation. "That date rings a bell. Like I have something else to do that day." He thought for a moment. "Whatever it is, I can't remember right now. But *this* sounds awesome. And maybe we *will* get to meet Ginsberg. RSVP for four."

Four? I wondered who would be joining Jay, Zahra and me but before I could ask, Jay had gone.

19

I WAS READING THE *NEW YORK TIMES* in my office the next morning when Jay strode in, smiled and, with a single flourish, sent a twenty-foot paper scroll sailing across my desk.

"*This,*" he said proudly, "is The Greatest Poem Ever Written."

On the scroll was a long column of jagged text that cascaded downward and disappeared from sight behind the ten or twelve inches at the end that remained rolled.

"I took all of the poems I've written over the past twelve months and arranged them chronologically to tell the story of the last year in my life," he explained in answer to the question on my face. "I typed it on my dad's old electric typewriter. Let me know what you think."

I eyed the scroll as Jay left. "But it will be impossible to edit!" I yelled after him.

I heard him laughing in the hall as I read the first few words: "...sitting facing her." Dot dot dot. Very carefully, I re-rolled the manuscript, wrapped a rubber band around it and put it in my backpack. At the end of the day, I walked to the art department to say goodbye to Jay and tell him I was looking forward to reading his scroll that evening. On the way back to my office, however, I heard him call my name.

I stopped in my tracks. "What's up?"

"I wanted to talk to you about something. In private." He pointed to my office, so serious I wasn't sure what to expect. My heart started to pound as he paused and cleared his throat. "Remember Bobby?"

"Bobby?"

"Bobby. You met him at..."

"Zahra's exhibit, oh, right. The guy who used to live above Ginsberg."

"Yeah," Jay continued. "Well, he enjoyed talking with you. I mean, Zahra told me he enjoyed talking with you." I'd never seen Jay so tongue-tied. "Anyway, Bobby asked me... he was wondering if... if we could hang out on Thursday. You know, Zahra and me and you and him."

"This Thursday? You mean at the *United States of Poetry* party?"

"Uh, yeah," said Jay, more nervous than ever. "Unless there's someone you wanted to ask to go with you. Is there?"

"No, Jay, there isn't. When you told me to RSVP for four I wondered who you..."

"Do you mind if Bobby comes along?" he interjected, smiling awkwardly.

"No, I don't mind at all," I assured him.

"Good, then we'll all hang out together," he said with an audible sigh of relief. "He said he'd bring his keys."

"Keys?"

"You know, the keys to Ginsberg's apartment building. If Ginsberg's there, Bobby can introduce us." He paused. "I mean, I know we would introduce ourselves to Ginsberg, but," he added, laughing just a little, "Bobby will make it easier."

A second after Jay left it suddenly hit me—I had just been fixed up. Jay, the guy whose life I had needlessly complicated by falling in love with him, had just arranged a date of sorts in the hope that I might get to know someone who was at least capable of the same feelings I felt. I was so moved that I had to close my office door, overcome by the realization that I wasn't alone in my efforts to set things right. Is it any wonder, I asked myself, why I fell for him in the first place?

At home that night, I read The Greatest Poem Ever Written.

Everything Jay had ever talked about with me was there on that scroll, including the two poems he'd shown me a few months earlier. There was one section, though, that really struck me. Just a few lines. But they seemed to speak of a dark event that Jay had never discussed. I decided to ask him about it the next day.

"I've got two things to tell you," announced Jay at Star Burger the following afternoon. "First, I ran down to Martin's this morning and gave him the money to overhaul my typewriter. And, second, Sil finally got back to me about my portfolio. He really liked it and asked me to sit tight for a few weeks while he works everything out."

"Jay, that's great! It sounds like you pretty much have the gig," I said.

"Yeah," he agreed. "I'm keeping my fingers crossed. So," he continued, changing the subject, "my scroll. What do you think?"

I told him what I thought. That it was amazing, that it contained some of the most beautiful and touching and heartfelt writing I had ever read, and that, despite my initial concerns, the impact of the individual poems wasn't diminished in the context of a larger work.

"They hold up," I assured him. "They create rhythms, ebbs and flows."

"It's really a rough draft," said Jay. "I have to go back and do some work on it. But it's finished in the sense that I'm not going to add anything. I had to take out the titles of the individual poems, and, in some cases, I worked them into a transition. Do you think they work?"

"Yeah, they work very well. They're minimal, but that's all you need. Speaking of titles, are you going to give the scroll one?"

"I suppose I should," he said thoughtfully. "You know, I haven't even read it yet, Har. You're the only one who has. I'm going to show it to Zahra tonight."

I was touched that he had shown it to me before Zahra, but reminded myself not to make it mean something it didn't. "I'm sure she'll feel the same way about it as I do," I said. "I read it five times."

"Really?"

"Yeah, really. There are even a few lines I know by heart."

"Such as?"

"'I love you. I need you in this obscure space of life. A soul connection surrounded by pink and blue is...'"

"'...a calming idea,'" Jay chimed in. "Zahra wrote that."

"*Zahra?*"

"When she gave me the typewriter on my birthday, I asked her to sit down and write something off the top of her head and that's what she wrote. Any other lines you really liked?"

"Actually, yes. My favorite section." I cleared my throat. "'Today love abounds. There is nothing but extreme, unselfish, undying love. Yesterday was black and death was in the air. Today love abounds...' It's really beautiful."

"I wrote that after my father died," said Jay. "When he passed away, all I wrote about was death. I was obsessed with death. 'Love Abounds' is about a day I seriously considered jumping off a bridge. I might have, if it weren't for Zahra."

I didn't know whether to be more shocked by his disclosure or his matter-of-fact delivery. "Wait a second, Jay. You were thinking of killing yourself?"

"Yeah, I was pretty bad off for a long time. My father was taken away, so suddenly. He was there one day and gone the next. I had a hard time believing that anything mattered. I couldn't help thinking, 'Why am I here if he isn't?' I was crazy. I felt like I had a huge hole in my heart. Zahra helped me fill it."

I was stunned. "I'm so sorry you went through that, Jay. I didn't know. You never said anything about it."

"I thought about telling you a few times but there was never a right time, and it's not something I like to talk about, anyway, so I told you about it in the poem. Just like you've told me a few things in your stories that you couldn't talk about."

"If you don't mind me asking, what made you change your mind?"

"I realized that one death was enough. Life is too precious, no matter what you're facing, to ever throw it away. Even if your life doesn't feel precious to you, you can never forget how precious your life is to someone else. Like Kerouac wrote in *On the Road*, 'Nobody knows what's going to happen to anybody besides the forlorn rags of growing old,' you know? Anything can happen. And even growing old is something to look forward to, despite what Kerouac wrote. As long as you have someone in your life, as long as you have love, your life will never be forlorn."

I debated whether to tell him that I, too, had nearly jumped off a bridge—in a manner of speaking, anyway. Since my situation ended far differently, however, I decided not to tell him then and there. I didn't want to burden him with the knowledge. Maybe some other time, I told myself. Maybe some other time I would tell him the final chapter of the Matteo and Harry story. But that would be getting ahead of things.

20

FOR ONE YEAR AFTER we spent the night together, Matteo and I were an inextricable part of each other's lives. It was a relationship based on our needs at the time. He needed someone to look out for him. And I needed someone who needed me. The last person I loved didn't.

I had always believed that Konrad and I would be together forever. For three years we lived in the kind of relationship our friends often wished they had. But we'd met when we were young, when it was easier to focus on what we had in common than what we didn't. Inevitably, time caught up with us and our differences became more apparent. We each reacted in our own way. I withdrew, hoping to minimize the gulf between us by minimizing myself. As I looked inward, however, Konrad looked out. I was crushed when he confessed to the affair. In the space of the few short seconds it took him to tell me what had happened, everything I had believed in, everything I had held to be true, suddenly came crashing down all around me. My world fell apart and so did I. I never felt more lost and alone in all my life.

He asked me to forgive him and I did, after I convinced myself that the heartache of living without him would be greater than the heartache of living with the knowledge of what he'd done. I wanted to believe that we still had a future. But I was wrong. About him. And about us. Though the second affair was less of a shock than the first, it hurt even more. The third affair was his final affair, on my watch, anyway. After that one, Konrad told me that he had finally decided he really loved me. I told him that in the time it had taken him to decide he really loved me, I had decided that I no longer loved him.

A part of me wished it were otherwise, but it wasn't. We'd both made decisions we needed to make and there was no going back. He flew off to Seattle to find a new life and a new love. I kept the cat and the house in Philadelphia, a house I shared with the ghost of a love that was no longer.

Until Matteo moved in.

The day after Matteo had spent the night, he called to tell me that the guy who ran the group house where he lived had given him an ultimatum: Pay the back rent he owed or leave. Matteo was beside himself. "Harry, I don't know what to do."

"You can stay with me," I offered with no hesitation.

He was quiet for a moment. "I would like that," he said finally. I interpreted Matteo's acceptance to mean that he felt what I felt. I had fallen for him. He showed up at my door at midnight carrying all his belongings in a single large duffel bag slung over his shoulder. I cleared a space for his citizenship study guides on the table in the living room. Upstairs, I emptied a few drawers in my dresser for him and after he unpacked we hit the sack. In bed, we were affectionate but not intimate. Matteo smiled and said he had too much on his mind. I said I understood.

When we awoke the next morning, however, Matteo lit a cigarette and stared at the ceiling for several minutes, deep in thought.

"Harry," he said finally, "I have feelings for you but I'm not sure they're the same feelings you have for me."

A million things went through my head but only a single word came out. "No?"

He looked at me. "No."

My face fell. "What about *this*?" I asked, indicating the obvious.

"*This* is good," he said slowly. "I like you. A lot. But it's not what you're thinking. You're a great guy but you're not my type. I wish you were. But you're not."

"No?"

"No."

He saw the light in my eyes flicker and then go out.

"Ah, I'm not exactly a good catch right now, anyway, Harry," he offered. "I smoke too much, I drink too much, I'm out of work, I'm broke and I'm crashing at your place."

"I'll look out for you," I responded instinctively, as if that could somehow change his feelings.

"Nah, Har," he said gently, "I don't need anyone to look out for me." He sighed as he exhaled a long stream of white smoke. "Then again," he added with a laugh, "maybe I do."

I did look out for Matteo. He had given me just enough to hang my hopes on and I looked out for him in the belief that if I showed him how much I was willing to do for him, he would realize how much I loved him and, in turn, how much he really did love me. I *was* his type. I just needed to prove it. I had tried and failed to convince Konrad that I was the one—while I still wanted to be the one, anyway—but I was determined to convince Matteo. Or die trying. I didn't know how close I would come.

We went out drinking every night, usually to the Car Bar. That was our routine. When I got home from work, Matteo would close his history, geography and government books and we would hit happy hour. I would throw a twenty on the bar and we would down as many giant mugs or pitchers as possible at happy hour prices. I had never drunk so much and so often in my life, but it was what Matteo wanted to do and I would have done anything for Matteo. By early evening, we would both be buzzed, laughing and joking, playing pool and shooting darts with the rest of the Car Bar regulars. Many of them supposed that Matteo and I were lovers. They saw us arrive together. They saw us hang out together. And, at closing time, they saw us stumble out into the night and head home together. Matteo would sometimes try to set the record straight but few believed him. On top of everything else, they saw how I looked at him.

I derived a measure of hope, however irrational, from all the assumptions. If Matteo and I *seemed* like lovers, I reasoned, then it followed that we would *become* lovers. We were already more than friends. Every night when we got home, we would climb into bed and, under the covers, Matteo would ask me to hold him. I would lock my arms around him and pull him into my chest. He would laugh and yell, "Not so tight!" And I would loosen my grip. Just a bit. By morning he would be holding me.

It was all so incredibly reckless and romantic, so contrary to the picture-perfect picket-fence existence Konrad and I had carved out, that, in the end, was not so perfect. With Matteo, I willingly lost myself in a whirl of idyllic lost weekends and weeks, choosing to believe that every beer I bought him brought us closer together while choosing to forget that Matteo had said we could never be as close as I wanted. It was only a matter of time, I told myself, before everything fell into place. It was only a matter of time, however, before everything fell apart.

I came home from work one day to find a note on the fridge. "Happy hour started early," it said. "Meet me at the Car Bar." It was the first of many similar notes. At that point, Matteo had been unemployed for three months and it was beginning to weigh on him. He had put aside his citizenship studies to look for other work, but looking for work was equal parts actively searching and patiently waiting and Matteo wasn't good at waiting. With too much time on his hands, he grew anxious and restless. In need of something to ease his anxiety and fill all the empty hours, Matteo started drinking earlier in the day. Every evening, by the time I found him, he would have more beers in him than we would normally down in an entire night and he would greet me with an exaggerated grin and a sloppy, slurred affection. For a while, I could convince him that it was time to go home after I'd had a single beer. I saw what was happening and I was worried about him. One night, however, he didn't want to leave.

I had arrived at the Car Bar to find three empty shot glasses and a half-empty pitcher in front of him on the bar, courtesy of a generous stranger who had already departed. I stood next to him for several moments before his eyes focused and he realized who I was.

"Harry!" he yelled, slipping from his barstool and falling into my arms. He laughed as I tried unsuccessfully to stand him upright. "I need to *sit!*" he said, grabbing his stool. When he was finally stable, I suggested we get something to eat. "Nah, not hungry," Matteo replied. "And," he added, tapping the pitcher, "we're not done drinking. Get yourself a mug."

I got myself a mug but sipped my beer. Matteo seemed distracted and repeatedly disappeared into the crowd around us, returning from time to time to take another swig. The fourth or fifth time he returned with a bewildered young blond in tow.

"Harry, this is Joey," he said, wrapping an arm around Joey's waist. Joey smiled awkwardly at me.

"Hi, Joey," I said, extending my hand. "How do you guys know each other?"

Joey looked at Matteo.

"Joey and I just met," Matteo explained. Joey leaned over and whispered something in Matteo's ear. "Sure, I'll be right here," said Matteo. "See you in a few." Joey headed off into the darkness.

"Matteo, what do you say we get out of here?" I asked as soon as he'd gone.

Matteo frowned. "Harry, I'm going home with that kid."

I blinked. "What?"

Matteo studied my face through his bloodshot brown eyes. "I'm going home with him. You don't mind, do you?"

I felt like I had just been stabbed in the heart. It obviously showed.

"I won't be out all night," Matteo assured me. "I'll see you later, okay?"

I nodded weakly, too stunned to do anything else.

Matteo leaned close and put his arm on my shoulder. "Do you think you could lend me a twenty?" he asked. "I'm all out and I want to buy him a drink before we leave."

I stared at the floor for a moment, shattered. Matteo and I weren't lovers. No matter how many people thought we were. I wasn't his type. I handed him a twenty and left.

Matteo came home in the dead of night. The sound of the front door opening and closing woke me up. I listened, expecting him to come upstairs, but when several minutes passed and he still hadn't, I got out of bed to see why. I found him lying on the sofa in the dark, smoking a cigarette.

"You all right?" I asked, sitting down next to him.

He exhaled and sighed at the same time. "Yeah, I'm okay."

"Come to bed."

He looked at me. "I think I'm going to sleep here from now on."

"You don't have to do that."

"Yeah, I do. It's better. For both of us."

"No, it isn't," I stammered. "You can sleep upstairs."

"Harry, I don't want to give you the wrong idea about us. I was even thinking that maybe I should find someplace else to live."

"Please stay," I said, trying not to choke up. "I like… you… being here."

"I like being here, too. You just need to understand where I'm coming from."

I swallowed. "I understand."

Matteo looked doubtful. "You sure?"

"I'm sure," I insisted, although I really wasn't. The only thing I was sure of at that moment was that I wanted him to stay and I would have said anything to convince him. If he left, I would lose him. If he stayed, I still had a chance.

"Okay, good," he said, rubbing my hand and smiling tenderly. "Let's get some sleep."

"All right," I replied. I hesitated for a moment, searching for words I couldn't find, before finally heading to bed by myself. I was still awake when the sun came up.

21

"**W**HAT'S HAPPENING?" asked Cliff, stopping by my office to see if I had any intriguing story ideas. Cliff had been editor-in-chief for a month and I had already become familiar with his likes and dislikes, so I had a feeling that selling him on my latest idea—an article about *The United States of Poetry*—wouldn't be easy.

I had watched the series the night before and been struck by the concept: "Poetry as television. Television as poetry." Poets were presented like rock stars, performing their works in MTV-inspired videos. There was Henry Real Bird reflecting on the wanderlust inspired by the wind, the sky and the stars from a rocky hilltop, Tracie Morris rapping about the grace and presence of a Project Princess in East New York and Lois-Ann Yamanaka rhapsodizing about a box of Raisinets beneath a South Pacific palm. And then there was Sparrow, "a self-described 'renowned street poet.'" From a sea of multicolored umbrellas on a rainy Manhattan sidewalk, a manic, bearded, long-haired Sparrow rose, with his arms outstretched, to address his fellow citizens in "A Testimonial."

"I have lived in this city / 25 years / and all that time / I have dropped things. / I've dropped / tissues, / letters from women / in Santa Fe, N.M., / money, / the keys to my house, / books by / Jacques Prevert. / And all this time, / you, / the people of this / city, have pointed / to me, and said, / "Hey!" "Sir!" "You! / You dropped something!" / and then I've picked it up. / You have watched / over me all these / years, / and I've waited till / now to thank you."

A finger bell and bongos announced Ginsberg's segment. Allen appeared, bearded, bespectacled and balding, dressed in baby-blue pajamas and seated on a red meditation mat in lotus position. The camera cut to the tip of a fountain pen scribbling in a notebook and then pulled back to reveal Ginsberg as the scribbler. The scene shifted to grainy black-and-white footage of him and a young hunk parading around an apartment in their boxers, looking at books, hanging laundry and making tea as Ginsberg, in a voice-over, intoned "Personals Ad."

"Poet professor in autumn years / seeks helpmate companion protector friend / young lover with empty compassionate soul / exuberant spirit, straightforward handsome / athletic physique & boundless mind, courageous / warrior who may also like women&girls, no problem…"

Next up was Johnny Depp, the only one in the entire series performing a poem written by someone else—the "113th Chorus" of *Mexico City Blues* by Jack Kerouac. I remembered that he had bought Kerouac's raincoat for ten thousand dollars. With a cigarette dangling from his goateed lips, Depp delivered Kerouac's words in a smoky whisper over a driving electric guitar.

"Got up and dressed up / and went out & got laid / Then died and got buried / in a coffin in the grave…"

As I pitched my story idea to Cliff, I played up the celebrity angle and the MTV influence in an attempt to convince him that the show was, as Donal, the managing editor, liked to say, hip, hot and happening. Much to my surprise, Cliff nodded when I was through.

"Sounds good."

Taken aback by his quick approval, I decided to really go out on a limb. "What would you think if I asked Ginsberg to write an original poem to go with the article?"

"I'd love it," Cliff replied immediately. "I went to a Giants game when I lived in San Francisco and Ginsberg did a reading before the teams took the field. The guy I was with said, 'What the hell is *this*?' But I thought it was great."

I called Ginsberg's office and got his assistant, Bob Rosenthal, who immediately recognized my name.

"You're the guy who sent that fax."

"Uh, yeah," I said, slightly embarrassed.

"Allen was very touched by your invitation and he did consider meeting you guys, but he's been very busy and a little under the weather."

"Really?" I said, impressed that he had even looked at the fax. I explained the reason for my call.

"For a poem, you'll have to contact Allen's literary agent, Jeffrey Posternak," said Rosenthal. "But I can help you set up an interview with Allen if you'd like."

"I'd *love* to talk with Allen," I replied, a little too enthusiastically.

"Maybe you'll get to meet him after all," he said. "In the meantime, give Jeffrey a call."

I did as he suggested right after I hung up.

"Allen gets lots of requests for commissioned poems," said Posternak. "He's never accepted one. Still, you never know. I'll run it by him. Would you be interested in one of his unpublished poems? He might be more likely to provide you with one of those."

"Definitely," I assured him, "although, obviously, I'd prefer an original."

"I'll be in touch."

I hurried to tell Jay the news. "Ready for lunch?" I asked when I was through.

"Actually, Har," he said, "I'm meeting Zahra to go shopping for a birthday present for my mom. Her birthday is October fifth—the date of *The United States of Poetry* preview party. That's the reason the date kept ringing a bell. I'm really bummed, but I'm not going to be able to make it."

Jay didn't say whether Zahra and Bobby would go if he didn't, and, for some reason, I didn't think to ask. Even if they did go, it wouldn't be the same without him.

"I'll walk out with you," I said.

Zahra was standing on the plaza out front. She gave me a hug and a kiss on the cheek. She gave Jay a hug and a kiss on the lips.

"I'll see you two later," I said, turning to go.

"Aren't you coming with us?" asked Zahra. "Come with us."

I looked at Jay, looking for an answer. He hadn't invited me along earlier and I assumed there was a reason. I really wanted to just leave the two of them on their own.

"We'll eat first, and then Zahra and I will shop afterward," he offered as a solution.

I frowned, still reluctant. I felt like Jay was once again being pulled in two different directions and I didn't want to be one of them.

"It's okay for you to join us," Zahra insisted.

"I was just trying to take everyone's feelings into consideration," I explained.

"Oh," she said, turning to Jay, "we see enough of each other. Don't we?"

"No," he answered with a smile. He took her hand in his as we began walking—a gesture, I assumed, intended to pre-empt any doubts about who was with whom. "Hey, Har, tell Zahra about Cliff and Ginsberg."

I related my conversation with Cliff on our way to Star Burger.

"You must be a good salesman," Zahra observed when I'd finished. "So, do you want to go to the poetry party with Bobby?"

I hesitated.

"I know all four of us originally planned to go," she continued as we ate, "but we can all go out together some other time. You don't want to go alone."

"You'd just be hanging out together," said Jay. "It's nothing serious."

He sounded so hopeful. I remembered how nervous he had been when he first told me about Bobby.

"Sure, we can hang out," I said. "Give Bobby my number."

Bobby called a little later. "So, this is okay with you?" he asked.

"I mean, that Jay and Zahra aren't going to be there with us?"

"It's okay with me if it's okay with you."

We agreed to meet at the Coffee Shop on Union Square, where the party was being held. I was planning to arrive at six-thirty, but he couldn't make it till seven.

"You remember what I look like, right?" he asked anxiously.

"Of course."

Jay stopped by my office at six, sporting his vintage leather. "I'm on my way to Long Island," he said. "Look what I got for my mom." He held out a small, embroidered jewelry box and opened it to reveal a beautiful rose and ivory cameo.

"Nice, Jay. I'm sure your mom will love it."

"Yeah, I think she will, too. Hey, have a good time tonight. I want a full report tomorrow. And if you meet Ginsberg, tell him I'll catch him next time."

I LEFT WORK TEN MINUTES later, heading to the Times Square subway station in a windy downpour that defied my best attempts to stay dry, even with an umbrella. By the time I was underground, I was soaked from the waist down, a situation that would not have been quite so apparent had I not been wearing khakis. Jay had observed on more than one occasion that I always seemed to be wearing khakis whenever it rained, and, unfortunately, he was right. I settled into a soggy ride on a downtown N-train and got off at Union Square. Though I'd never been to the Coffee Shop ("It's where all the unemployed actors and models hang out," cracked Jay), I found it easily enough, at the corner of Sixteenth and Broadway, and, after a brief look around the main bar that seemed to confirm Jay's appraisal, I made my way to a private room in the back where the *United States of Poetry* party was already in full swing. Oscar Morrison, the publicist for the series, was standing at the door to greet new arrivals. Oscar and I had spoken about various projects on the phone for years but had never met.

"Harry!" he enthused after I introduced myself. "It's so nice to finally put a face with the voice."

"Yeah," I agreed as he handed me a press kit. "Hey, Oscar, is Ginsberg here?"

"No," he replied, slightly disappointed. "And given the weather, I'm not sure he's going to show. But the producer and director are here—Bob Holman and Mark Pellington. And a few of the poets. I'll introduce you to them if you want. In the meantime, get a drink. It's open bar."

Just inside the door, sitting on a stool, was a wicker basket full of black metal buttons. I picked one out and read the words inscribed on its surface. *The United States of Poetry*, it said around the perimeter, and, in the center, "If it ain't a pleasure, it ain't a poem," a quote by William Carlos Williams featured in the show's opening credits. I grabbed another, shoved both in my pocket and headed for the bar, where I ordered a Heineken and then turned to study my surroundings. The place was packed with more than a hundred downtown types, nearly every one of whom was dressed in black from head to toe. I glanced at my wet khakis. Hard to believe that a pair of tan pants would ever make someone stand out in a crowd.

Across the room, I spotted a familiar face, or, more accurately, a familiar hat. It was a distinctive brown leather fedora, and although I couldn't remember the name of the guy who was wearing it, I recognized him—and his hat—from MTV's *Spoken Word Unplugged*, on which he had performed a year earlier. I made my way through the crowd, figuring I could strike up a conversation about his *Unplugged* appearance.

"Harry Charity from *Element*," I said.

"Bob Holman," he replied, grabbing my hand and pumping it vigorously.

"Bob Holman?" I repeated. "You're the producer."

"Bingo!" he yelled. "Co-producer, actually. Glad to see *Element* is interested in *The United States of Poetry*."

"Well, *I'm* interested," I said. "And I've managed to interest my editor. He gave me the go-ahead on an article."

"That's terrific!" Holman raved. "*Do you* write poetry?"

"Prose, mostly. But I have a friend who writes poetry."

"Do you guys like to perform? I emcee a weekly poetry slam every Friday at the Nuyorican Poets Café in the East Village. I could add the two of you to the lineup some night if you'd like."

"Thanks for the vote of confidence," I said. "You haven't even seen our stuff."

"Doesn't matter," he said with a shrug. "It's an unwritten rule that the best poem never wins!" He grinned, clearly amused by such an ironic inevitability, and then wrote down his phone number as I handed him my card.

"Mr. *Charity*," he read, delighting in my surname. "Call me any time."

Just then, I spotted Bobby standing a few feet away, looking a little lost. I called his name and made my way over to him. "So, you made it," I said.

He nodded and looked around. "Do you know a lot of these people?"

"Not a lot, but a few."

He smiled weakly. I got the feeling he didn't want to be there.

"Would you like to have dinner?" he asked, confirming my suspicions.

"Sure."

Outside, we wandered aimlessly in the pouring rain for a half-hour before finally ducking into a diner on University Place. I ordered a burger and fries; Bobby had a salad and soup.

"So, how long have you known Jay and Zahra?" he asked as we ate.

"About six months, although it feels like a lot longer."

Our conversation was self-conscious, each of us attempting to find some common ground. He volunteered that he was an art teacher. While he was at Pratt, he had constructed a life-size doll-house from appliance crates and populated it with mannequins styled as Joan Crawford, Bette Davis, Mae West and Zsa Zsa Gabor.

"Do you like Joan Crawford?" he inquired.

I didn't like or dislike her, but I didn't want to tell him that.

"She's all right."

"Have you seen any of her movies?"

I thought for a moment. "I'm not sure."

"*The Women?*"

"No."

"*Johnny Guitar?*"

"No." I suddenly remembered something. "But I *did* see Mom-*my Dearest.*"

His eyes dropped to his salad. "Oh."

An awkward silence descended. I stared out the window at a woman without an umbrella desperately trying to hail a cab in the driving rain.

"So, would you like to get together again?" he asked as we walked through the rain back to Union Square where he could catch an L-train to Brooklyn.

"We'll be in touch," I replied, trying to sound upbeat. I felt bad for not really answering his question but I didn't feel any chemistry between us, and because he seemed like a genuinely good guy, I felt bad about that, too.

"HOW WAS THE PARTY?" asked Jay first thing next morning.

"It was great," I replied, handing him one of the buttons I'd picked up.

He eyed the inscription and smiled. "I was hoping you wouldn't say that. I mean, I'm glad it was great, but I really wish I could have been there. Did Ginsberg show?"

"Unfortunately, no."

"Did you have a good time with Bobby?"

"Yeah," I said slowly. "We grabbed dinner afterward."

Jay smiled, pleasantly surprised. "Do you think you'll see each other again?" he asked hopefully.

I hated to let him down. "Maybe. I'm not sure. He's a nice guy, but..."

Jay sighed and nodded. "But not your type. Can't do much about that."

"I'm sorry, Jay. I really appreciate what you did."

"No big deal," said Jay. "You're both good guys, just different kinds of guys."

"Yeah," I agreed, somewhat reluctantly. "By the way, Jay, Bob Holman, one of the producers of the poetry series, asked if we would like to read at the Nuyorican Poets Café."

"Really? Do you think he was sincere? Or did he just say that because you're a magazine editor?"

"Oh, he was sincere," I assured him.

"Then we should definitely check out the Nuyorican some night."

"So you can see what it's like before you read there?"

"Before *we* read there. And I'm going to have lots to read. While *you* were out on the town last night, I picked up my typewriter from Martin. It's like new! I hit a key and it just goes... *click!*"

"So, you'll be writing some new poems soon?"

"*Very* soon. But you're going to need something to read at the Nuyorican, too. When are you going to start writing your book?"

"Like I said before, I'm waiting for something to happen."

"What?"

"I don't know. A reporter once asked Kerouac what he was waiting for and he said, 'I'm waiting for God to show his face.'"

"Is that what you're waiting for?"

I shrugged. "Maybe. I'll let you know when He does."

"In the meantime, there's always the continuing saga of Matteo and Harry," suggested Jay.

"Yes," I agreed, "there is."

22

WHEN MATTEO BEGAN an endless string of one-night stands, my hopes for him and me did not diminish. Even when a one-night stand occasionally stretched into a two- or three-night stand. Though he had made it easy for me to get over my feelings for him, I actually became even more single-minded in my pursuit. I considered his repeated rendezvous with other guys as something I just had to deal with. Everyone who ever loved anyone had something to deal with, right? At least Matteo didn't lie to me, as Konrad had. At least Matteo was honest about what he was doing. That meant something, didn't it? And Matteo always came home. He might spend a few hours a night with other guys but he spent the majority of his time with me. That alone proved how he really felt. Even if we no longer slept in the same bed.

My rationalizations piled up precariously. Whether I simply didn't see them or simply chose to ignore them, they slowly but surely whittled away at any lingering feelings of self-worth that had survived the circumstances of my split with Konrad.

Every night brought a new rejection. Every night, Matteo and I would spend the first few hours joined at the hip. Every night, I would cling to the hope that we would go home together, as we once had. But, come last call, Matteo would wander away and, within minutes, return with a guy he'd just met. He would whisper to me that they were going back to the guy's place and ask me for a five, a ten or a twenty so he could buy the guy a drink and catch a cab back to my house later, when all was said and done. It was as if I was good enough to hang out with, good enough to have a few beers with, good enough to shoot pool with, to talk with, to share secrets with, to live with, to do just about everything with, but as soon as someone appeared who was good enough to sleep with, I didn't matter. I was just someone to pass the time with between hookups. Hookups that didn't mean anything. And I was supposed to understand that, to feel like it was no big deal, to not be hurt. But I *was* hurt. Every time. At home, alone, I would lie in bed and torture myself by imagining what Matteo was doing while I waited to hear the click of his key in the door.

We rarely spoke of the other guys. I didn't want to believe they even existed, so I never asked. And if Matteo did mention them after the fact, it was only to say that nothing notable had transpired or that he'd passed out shortly after they arrived at the guy's apartment and couldn't even remember if they'd actually done what they'd gone there to do. I learned to recognize Matteo's type. The type of guys he wanted to spend a few hours with, anyway. They were soft. Pretty. I could pick them out of a crowd the moment we walked into a bar. Sometimes I knew whom he was going to end up with even before he did. And certainly before they did.

I always gave Matteo the money he requested. I told myself that if I demonstrated just how far I would go to make him happy, even help him hook up with someone else, sooner or later, hopefully sooner, he would realize who really made him happy. And I could wait. I was patient. Eventually Matteo would see his flings for what they were and see me in a new light. Such were the delusions born of desperation.

Matteo actually didn't pick someone up every night. Some nights, he was simply too drunk. Too drunk to fuck. Too drunk to even think about fucking. On those nights, something else happened. Matteo's demons surfaced, the demons that he tried to drown night after night without success, the demons that clawed at his soul, tearing open an aching wound and triggering an ugly anger. I knew what was weighing on him. I could give him a roof over his head. I could give him money. I could buy him beers. But he wanted to stand on his own two feet. Even more importantly, he wanted to be accepted for who he was by his father. Though he downplayed his feelings for him, it was obvious that what his father thought of him had a significant effect on what he thought of himself. He was less than perfect in his father's eyes, so less than perfect in his own.

The smallest thing could summon Matteo's demons when he drank more than he could handle. His easy-going temperament would make a hairpin turn and, without fail, even the most innocent of situations could spin wildly out of control without a second's warning.

He told me he was hungry one night. We were at the Car Bar. He had been drinking heavily. Out of the blue, he wanted something to eat. It was only one o'clock, relatively early for Matteo to call it quits, and I took it as a good sign. Maybe it was a turning point, I thought. It was, but not the kind I'd hoped for. We headed to a twenty-four hour diner off Locust. A waiter took our order and we were relaxing over a cup of coffee when high-pitched laughter erupted at a table behind us to our right. I glanced over, expecting to see a couple of young girls, and was taken aback when I saw, instead, two extremely muscled black guys, each of whom had to be close to three hundred pounds. For a moment, I thought the laughter I'd heard had to have come from another table. But then one of the guys leaned in to his companion, threw his hands in the air and said something in a voice that seemed about three octaves too high and once again the two of them let loose with the same incongruous laughter I'd heard before.

Matteo scowled and set his coffee cup down with a loud clink.

"Were you born with a dick between your legs or a pussy?" he muttered under his breath but loud enough for everyone in the place to hear.

The two guys stopped laughing immediately and glared at Matteo and me.

"*What* did you say?" asked one of them incredulously.

"I *said*," repeated Matteo, much more loudly than the first time, as he turned defiantly to face them, "were you born with a *dick* between your legs or a *pussy?*"

I was sober. I had been drinking nonstop for six straight hours but in a split second I was stone-cold sober. As I struggled to find the words that would undo what couldn't be undone, from another part of the diner came an unexpected response.

"What's *wrong* with being born with a pussy between your legs?" demanded a woman from a table of five women behind us.

"He didn't mean it," I stammered. But it was futile.

"Oh, yes I did," insisted Matteo. "I meant *every word*."

The two guys jumped up. "You wanna take this outside?" one shouted.

"Sure," Matteo shot back without missing a beat. "*Outside!*"

In a second, Matteo and the two bodybuilders bolted through the door. I followed as fast as I could, not knowing what I could possibly contribute to the situation but still hoping that I could somehow defuse it.

Outside, Matteo and one of the guys were already squaring off, taunting each other with four-letter epithets as they simultaneously stripped off their shirts and tossed them aside. I made a last-ditch effort to grab Matteo and pull him away, but the second guy grabbed me instead and pinned me to a car.

"It's between *them*," he insisted.

I watched helplessly and in horror as his friend swept the sidewalk with Matteo. Inside the diner, the table of women also watched, lining up at the window to cheer Goliath on as he beat David to a pulp.

It was all over in a minute. Matteo escaped with only two black eyes. The guy had actually gone relatively easy on him, considering the damage he could have effortlessly inflicted. But as the guy turned to go back inside the diner and his friend finally let me go, Matteo pushed his luck just a little too far.

"Is that all you got?" he scoffed as he pulled his shirt back over his head. "I *knew* you had a pussy between your legs."

The guy looked at him in disbelief and then, with as much thought as it takes to swat a fly away, he walked up behind Matteo, placed a hand on his shoulder, spun him around and landed one last punch that sent Matteo sailing ten feet though the air and crashing down on the sidewalk in a heap. He sat there, stunned, as blood gushed from his nose and mouth and turned his white cotton shirt scarlet.

I rushed over and picked him up, pulling off my own shirt and wrapping it around his face. "I'm taking you to Pennsylvania Hospital," I said, dragging him down Thirteenth Street. Matteo started to say something but I shook my fist at him. "One word, just one word, and I'll flatten you myself."

I couldn't imagine what we looked like sitting in the emergency room, Matteo a bloody mess with two black eyes and me in a filthy white tank. While we waited for a doctor, I stared at an overhead TV that was showing *Benji*, of all things. As Matteo dabbed at his mouth and nose with my shirt, I silently shook my head in disbelief. For the first night in memory, Matteo had left the Car Bar with me rather than a stranger and instead of going home together we had ended up in an ER.

"Sucker punch," Matteo mumbled after a few minutes.

I looked at him. "*What?*"

"He didn't have me till that last punch," he ventured. "And it was a sucker punch."

"*You're* the sucker," I countered.

We were both quiet for a moment.

"Yeah, I guess I am," Matteo said finally. "Why do you put up with it, Har?"

"Because I'm a sucker, too," I said.

"For a pretty face?" asked Matteo, with as much of a smile as his injuries allowed.

"Yeah, and you're lucky this isn't the first time I'm laying eyes on yours."

Matteo stood and checked himself in a mirror. "I'm pretty messed up," he observed.

I glanced at his reflection. "Are we still talking about your face?"

He laughed and then immediately winced. "I wish we were."

23

ON NOVEMBER NINTH, Jay and I took off from work to attend the press preview for the Beat Culture exhibit at the Whitney—officially titled "Beat Culture and the New America, 1950-1965"—an event we had been eagerly anticipating since we first heard it was in the works several months earlier. I agreed to meet Jay and Zahra at the museum at eleven o'clock. I was glad Zahra was joining us. I had grown fond of her after clearing the air at her own exhibit, and I enjoyed hanging out with the two of them. Her presence also helped me to keep my feelings for Jay in perspective, even though I knew full well I needed to do that on my own.

I arrived fifteen minutes early and as I waited on the pavement out front, I became aware of a guy sitting at a rickety card table about twenty feet away. Hanging from the front of the table was a piece of cardboard with a neatly lettered message written in black Magic Marker that said, "Down with the Beat Veneration." My curiosity aroused, I approached, recognizing the guy in the olive green army field coat behind the sign as one of the poets in *The United States of Poetry*.

"Excuse me, are you... Sparrow?" I felt funny saying his name. It didn't seem to go with his long bushy beard and shoulder-length light brown hair or his incongruously stylish red-framed eyeglasses.

He looked up and smiled, pleasantly surprised that I knew who he was even if he didn't know who I was.

"Yes, I'm Sparrow," he replied. "Mind if I ask how you know me?"

"I saw you in a TV show."

"Really? How'd you do that? The only TV show I've been on hasn't aired yet."

"I'm an editor at *Element*," I explained. "I got an advance copy."

"Ah. What did you think?"

"I loved it."

"Great. I don't suppose *Element* is going to publish an article about it."

"Actually, *I'm* writing one."

"Wow, I wouldn't have thought," he said.

I shrugged and gestured to the table between us. "So, what's all this about?"

He cleared his throat. "We're protesting the Beat Culture exhibit."

I looked around. "We?"

"Well, me and this group I'm with, the Unbearables."

"The Unbearables?"

"Well, we used to call ourselves The Unbearable Beatniks of Life," he continued, "but we dropped the embarrassing 'Beatniks of Life' part because mostly what we do now is protest the *real* beatniks. So we certainly don't want people to know our original name."

"Where are your comrades?"

"We're protesting in shifts. Poetry doesn't pay the bills. Some of us have day jobs—including me."

"Really?" I asked. "If I remember correctly, the press kit for *The United States of Poetry* says that you describe yourself as a, quote-unquote, *renowned street poet*."

"Hmmm," he mused. "I don't *think* I ever described myself as a *renowned street poet*. For one thing, I didn't know street poets could *be* renowned. I'm a program director at the Ninety-Second Street Y. I'm actually an establishmentarian fellow. I mean, I work part-time and I'm poor, but I have an MFA in writing. And a family. I took a personal day to do this."

"And what *is* this, exactly? Why are you protesting?"

"You know," he answered, "to be honest, I wasn't sure myself, initially—there's a Marxist element to the Unbearables. Our view is that the Beats are sanctioned rebels. They're the official mythic rebels of the society. But what are they rebelling against? The moment I saw a full-page ad in *Paper* magazine promoting AT&T's sponsorship of the Beat Culture exhibit, I knew we *had* to protest. The ad said, 'Communication: Whether it's poetry, jazz or your grandmother calling you for Christmas, we're involved. AT&T.' Or something to that effect. After I saw that ad, I wrote this flyer," he continued, directing my attention to a pile of papers. "I mimeographed it myself at St. Mark's Church."

I read the flyer aloud. "'We would like to thank AT&T for generously supporting the Beat exhibit. This demonstration against the exhibit is brought to you by Pepsi, the drink that *demonstrates* its taste again and again. Give the gift of life, give Pepsi.'"

When I finished, Sparrow pointed to another pile. "I wrote this second flyer to explain the first one," he continued, picking one up and reading it himself. "It says, 'I envision a future where not only cultural rebels are underwritten by corporations, but the rebels *against* the rebels are similarly sponsored. Thus, rivalries between schools of art are actually advertising wars.' Basically, most of us are protesting the idea that AT&T could sponsor this exhibit by the big rebels against American culture. What are they rebelling against? Un-hipness?"

"But the Beats have no control over the fact that they're being underwritten by AT&T?" I countered.

"They could *all* be protesting it," he insisted. "I mean, there was a big party last night and they all came! They could publicly write a letter defying their sponsorship. They could refuse to participate. I'm not saying that they *should* do that. I'm just saying that you can't have it both ways. People are saying, 'Oh, the Beats were never rebels. They were just a school of poetry.' This is the American fucking amnesia. Maybe they *were* a school of poetry, but everybody *thought* they were rebels. They certainly *gave out* that they were rebels. So, what was it really? They were just smoking pot? The point is, if a person's rebelling against American society, and all they're against is Norman Rockwell paintings, well, fine. But that's not much of a protest." He looked down at his fliers and card table. "I guess this isn't either, but at least it's *something*."

"Interesting," I said. "I never thought of it that way. I'm not sure if I should admit this but I'm actually here to see the exhibit."

"Oh, I plan on seeing it, too," he said. "The Unbearables are protesting en masse on Thursday evening. It's the first free night of the exhibit, so I'll go inside after our protest."

Glancing at the museum, I spotted Jay through the glass doors, in the lobby gift shop.

"Well, I see my friends are already here," I said. "Do you think I could interview you for my article on *The United States of Poetry*?"

He seemed skeptical. "You want to interview *me*? In the pages of *Element*?"

"Yeah."

"Well, sure," he said. "Let me give you my number." He wrote it on the back of one of the fliers.

"I'll call you next week," I assured him, though I could tell he was unconvinced.

Inside the Whitney, I walked up behind Jay and tugged the sleeve of his coat.

"Hey, Har!" he yelled, excitedly patting me on the back. "Look at these!" He pointed to a rack of postcards featuring black-and-white photographs of the Beats, classic shots of Kerouac and Burroughs as well as one of Ginsberg and companion Peter Orlovsky standing naked in a shower, smiling demurely and hiding their privates behind their crossed hands. "Zahra is buying a set," he said just as she appeared, greeting me with a hug and a kiss.

"Shall we go in?" she asked.

"We've waited long enough," I said, leading the way to the check-in table for the press.

"What publication are you with?" asked the woman manning

the table.

"*Element*," I replied as she scanned a long list. "Jay Bishop and Harry Charity."

She checked off our names and then looked at Zahra. "And you are?"

It was time for a little triage on my part; the invitation only admitted two. "She's not on the list but she works in the art department of *Element*," I bluffed.

"I'll mark it down as 'plus one,'" said the woman, handing us each a press kit. "Would you like to listen to an audio tour of the exhibit narrated by Allen Ginsberg? We have portable tape recorders and headsets."

Jay and I looked at each other. "No thanks," I replied. We just wanted to get going.

She pointed behind her. "The exhibit is on the third floor. You can either wait for an elevator or take the stairs."

"The stairs," said Jay, laughing as he ran ahead with Zahra and me right behind him.

Just inside the archway on the third floor, the Beat Culture exhibit began with a large plaque suggesting that the Beats were distinguished not only by the range of their collective artistic output—from prose, poetry and performance to painting, photography and film—but by their individual experimentation in more than one medium.

Arranged on the wall to the right were a dozen or so large prints of black-and-white photographs taken by Allen Ginsberg, each one with a long, hand-written caption.

"This is my favorite picture of Kerouac," said Jay, pointing to a stark and striking image of Kerouac on a fire escape in the East Village. "Look. He's got the Brakeman's Manual in his coat pocket from when he worked on the railroad in California with Neal Cassady."

"Ginsberg calls it the *Heroic Portrait*," I offered, not sure where I'd picked up that piece of information.

"Look at this one," said Zahra, moving on to a portrait of Burroughs, his eyes heavy and vacant beneath the brim of the gray Stetson he was nearly never without.

I read the caption aloud. "William Burroughs, slightly zonked."

"Maybe that's why he always wore the hat," said Jay with a laugh.

Just past the photos were a series of paintings by Kerouac, highlighted by an oil of a radiant, blissful Buddha. Just beyond the Buddha, bolted to the wall, was a Plexiglas box that contained an artifact Jay and I had seen before, under more intimate circumstances—the scroll manuscript of *On the Road*, with the first nine inches exposed. As Zahra studied the scroll, Jay and I studied her, watching as she squinted at the words with a contemplative reverence that was quite unlike the awestruck exhilaration we'd exhibited the first time we had laid eyes on it.

"What do you think?" Jay asked her finally.

"It has a sort of power," she allowed. "A definite aura."

"Har, look!" yelled Jay suddenly, pointing to a rather large crevice near the top of the manuscript. "That piece wasn't missing when we saw it at the Library."

"And neither of *us* has it," I said.

"Well, *someone* does," said Jay as we continued on our way. "Someone has a very nice little piece of the scroll manuscript of *On the Road*."

Just around a corner, in a long glass case, we discovered the original manuscript of Ginsberg's "Howl." Like *On the Road*, it, too, was typed, but on three separate pieces of letter-size white paper. And, like Kerouac, Ginsberg had typed a first draft that was very close to the published poem. There were only a few revisions, including one penciled-in by Kerouac, who suggested changing the word *mystical* in the first sentence to *hysterical*. "I saw the best minds of my generation destroyed by / madness, starving hysterical naked..."

Next to "Howl," in the same glass case, was an array of vintage literary magazines.

"*Beatitude*," said Zahra, reading the title of one of them.

"Doesn't that have a Christian significance?"

"Yes, it does," I replied, recalling my parochial schooling. "The Beatitudes are the blessings that Jesus described in the Sermon on the Mount—you know, 'Blessed are the poor in spirit, for theirs is the Kingdom of Heaven, Blessed are they that mourn, for they shall be comforted, Blessed are the meek, for they shall inherit the Earth.' But *beatitude* was also the word Kerouac used to describe the *real* meaning of *Beat*. He felt that *Beat* meant *beatific*, not down and out. To be Beat was to be in love with life, to exist in a state of beatitude, to exist in a state of unconditional bliss."

"Do you think unconditional bliss is *attainable?*" asked Zahra thoughtfully.

"I'd like to hope so," I replied.

We pored over the other magazines for a few moments and then Jay and Zahra drifted away in opposite directions, gradually growing farther and farther apart as they explored the exhibit alone. I looked from one to the other, trying to decide whom to follow, and finally set off by myself.

The central hallway, where the literary achievements of Beat culture were chronicled, was surrounded by several galleries devoted to the visual achievements, assembled in an attempt to illustrate that the spiritual essence of Beat Culture was evident in everything from Jackson Pollock's *Number 27* drip painting to Robert Rauschenberg's *Mother of God* collage, from Bruce Conner's *Portrait of Allen Ginsberg* (constructed of "wood, nylon, tin can, candle, wax, spray paint, and assorted detritus") to Dennis Hopper's black-and-white photographs of bikers and Robert LaVigne's pen-and-ink sketches of Kerouac, Ginsberg and Peter Orlovsky.

I wandered from one to another, trying to decide if I agreed with the premise. Sometimes it made sense, other times it seemed a stretch. Eventually I arrived back at the beginning of the exhibit, where I came upon a glass case I hadn't noticed previously that was filled with first editions of Kerouac's books. As I went to inspect them, I realized they were arranged chronologically and that I was at the end. I followed the case around a corner and, at the very beginning, found what I was looking for, a first edition of *On the Road*—in only slightly better condition than the one I'd bought from The First Edition Finder, I noted happily—along with a first edition of Kerouac's first book, *The Town and the City*, written by a pre-spontaneous-prose *John* Kerouac.

On the wall opposite the books was a series of black-and-white photographs. One of them caught my eye, a picture of Kerouac reading from *On the Road* to a small crowd in the Artist's Studio in 1959. He was standing on a stepladder, arms outstretched, like Christ on the cross.

As I studied the picture, I became aware of someone standing next to me. I turned and recognized him instantly—Allen Ginsberg. He was wearing a pair of headphones and staring at a photograph of himself as a wide-eyed young man pointing to Moloch, a monolithic Manhattan skyscraper rising behind him in the night. It was the very same skyscraper he had glimpsed in a terrifying vision and transformed into a modern symbol of inhumanity in Part II of "Howl" ("What sphinx of cement and aluminum bashed open / their skulls and ate up their brains and imagination?").

I saw Jay a few feet away, pondering a Rauschenberg, and ran over to him. "Jay! Jay! Did you see who's here?"

"Who?" he asked, not sure where to look.

"Ginsberg," I answered, nodding in his direction. "And he's listening to his own audio tour of the exhibit!"

"Think we should talk to him?" asked Jay.

"I'm not sure. Maybe he's wearing headphones so nobody bothers him."

Just then Zahra walked up, discreetly pointing in Ginsberg's direction. "Is that...?"

"Yes, it is," I replied.

"Let's go talk to him," she suggested.

"Not yet," I said. "Let's see if anyone else does."

Jay smiled and wandered away, happy to see Zahra and me in cahoots. A minute later, we watched as a man maneuvered next to Ginsberg and touched his arm. Turning to face him, Ginsberg removed his headphones, and the guy introduced himself. Ginsberg smiled warmly and shook his hand. "Nice to meet you," he said. Zahra and I looked at each other. A good sign.

"Now's as good a time as any," I said. I called to Jay. "Coming?"

"In a minute," he answered.

Zahra and I each took a deep breath and a single step toward Ginsberg, only to be intercepted by an older man with close-cropped white hair who got to him first.

"Allen, I used to be with the *Post*," he said.

The two chatted for a moment, obvious acquaintances, and as Ginsberg said goodbye and walked past Zahra and me, I extended my hand.

"Mr. Ginsberg, my name's Harry," I began. "I'm an admirer of your work. And this is Zahra. So is she."

He shook my hand, then Zahra's, and then abruptly pulled back. "I'm here to see the exhibit," he said tersely. He turned to go but before he took even one step another man and woman approached, members of the press, both brandishing pens and notepads. "Allen," said the man, "could you tell us about your involvement with the show?"

"Certainly," answered Ginsberg, who proceeded to elaborate for five full minutes as they studiously scribbled his every word. Zahra was in shock. "Do you believe that?"

Jay, who had observed our brief encounter from a few feet away, joined us. "What'd he say?" he asked eagerly.

"He told us he's here to see the exhibit," I replied.

"He was *rude*," said Zahra, staring after him.

"He obviously wouldn't have acted the same way if I'd told him we were with the press," I said. "But I didn't want it to seem like that's the only reason we were here, to cover a story. I wanted him to know that we were here because we appreciated his poetry."

"It's unbelievable," continued Zahra. Jay tried to defuse the situation. "Hey, did you see this?" Still smarting, Zahra and I followed him to the Kerouac case. "A first edition of *On the Road*. I guess this is as close as I'm ever going to come to one."

"You never know," I said.

"I've searched all over the place," said Jay. "Every time I pass a table of books for sale on the street, I stop to look, hoping I'll find one."

"Maybe when you stop looking, one will find you," said Zahra. I looked at her, wondering if she really could see into the future.

"You know," she continued as we made our way to the lobby, "the more I think about Ginsberg, the madder I get. I'm going to write him a letter. And I'm going to send it to his house. Bobby will give me his address."

"I know who you are and I know where you live," cracked Jay.

"I'm with you, Zahra," I said. "I could understand if we had tried to talk with him at a restaurant, or on the street, *but he was at the press preview for the Beat Culture exhibit!* Of course people were going to approach him! His response really was inappropriate. Basically, he told us to fuck off." I thought of what Sparrow had said—"you can't have it both ways"—and I had a sudden insight. "Jay, you know what I just realized? After months and months of us talking and thinking and writing about the Beats..."

"This is the payoff," said Jay.

"Yeah, *this* is the payoff," I repeated, shaking my head. "Write that letter, Zahra."

On the way out, Jay noticed a flyer by the gift shop announcing a reading by Ginsberg a few nights later at MoMA. "Should we?" he asked cautiously.

"Of course we should," I said.

"We *must*," agreed Zahra. "He's still Allen Ginsberg."

24

T HERE WAS A FAMILIAR FACE on the cover of the new issue of *TimeOut New York* on my desk. Henry Rollins. I had interviewed the former Black Flag frontman a few months earlier for an article about the publishing company he'd founded, 2.13.61, named in honor of his birth date. There were very few celebrities I looked for an excuse to interview, but after reading a few of Henry's confessional, confrontational and cathartic tomes—in particular, his brutally heartbreaking account of losing his best friend in *See a Grown Man Cry, Now Watch Him Die*—I had to talk with him. A loner who sought physical strength in pumping iron and psychic strength in sticking to himself, Rollins lived by a set of rules he dubbed the Iron Reminders. Rule Number One: "Do not attach. To anything or anyone." I empathized with his resolve.

Splashed across the photo of Rollins was a headline, "Punk hunk Henry Rollins has phone sax with jazz great Sonny Rollins." But beneath that was another headline, "Reheating the Beats: Attack of the Kerouac Pack," which trumpeted an article about the new popularity of the Beats, as evidenced by the Whitney exhibit. The piece contained very little I didn't know, with the exception of the observation that "almost everyone who slept with Kerouac has found a way to get that fact out there, the latest being Gore Vidal in his memoir, *Palimpsest*."

I scanned the shelf in my office for the copy of *Palimpsest* I'd received, unrequested, a few weeks earlier. A check of the index revealed a whole chapter devoted to Kerouac titled "Now You Owe Me a Dollar," in which Vidal recounted the night they ended up together at the Chelsea Hotel. Kerouac had detailed the same night in *The Subterraneans*, with one glaring omission—the fact that he and Vidal had slept together. Determined to set the story straight, Vidal took the man known as Memory Babe to task about his convenient memory loss, describing in great detail exactly what had happened in the Chelsea that night and who did what to whom. It was not a very tender reminiscence, right up to the very end, when, many years later, Vidal confessed to a young boy wearing a Kerouac T-shirt that he had been in love with Kerouac—"for a few minutes, anyway"—and quipped that Kerouac never returned the dollar Vidal had lent him for the subway.

I was still marveling at the seemingly random connections between Henry Rollins, Gore Vidal and Jack Kerouac when Jay stopped by and handed me a purple folder without saying a word. Inside was a typewritten manuscript titled *Elliptic Veracity I…and other poems*. Jay's initials, *JB*, hovered in the lower left corner.

"What's this?"

"My scroll, re-typed on separate pages, and four new poems. I'm sending them to a competition I saw in here." He held up a newsprint publication called *The Poetry Calendar*. "I found it at a coffee shop near Zahra's apartment."

"You know you have my vote," I said.

"I also came up with a new word to describe my writing."

"And what word would that be?"

"*Prosetry*."

"Actually," he continued, "I came up with another word, too. *Proems*."

"Proems…" I repeated, trying it out.

He turned to go. "Take a look at the new poems. They're really different from anything I've written before."

I started reading the moment he left. "Zahra's Dreamscape" was a lighthearted, dreamy dialogue between Zahra and Jay, with Zahra contemplating the simple sensual pleasures of Fiji in the

South Pacific, and Jay pragmatically pointing out that the island had little else to offer ("Exactly…"). "Midnight" was a dark, disturbing description of a breakdown by someone Jay held close and Jay's effort to pull him back from the brink ("Helter Skelter feller…"). "Shade" was a study in contrasts ("In my dreams / I had the gift of flight. / White. / In the dismal rain a little boy leaves… / and he ain't ever comin' back / black."). And the final poem, "Melancholy O' the Night," described the sadness just below the surface on his older brother Freddo's wedding day ("Classic black tuxes all on together in one room / and my pocket's ripped anyway. / Done, pictures, smile, food, limos late— / my mother's a wreck. / Cool Fall afternoon 'round 3pm, / take formal picts at gazebo / in front of boats / and green grass, flowers and the bride. / If you stand in the middle and hold your head back / and yell, / you'll hear IT yell back… / Look beyond the reflectance of the mirror / and you'll see the melancholy o' the night.").

When I'd read them all, I was overwhelmed. By the honesty and the intensity. By the fact that those words had been written by the man who meant more to me than anyone ever had. I sat there, unable to do anything else for a good ten minutes, before I finally put the poems back in the folder. Then I walked to the art department and handed Jay a folder of my own.

"My turn," I said.

IT WAS THE SADDEST BAR I'd ever seen, one flight down from street level, off an alley that was off an alley in a no-man's-land of grated pawnshops, twenty-four-hour check-cashing joints and neon-lit peep shows. Walk a few blocks away from the bright lights of the casinos and boardwalk in Atlantic City at four in the morning, however, and that's where you ended up.

That's where Matteo and I end up, anyway. We'd spent the night at the Car Bar and Matteo hadn't hooked up. No one had caught his eye so he focused on drinking instead. Thanks to my generous tip, the bartender had let us hang out for one last mug after he'd sent everyone else home at two and locked the doors. But when we were finally ushered out a half-hour after closing time, Matteo said he wanted more.

"There's no place else to go," I said as we staggered to my car. "All the bars are closed."

"In Philly," he said. "But they're open all night in Atlantic City."

"Matteo, that's an hour away."

"I know." He managed to sound sympathetic and hopeful at the same time.

"And it's two-thirty."

He looked at me and smiled with just the slightest trace of disappointment in his eyes. "Okay, Har. Let's go home."

Fifteen minutes later we were already in New Jersey, flying down the Atlantic City Expressway with the radio blasting and all the windows open.

Our first stop was a casino. I didn't know which one; they all looked and sounded the same. Garish, loud and lit to mimic daylight to confuse internal clocks. We played a few rounds of twenty-one for the free drinks and actually won fifty dollars, at which point Matteo said we had enough money to pay for our own alcohol and we took off, heading to a bar recommended by a pair of older guys in matching pastel polos sitting next to us at the blackjack table.

They hadn't told us the name, only how to get there, and as far as I could tell when we arrived, the place didn't have a name. Or didn't deserve one. Spongy shag carpeting, Tiffany lamp knock-offs, tattered St. Pauli Girl posters and cheap wood paneling that was peeling off the walls either contributed to its charm or pegged it as the most pathetic Jersey shore dive Springsteen never sang about. One look at the clientele, a catalog of the beleaguered, busted and broken hunched over highballs and Old Fashioneds, and I concluded the latter was more likely.

Matteo and I settled on two stools where we quickly drew stares from several guys in our vicinity.

"Nice place," muttered Matteo as he sipped a Bud and looked around skeptically. "I thought you were taking me to a classy joint, Har."

"We're in AC," I said. "There *are* no classy joints. Be right back."

In the men's room, a guy walked in right behind me, lurking in the shadows while I had my hands full. As I washed, he spoke up.

"Forty bucks for a blowjob."

I scowled in his direction. "Not interested."

"A hundred?" he shot back.

"Huh?"

"A hundred if I get to blow the both of you."

"We're not..." I didn't finish.

Back at the bar, he took a seat directly across from Matteo and me, squinting at us and nodding suggestively whenever one of us happened to glance his way.

"We seem to have an admirer," said Matteo.

"More than you know."

To my left I saw a hand tap Matteo on his back. He whirled around and jumped off his stool. The guy who tapped him took a step back.

"I'm sorry," said the guy, a tanned, athletic twentysomething in a Bugle Boy shirt. "I didn't mean to scare you. I was wondering if I could take a picture of you guys." He held up a Polaroid camera.

"What for?" asked Matteo.

"For... inspiration," the guy replied.

"Oh, okay," said Matteo, although I wasn't sure he realized what the guy meant. "But only if you take one for us."

"No problem."

Matteo slid onto my stool, wrapped his legs and arms around me and rested his chin on my shoulder. I felt his breath in my ear and held my own breath in response.

"Anytime you're ready," he told the guy.

A second after the flash went off, the picture slid out of the camera. The guy immediately took another and handed it to Matteo, who didn't move from the stool we were sharing. Instead, he held the photo in front of me, pressing close and watching over my shoulder as it slowly developed.

187

"That's a good one of us," he said when it was finished. "You keep it, Har. I'll only lose it."

I slipped the picture into a pocket as he slipped off my stool. A beer or two later, it was Matteo's turn to hit the men's room. He returned with the photographer.

"Harry," Matteo began, "Tommy here made me a proposition."

I stared at the two of them, knowing where the night was about to go.

"He wants to spend the night...."

I swallowed, steeling myself.

"...with us."

"Huh?"

"He thinks we're hot. Right, Tommy?"

Tommy nodded. Matteo could tell I was confused.

"Tommy, give us a minute," he said, waving him away. Matteo leaned in close, putting an arm on either side of me. "What do you say, Har? It could be fun, right? And we get a place to sleep out of the deal so we won't have to pay for a hotel or sleep in the car."

I looked at the guy again. He wasn't my type. And he wasn't exactly Matteo's type, either. Maybe somewhere in between. I didn't particularly want to sleep with him, but if sleeping with him meant I got to sleep with Matteo, then so be it. And maybe, I thought, maybe this was Matteo's way of letting me in, just a little.

His face hovered only inches away from mine. I studied his eyes and his lips. I so wanted to kiss him, I could so easily have kissed him, but I didn't. Instead I imagined kissing him later, in the heat of the moment, when it would be a natural extension of everything else that was going on.

"Let's go," I said.

He broke into a huge grin. "Really? All right, Har!"

Tommy started to strip the second we were in his apartment. Matteo did likewise, pulling his black tank top off in one quick move and tossing it aside as he followed Tommy to the bedroom. I did the same, but they were way ahead of me, ripping off their jeans and diving on to the mattress even as I unbuckled my belt.

I joined them a few seconds later. I'd never been in bed with two other bodies. So many moving parts. So many possibilities. So many things that fit or could be forced into so many openings. But just as things started to heat up, I pulled away, wondering what I was doing there. I didn't want to be there. I wanted to be with Matteo, yes, but not with Tommy. And I really didn't want to be with the two of them.

I got up and went to the living room, closing the bedroom door behind me. Covered in a nervous sweat, I sat on the sofa and soon drifted off, only to be awakened a short while later by Tommy, still naked, who smiled and leaned in to kiss me. I pushed him away. He shrugged and motioned for me to go to the bedroom as he took my place on the couch.

Matteo was tangled up in the sheets and sound asleep. I lay down next to him and gazed at his face, watching the rise and fall of his chest as he breathed. Sensing a presence, he opened his eyes and looked into mine. "Harry, will you hold me?"

I put my arms around him and pulled him close. He woke for a moment, smiled and went right back to sleep. We were both soaked and sweat pooled where our chests touched, occasionally slipping down our stomachs in warm rivulets. I was wide awake, part of me lost in a make-believe moment, part of me trying to figure out what it all meant, if anything.

At first light, Matteo stirred and cracked one eye. "Fuck," he growled.

"Is that a request?" I asked, trying to sound like I was kidding and serious at the same time.

He smiled. "Let's get the hell out of here."

We pulled our boxers and jeans on in the bedroom and scooped our shirts up from the floor of the living room where Tommy was out cold.

At a diner we grabbed coffee to go, drove back to the center of town and made our way to the beach. The sun had just come up and we were the only two in sight. A few minutes after we finished our coffee, we were asleep again, side by side on the sand.

I awoke in a few hours to discover that we were surrounded by blankets full of beachgoers. I couldn't imagine what they'd thought of Matteo and me, passed out in their midst, still wearing our street clothes. I stared at the horizon for several minutes, listening to the sound of the surf and drawing more than a few damning looks. Matteo yawned and stretched a few minutes later, shaking his head as he propped himself on his elbows and looked around.

"What are these people doing in our bedroom?" he asked, squinting in the sun as he lit a cigarette.

"Our bedroom? I like the sound of that," I said, feeling hopeful.

Matteo smiled. "I need coffee," he said. "Actually, I need a beer. It's gotta be close to happy hour."

We returned to the nameless bar, where a steam table with hot dogs was set up as Sunday brunch. Perfect, really. Matteo and I each grabbed two and ordered Buds at the bar. As we ate, Tommy approached, this time with a friend who looked vaguely similar.

"Tommy said he had a great time with you guys last night," he began. "We were wondering if the two of you would like to go home with the two of us."

Matteo glared at the guy and then at Tommy. "Stop talking shit about us," he said menacingly. "It never happened." And then, to the other guy. "We would *never* go home with you. *Either of you.*"

"But I have this," said Tommy, holding up the Polaroid he'd taken as some sort of indirect evidence.

"No you don't," said Matteo, snatching it away and ripping it up. "I told you—it *never happened.*" He tossed the pieces into the air and turned his back on them. "I think it's time to blow this joint," he said to me.

A few hours later, after we'd showered and changed at my house, we were playing pool at the Car Bar. I was still thinking about the weekend, smiling affectionately at Matteo every time our eyes met. In between games, however, he went off to refill our mugs and came back to tell me that he was going home with someone.

"Just you?" I asked.

He winced. "Yeah, Har, just me."

I left shortly after he did.

At home, I looked at the Polaroid I had tucked into the edge of the mirror above my bureau, the picture of Matteo and me, his arms wrapped around me, holding me close.

It never happened, I told myself. It never happened.

25

JAY AND I LEFT THE OFFICE at five-thirty, making our way to the Allen Ginsberg reading at MoMA through a downpour that had done nothing to deter a hundred other Ginsberg fans from getting there before us and lining up behind a red velvet rope. Thankfully, Zahra had been among the first to arrive. Jay spotted her near the very front of the line and we skirted the crowd, ducking under the rope to join her. "My two favorite guys," she said, giving Jay a kiss and then me. The couple behind us stared as she did so, looking from Zahra to Jay to me and then back to Jay in an obvious attempt to determine who was with whom.

"How are *you*?" Zahra asked me.

"I'm good," I replied. "And you?"

She spoke so softly that I couldn't quite hear her answer, but instead of asking her to repeat it, I just nodded, which was obviously an inappropriate response.

"Boy, everyone's grumpy today," she said. "It must be the weather."

"I'm sorry," I said, realizing my faux pas. "I didn't hear what you said."

"It's no big deal," she said. "I'm going outside to have a cigarette."

Jay lifted the rope for her and after she'd gone I explained that I had trouble hearing her sometimes. "You don't seem to have that problem," I said.

"I'm used to it," he said. "And I can also read her lips."

Zahra returned a few minutes later. "I don't know what it is," she said, "but smoking a cigarette in the winter isn't as satisfying as smoking a cigarette in the summer. Especially in the rain."

Jay extracted a large white plastic bag from his backpack. "Here," he said as he handed it to her. "I got you a present."

Zahra opened the bag and pulled out a pad of graph paper. "Oh, thank you!" she said. "I was just about out."

She smiled and gave him another kiss, a real kiss, finally clearing up any lingering confusion the couple behind us might have had, just as the line began to move. We filed into an auditorium that was set up café style, with small tables surrounded by several chairs. Since we were among the first to enter, we scored a table at the front of the room, only a few feet away from the podium where, presumably, Ginsberg would soon perform.

"Would either of you like something to drink?" asked Jay, noticing a bar in the back as we settled into our seats. "I think they're selling beer and wine."

"I'd like a glass of wine," said Zahra. "Red, if they have it."

"I'll have a beer," I said. "But I'll go with you to help carry everything."

When we returned, I noticed a heavy-set older woman in a long, electric-blue dress and a string of enormous pearls seated at a table behind the podium, facing the audience. Her lashes were thick with liner, her face caked with powder and her snow-white hair swept around her head in a smooth, tight coil. For some reason, she couldn't seem to keep her eyes open and she looked, to use Zahra's word, grumpy.

"There he is!" said Jay suddenly as Allen Ginsberg appeared. He strolled over to the sleepy-eyed woman and chatted with her for a few seconds before taking a seat off to the right. Just as he did, a young woman with brown hair and horn-rims approached the podium.

"Welcome," she said, "to another evening of poetry at MoMA sponsored by Lita Hornick, who has been sponsoring poetry at

MoMA for thirty years." She turned to face the woman seated behind her and clapped in appreciation. The audience followed suit. "Reading tonight, in this order, are Bob Rosenthal, Eileen Myles and Allen Ginsberg." Ginsberg stood to whisper something in her ear. "I'm sorry," she continued. "There's been a change. The order will be Bob Rosenthal, Allen Ginsberg, Eileen Myles. There will be short intermissions between each."

"Bob Rosenthal is the guy I talked to in Ginsberg's office," I said to Jay.

Rosenthal walked to the podium, tapped the mike and smiled enthusiastically. "Thanks for coming out on such a wet night," he began. "This is something I've *always* wanted to do. I had an odd poem that I couldn't place anywhere because it was self-deprecating. In the end, my friend Ted Berrigan said, 'Why don't you just put it in the beginning and get it out of the way?' I think you'll see why I want to read it tonight. It's called 'MoMA.' He paused and then recited a haiku from memory. "'Gray cafeteria off rain garden... / All my poems... / look *bad.*'"

The audience laughed along as he laughed at himself, skillfully turning his status as a warm-up act on its ear.

"I think that was written at one of these readings many years ago," he recalled before launching into his next poem. "'I Used to Be but Now I Am.' First I was called Little Oedipus. / Then I was called psycho neurotic. / Then I was called schizophrenic. / Then I was deemed learning disabled. / Then I brought a girl home / and I was considered pretty okay.'"

Again, the audience laughed, but just barely, and as Rosenthal continued, it became increasingly apparent that the room was growing restless for the main attraction. His poems didn't look bad so much as they were in the way. Twenty minutes later, he finally wrapped it up, stepping out of the spotlight amid a polite modicum of applause. During the intermission that followed, Ginsberg stood and surveyed the crowd, wandering near our table when he caught sight of someone he recognized. En route to his destination, however, he was waylaid by an older academic type holding two books of his poetry.

"Mr. Ginsberg, would you please sign these?" the guy asked.

Ginsberg stopped only to glower. "Not now," he replied with a dismissive wave, immediately turning his attention to a boyish blond. "Hello!" he said, brightening visibly. "You're looking well."

Zahra was beside herself. "Did you see that?"

She was still fuming a few minutes later when the intermission ended and Lita Hornick introduced Ginsberg without getting up from her table.

"Allen Ginsberg will read next," she announced with not a little effort. *Selected Poems*, HarperCollins, is just out." She paused, gathering strength to continue. "Photographs are currently at the Whitney Museum. I think Allen needs no further introduction. Thank you."

Ginsberg advanced to the microphone. "Lita Hornick has been sponsoring readings here at the museum for decades now," he began, "so she really has been one of the great patrons of poetry since the early sixties, when she helped found *Kulchur* magazine, and has been very helpful to many, many poets who otherwise would have been more indigent than they already are and have fewer places to read as distinguished as this and fewer places to publish. However," he added, frowning severely, "she makes mistakes..." There was a bit of confused laughter from the audience and Hornick's eyes grew very wide. Ginsberg smiled as he continued. "My *Selected Poems* is just finished but it's not out yet. However, *Collected Poems* is. So, what I'll be reading now is poems of the last couple years that are not published in books, including and finishing with a poem that's in this week's *Nation*. Beginning in 1993."

He launched into his first poem, "After the Party," instantly transmogrifying from a fragile septuagenarian to a sly and spirited observer, eyes twinkling, knowingly wringing every ounce of irony from his description of assorted *artistes* gathered for cocktails and the eighteen-year-old window-washer escort amongst them who caught his eye: "I'm / happy to guess he'll show his / naked body in bed / where we talk the refined old doctrine, / Coemergent Wisdom.'"

"Dream of Carl Solomon, January 1955,'" he continued, after an indifferent smattering of applause. "I meet Carl Solomon / 'What's it like in the afterworld?' I ask. / He answers, 'It's just like in the hospital. You get along if you follow the rules.' / 'What are the rules?' / He answers, 'The first rule is, Remember you're dead. The / second rule is, Act like you're dead.'"

He paused for only a moment, cutting the laughter off in his enthusiasm to push on. "'Two American...' uh... 'Three American Sentences.' 'I felt a breeze below my waist and realized that my fly was open.' 'That was good! that was great! That was important!' 'Standing to flush the toilet.' 'Sun setting on their faces the diners chatter over plates of duck.'"

Shuffling through the pile of papers on the podium, he found what he wanted and started again. "'New Stanzas for Amazing Grace.' Tomorrow evening at St. Marks, many poets will do new verses for 'Amazing Grace' at the behest of Ed Sanders, head of the Fugs. We had this evening last year and we're repeating it because it was so pleasant and nobody ever got tired of the melody." He cleared his throat and began to sing to a familiar timeless tune. "I dreamt I dwelt in a homeless place / Where I was lost alone / Folk looked right through me into space / And passed with eyes of stone / O homeless hand on many a street / Accept this change from me / A friendly smile or word is sweet / As fearless charity / Woe workingman who hears the cry / And cannot spare a dime / Nor look into a homeless eye / Afraid to give the time / So rich or poor no gold to talk / A smile on your face / The homeless ones where you may walk / Receive amazing grace..."

Finally, the crowd gave Ginsberg his due, clapping enthusiastically for a full minute.

"'After Ted Berrigan,'" he began anew. "In the *mode* of Ted Berrigan. 'I'm too serious. I should be feminine, marvelous & tough / like other guys. I should fall in love with chicks. / I should get a tattoo on my ass and raise two kids... / I should stop jacking off. I should jack off more... / I should write more poems stop farting around / with rock & roll, I'm already a rock star, automatically..."

"'Is About,'" he announced. "'Dylan is about the individual against the whole of creation / Beethoven is about one man's fist in the lightning clouds / The Pope is about abortion & spirits of the dead... / Television is about people sitting in their livingroom looking at their / things...'"

Jay nudged my arm and nodded toward Zahra, who was obviously enthralled.

"Last poem," said Ginsberg a half-hour later. "'A Ballad of the Skeletons,' which is in this week's *Newsweek*—uh, not *Newsweek*, would it were. *Nation*. Ha. Smaller circulation."

"We have to remember to pick up a copy," Jay whispered as Ginsberg cleared his throat.

"'A Ballad of the Skeletons.' 'Said the Presidential Skeleton / I won't sign the bill / Said the Speaker skeleton / Yes you will... / Said the Buddha Skeleton / Compassion is wealth / Said the Corporate skeleton / It's bad for your health... / Said the Junkie skeleton / Can't we get a fix? / Said the Big Brother skeleton / Jail the dirty pricks... / Said the Mirror skeleton / Hey good looking / Said the Electric Chair skeleton / Hey what's cooking?... / Said the Talkshow skeleton / Fuck you in the face / Said the Family Values skeleton, My family values mace...'"

As he read his final poem, Zahra sketched a small likeness of him on the pad of graph paper Jay had given her earlier.

"There will be a brief break, five minutes, not as long as the other," said Ginsberg, after an extended appreciative applause had died down. "Let's all stay for Eileen Myles, who's an amazing, bold, innovative poet, one of the best in her generation, which comes right after mine."

Despite his request to the contrary, about half the people in the audience put their coats on and left. It was their loss. Eileen Myles lived up to the hype. Immediately after her reading, Ginsberg took a seat at the table directly in front of us and started signing whatever people handed him—books of poetry, napkins, newspaper articles.

"See? He *does* sign stuff," said Jay. "He was just waiting till it was over." He looked at Zahra. "You should get him to sign your drawing."

"No," said Zahra.

"Come on," urged Jay. "You *have* to."

"No," Zahra repeated.

"Then Harry will do it for you," said Jay.

"Yeah," I offered. "Give it to me."

I took the pad of paper from her and got in line. "Allen," I explained when it was my turn. "My friend sketched you while you were reading and I was wondering if you would sign it."

He considered the drawing for a moment, so devoid of expression that I couldn't tell whether he loved or hated it. I feared the latter when he began to scrawl what seemed to be a series of meaningless loops in the lower right-hand corner, but when he handed the drawing back to me I realized that it was actually his signature.

"Thank you very much," I said, quickly presenting it to Zahra and Jay, who pointed out that Ginsberg had written the letters "AH" in a circle beneath his name. "What does that mean?" I asked.

Jay shrugged.

"Would you like to have it?" Zahra asked me.

"No, it's yours," I replied.

"You can have it," she offered.

"It's yours," I repeated. "It's *ours*. *You* hold on to it for the time being."

Inspired by my success, Jay approached Ginsberg and handed him a copy of the *Elliptic Veracity 1* manuscript. Ginsberg looked to see what he was signing but signed it without asking any questions. "Thank you," said Jay, who promptly showed it to me.

"Cool," I said. "Is that your original?"

"Nah, I was afraid to bring it out in this weather."

We turned at the same moment to see Zahra talking with Ginsberg.

"What effect do you think you had on the current generation?" she asked.

"I hope," said Ginsberg, "that I didn't do too much damage."

"And what does the 'AH' under your signature mean?" she continued.

"*Ahhhhh,*" he replied.

26

"THIS IS GOING TO BE WORTH a lot of money someday," said Jay the next day, placing a thin hardcover volume on my desk. He opened it and pointed to the first page. It was the *Elliptic Veracity I* manuscript Ginsberg had signed the night before. "I had it bound at a copy shop," he explained. "And I also made one for you."

He handed me an identical volume, sans Ginsberg's signature.

"I want *you* to sign mine," I said, giving it back to him.

"Hmmm. I'll have to..."

"Hold that thought," I said as my phone rang. It was Lester from the Gotham Book Mart, calling to let me know that the first-edition paperback of *On the Road* he'd told me about was in the store. "Get your coat," I said to Jay.

A moment after we arrived at Gotham, Lester presented me with the well-preserved paperback in a clear plastic envelope. Jay was nearly speechless. "Wow!"

"Just like the one at the Whitney," I said as Lester wandered away to assist another customer.

"How much do you think he wants for it?" asked Jay. "A few hundred?"

"Let's find out."

I gave the book back to Lester when he returned. "How much?" I asked, winking at Jay. "I mean, how much for *me*?"

Lester slipped the book out of the plastic envelope and flipped through it. "I don't know. It's not in very good shape. Ten dollars?"

"Sold!" I yelled.

"Ten dollars?" said Jay, incredulous. "You don't have another one, do you?"

"No, but I'm sure I'll get one," Lester replied. "They turn up from time to time."

"Save it for me if you do," said Jay. "I'd love to have a first-edition paperback, because I doubt I'll ever get a first-edition hard-cover."

Lester glazed over for a moment. "We had a first-edition hard-cover about a year ago," he recalled. "It was in good condition, except for some minor tape damage to the inside front cover. We were asking three-fifty for it. A guy from England left a fifty-dollar deposit on it and said he'd be back later. I put the deposit with the book in the vault and when the guy returned I handed him both and watched as he walked toward the counter in the front of the store. At the end of the day, I said something to the clerk at the cash register about ringing up a three-hundred-fifty-dollar sale, but he knew nothing about it. The guy had walked right out of the store with the book *and* the deposit. That's the only first-edition hard-cover I've seen in three years," Lester added. "Nobody sells them unless they really need the money."

I opened my wallet and handed Lester eleven dollars, figuring there would be tax on the ten. But he handed a dollar back to me.

"Ten even," he said, putting the book in a white paper bag.

"I am so jealous," joked Jay as we headed over to our usual place for lunch. "Ten bucks? That's less than a *new* paperback of *On the Road*."

"I hadn't even thought of that."

"He probably gave you a deal because he sees us in there all the time. And he knows we're interested in the Beats."

"Yeah," I agreed. "I suppose that's it."

"Three hundred and fifty dollars for a hardcover first edition?" continued Jay. "I'd have bought it in a New York minute."

"And that guy *stole* it," I said in disbelief. "That takes..." Jay and I finished my sentence at the exact same time. "...*balls*."

"Let's see it again," said Jay as we sat down to eat.

I slipped the book out of the bag and he read the blurb on the back cover. "Buying cars, wrecking cars, stealing cars, dumping cars, picking up girls, making love, all-night drinking bouts, jazz joints, wild parties, hot spots...This is the odyssey of the Beat Generation, the frenetic young men and their women restlessly racing from New York to San Francisco, from Mexico to New Orleans in a frantic search—for Kicks and Truth."

Kicks and Truth, I repeated to myself. That would be a good title for a book. Maybe mine.

Back at work, I called Ginsberg's literary agent, Jeffrey Pasternak, to see if there was any word on the original poem I had inquired about.

"Allen is interested," he assured me. "But he was wondering if you could pay him just a little more."

"How much more?" Not sure what price to put on an original Allen Ginsberg poem, I had offered him a thousand dollars.

"Oh, say if you offered him twelve-fifty."

I considered it for a second, thinking about the thousands of dollars *Element* threw away on stories that were bought but never published because they were so badly written. "Okay," I agreed. "Twelve-fifty."

"I'm sure that will make a difference," said Jeffrey.

After I hung up, I went to clear the twelve-fifty figure with Cliff and returned to my office to find my bound copy of *Elliptic Veracity*, newly inscribed by the author. "Harry—Say all that you want to say... And when you're done, say more!"

I did.

A MONTH AFTER the publication of each issue of *Rittenhouse Square*, the magazine where I worked as a staff writer in Philadelphia, the editor-in-chief would award a blank restaurant gift certificate to the author whose article generated the most reader feedback. It didn't matter whether it was fan mail or hate mail. Any story that inspired a strong reaction either way was considered a success. Such was the case for a piece I wrote on the continuing controversy over the Rocky sculpture, the eight-and-a-half-foot bronze likeness of big-screen boxer Rocky Balboa commissioned by actor-director Sylvester Stallone for *Rocky III*. In the movie, the statue was placed at the top of the steps of the Philadelphia Museum of Art in tribute to Rocky's triumphant and iconic run up the steps in the original *Rocky*. When filming was completed, Stallone donated the statue to the city with the request that it remain in front of the Museum. And that's when all hell broke loose. Though the statue quickly became one of the city's top attractions, for residents and tourists alike, debate erupted between Philadelphia's cultured class and the fictional Rocky's own blue-collar compadres about whether the statue was art—and deserved a place at the Museum—or just an ugly movie prop that deserved a place at the bottom of the Schuylkill River. With no compromise in sight, the statue had been moved to a spot outside the Spectrum sports arena in South Philly, where it continued to be every bit as popular as the Liberty Bell.

With gift certificate in hand, I made a reservation for two at one of the most luxurious restaurants in Philadelphia, Elfreth's, atop the tony Hotel Belmont. I asked Matteo if he'd like to join me. It was another opportunity, I thought, to show him how much I cared. Maybe it would be the one that finally changed his feelings.

"Me? At the *Belmont*?" he wondered incredulously.

"You want to go or not?" I asked offhandedly.

"What am I going to wear?"

"You can wear something of mine."

On a Saturday evening, Matteo and I donned my two best suits. I wore the light gray pinstripe, he wore the brown—a close fit, but, I noted, it only accentuated his build. I drove us to Fifth and Walnut, where a valet took the keys to my car. Matteo rolled his eyes and whistled as we walked through the ornate lobby to the elevator. When the doors opened on the top floor, he didn't make a sound, dumbstruck by Old World opulence, from the Oriental carpets on the floor to the oil paintings on the walls and the lead crystal chandeliers overhead. The maitre d' silently escorted us to our table, where two waiters pulled our chairs out for us and, in the blink of an eye, expertly placed crisp white linen napkins on our laps.

"I need a cigarette," muttered Matteo nervously as he glanced around.

The dining room was filled with assorted diamond-studded Society Hill sophisticates and mannered Mainliners. They sat stiffly and conversed over their meals in low tones or waltzed mechanically around the polished hardwood dance floor in the center of the room to tastefully subdued tunes supplied by a jazz pianist. But even as Matteo placed a Marlboro in his mouth, a waiter materialized out of nowhere, flicked open a lighter and lit the cigarette, vanishing into the woodwork just as quickly as he had appeared. Matteo was in awe.

"I've never seen *anything* like this, Har," he said as he exhaled and tapped the tip of his cigarette in a Waterford ashtray.

In a split second, the waiter was back, trading the dirty ashtray for a clean one in a single skilled maneuver. Matteo's jaw dropped.

"Wait till you go to the restroom," I said with as straight a face as I could muster. "They even hold it for you."

"Hold *what?*" he asked, realizing even as he posed the question what I meant. He looked over his shoulder uneasily. "Nobody better hold anything they're not supposed to be holding."

We ordered cocktails—gin and tonics—and, for dinner, jumbo shrimp appetizers followed by filet mignon, lobster and a bottle of Dom Pérignon. Three bottles later, we were both blitzed, breaking into uncontrollable laughter every time we so much as looked at one another—Matteo and I getting bombed in Elfreth's. Our waiter laughed right along with us. In fact, all the waiters did. And why not? With every new bottle of Dom we ordered, even we could hear the *ka-ching* of a bigger tip on our ever-growing tab.

As the evening wore on, it became increasingly obvious that our neighbors at nearby tables had noted that there were intruders in their midst, a couple of raucous scruffs who had somehow managed to penetrate society's inner sanctum and didn't know how to behave. And judging by the frequent disapproving looks in our direction, our neighbors were not as amused by it all as Matteo and I were.

"These people need to loosen up," observed Matteo.

"Ah, we're giving them something to remember," I said.

Matteo looked at me conspiratorially and snuffed out his cigarette. "Let's give them something they'll *really* remember." He jumped to his feet, ran around to my side of the table and held out his hand. "Come on, Har. Would you like to dance?"

"Sure," I replied. "I'd *love* to."

Matteo grinned and grabbed my hand, pulling me onto the edge of the gleaming hardwood floor and nearly knocking several other couples out of commission in the process. I could barely see straight, let alone move my feet, but Matteo expertly took the lead, taking one hand in his, placing the other around my waist and waltzing us both around the floor several times surprisingly well, given that we were both in a lowered state of equilibrium. It was all a blur to me although I do recall the other duos falling all over themselves to get out of our way and the horrified look on one woman's face as we passed her table and her fork froze in midair, hovering between her plate and her awestruck open mouth.

A round of applause erupted as we returned to our table and collapsed in our chairs, laughing hysterically. But it wasn't the patrons who were clapping—they were all busy asking for their checks—it was the waiters, all of whom, it seemed, played for the same team as Matteo and me.

"More champagne?" asked one of them with a knowing smile.

"Sure," said Matteo. "Why the hell not?!" He looked at me and smiled affectionately, then placed his hand on top of mine. "Harry, you are so good to me. I can't tell you how much this means. I'll never forget it."

I fought back ecstatic tears, slipped my hand out from under his and locked our fingers together. He gripped my hand tightly and wouldn't let go. This, I thought, was the moment I'd waited so long for.

We never finished the fourth bottle of Dom. It finished us. When neither Matteo nor I could hold our heads up, I decided to call it a night and signaled the waiter that it was time to ask for the check. The waiter handed me a heavy fountain pen to sign the gift certificate but when I went to hand the pen back to him he waved it away.

"You can keep it," he said with a smile.

"So, what was the damage?" asked Matteo as we stumbled out.

His eyes grew wide when I told him. "Man," he said. "Damn right you can keep the pen."

At home, Matteo followed me upstairs where we stripped to our skivvies, haphazardly hung up our suits and slipped into bed. I rested my head on Matteo's chest, listening to the beat of his heart.

"Harry?" he asked.

"Yeah?" I replied.

A moment passed and he didn't answer. I lifted my head and looked into his eyes. He looked into my own.

"Buenas noches," he said finally, kissing my forehead. "Dios te bendiga."

27

THANKSGIVING ARRIVED EARLY. Or so it seemed, anyway. At some unknown point in the proceeding months, Time had resumed its normal ebb and flow, passing at a speed to which I had grown unaccustomed during my year of solitude. I would have liked to spend Thanksgiving with Jay, but that didn't happen. Jay told me that he and Zahra were spending the four-day weekend at his mom's house on Long Island.

"Have a good holiday," he'd said as he patted me affectionately on the back before heading to Penn Station after work on Wednesday afternoon. "Sorry I won't be around, but I have a lot of family stuff to do. Besides," he added, "you can use the time to catch up on your journal. Or start writing your book."

I had begun to think about my book—what it would be about, anyway—inspired by a line from *Visions of Cody*. It was one of the few Kerouac books I hadn't read, but I had listened to Kerouac read from it over and over again on one of the CDs in *The Jack Kerouac Collection*. "Of this world report you well and truly," said Kerouac. Could I possibly hope to do that? A pretty tall order, but I would try. I still wasn't quite ready to begin, however. As I'd told Jay when he asked me about it before, I was waiting for something to happen. I wasn't sure *what*, but I *was* sure it hadn't happened.

After saying goodbye to Jay, I stopped at a supermarket on my way home from work and bought a basket of groceries with all the makings of a generous Thanksgiving spread, including a perfectly portioned turkey breast. I spent Thursday morning and afternoon bringing my journal up to date. I also called my folks in Florida, where they had retired a few decades earlier. It had been many years since my parents and my three siblings and I had sat around a Thanksgiving dinner table, or any dinner table, for that matter, and not only because we lived different lives in different cities. I would have been welcomed at any of their homes at any time, but my recent past had left me feeling disconnected and I would not have wanted to make anyone feel ill at ease simply because I did. So, for the time being, I chose to spend holidays alone.

Or, almost alone. Flannery, my faithful companion, was with me. And as I shared half of my turkey with her, I reflected on everything I had to be thankful for, how much my life had changed in ways I had been unable to foresee. Nobody, *nobody* knows what's going to happen to anybody.

On Friday, after the gym, after a nap and after a delicious dinner of Thanksgiving leftovers, I sat in the chair by the bay window in my living room that overlooked Columbus Avenue and offered a small slice of the Manhattan skyline. Flannery was lying in my lap, purring contentedly and dozing on a full stomach of her own. As I stared at the street below, I thought of Jay, wondering what he was up to at that moment, wondering whether he would call that weekend, and then I caught myself, wondering whether I had made any real progress in my effort to change my feelings for him if he constantly came to mind. It was still a struggle not to think about him, still a struggle to replace what I felt with what I knew I should feel. If I let my guard down for even a second, I would find myself daydreaming about impossible and inappropriate scenarios. Immediately afterward, I would grow angry and frustrated, hating myself for my inability to completely control my thoughts and feelings, for allowing a primitive impulse to overpower a more evolved and enlightened one.

"What am I going to do, Flannery?"

She opened her eyes and looked up at me. "Well," she said, "for starters, you might want to consider going out and doing something on your own instead of moping around your apartment on a Friday night. Just a thought."

A minute later, I was on a subway to the Lower East Side.

THE NUYORICAN POETS Café was located on a particularly dark and desolate block of Third Street in a nondescript five-story red-brick row house. I was nearly past it before I spotted the small slate sandwich board by the door with the words "Friday Night Poetry Slam" scrawled on it in white chalk. Inside, the place was packed, overflowing with a loud, rowdy crowd looking for release after fraternizing with their families for two days. I squeezed through the mob at the bar in search of a seat, settling on to a vacant stool in front of the DJ booth, just on the edge of a large open area filled with café-style tables. To the left of the bar was a small stage covered by a threadbare Oriental. Surrounding the stage was a sea of new bohemians, relaxing over Rolling Rocks and rapping over an infectious Latin-flavored percussion track.

Marking my seat with my leather jacket, I wandered over to the bar, where I spotted Bob Holman in his familiar fedora, busily scribbling in a notebook. He looked up and smiled when I said his name.

"Mr. Charity! Good to see you. Hey, have you got a bad poem you'd like to read? This is our annual 'Friday After Thanksgiving Low-Ball Night'—the night the *worst* poem wins the slam."

"No," I replied. "I didn't come prepared."

"Well, then," he said, "get a beer and enjoy yourself!"

A moment after I returned to my seat, Heinekin in hand, Holman took the stage and explained to the audience what he'd already explained to me.

"We all know that the best poem never wins in a regular slam," he said, "but tonight, we don't have to worry about that. Let's give a hand to *United States of Poetry* poet Hal Sirowitz, who has graciously agreed to provide a sacrificial poem to get things started."

A tall gangly guy with thick curly hair and Buddy Holly glasses stepped into the spotlight. I remembered him from *The United*

States of Poetry for a hilarious poem about his overbearing mother that he'd delivered while lying flat on a psychiatrist's couch. Greeted by a familiar applause, he regarded his fans with a blank expression, an almost imperceptible smile tugging at the corners of his mouth.

"This is called 'Peeping,'" he announced with a deadpan reserve. Nervous laughter erupted at a few tables. He waited for it to subside before continuing. "I once went into this place, he said, / on Forty-second Street." His cadence was near psychotic, which elicited more laughter. "For a quarter / you could peep into this hole. / There was this naked woman, / and every time she bent over..." He paused, eyes dancing behind his Coke-bottle lenses. "...I could see her hemorrhoids." Half the audience groaned, the other half goaded him on. "She probably wasn't aware they were showing. / She had this advanced case." Even Sirowitz couldn't keep a straight face. "I wanted to give her some medical advice, / tell her the foods she shouldn't be eating."

The place went wild as Sirowitz grinned a naughty grin, acknowledging the applause with a nod and exiting stage left as Holman entered stage right.

"Well, if you didn't understand what we meant by Low-Ball Night before, you certainly do now," he howled. "Our first contestant once picketed *The New Yorker*, claiming his poems were just as bad as the ones they published. Let's give a big hand for the one, the only, the one-named Sparrow."

The guy I'd talked with outside the Whitney appeared at the mike.

"This is called 'I Love Ph.D's,'" he said, reading from a sheet of white paper. "I love flowers. / I love trees. / I love birds. / I love bees. / I love giraffes. I love Ph.D's. / But mostly I love Ph.D's." He paused for effect and began again. "I love opera. / I love G.I. Joes. / I love Darth Vader, particularly / without his clothes." Looking up from the paper, he addressed the audience directly. "I was amazed when Darth Vader took off his mask, how much he resembled one of the Three Stooges. But mostly I love Ph.D's." Back to the script. "I love China. / I love Belize. / I love vagina. / I love women on their knees." Another aside. "I'm sorry this poem has suddenly gotten so pornographic, Because mostly I love Ph.D's." He returned to his verse with renewed enthusiasm. "I love trauma. / I love depression. / I love suicide. / I love Catholics who kill someone, then go to / Confession. / But mostly I love Ph.D's. / I like baccalaureate degrees a little, / and master's degrees I like still more, / but there is only one degree / that I have a real love for; / And that is Ph., Ph., Ph..." The audience was getting anxious, the big D on everyone's lips. "Wait a moment now, / and I will add the last letter; / I'm sure I know how. / Ph., Ph., / Say it along with me..." Everyone joined him, shouting. "Ph., Ph., / Ph.D!"

With a modest bow he departed the stage, buoyed by an immodest ovation. I got up to get another beer and noticed him standing next to me at the bar.

"Good poem," I said, "although maybe that's not the right thing to say."

He squinted at me, then smiled in recognition. "*Element.*"

"*The New Yorker?*"

"Right. Was that true what Holman said about you picketing *The New Yorker?*"

"Yeah," he replied. "But there's sort of like this whole evolution of the story."

"I've got time."

"Well," he began, "some years ago I got this idea to translate the poems in *The New Yorker* into English. To rewrite them the way someone who spoke English would talk. Something like 'the dinghy sped merrily over the waves' became 'I rode in a boat.' Later, I was talking with one of my friends in the Unbearables and, as a joke, we had this idea to protest *The New Yorker* and to present the editors with the translations. The idea for the protest grew and grew until everybody started asking, 'Well, when are we going to do it?' We chose Pearl Harbor Day two years ago and we descended on *The New Yorker* with picket signs, protesting, shouting slogans."

"What was written on the signs?" I asked.

"One of mine said, 'I'm Dorothy Parker with a Magic Marker.' Another said, 'We reject rejection.' The slogans we shouted were things like, 'Put their verse / In a hearse,' and, 'Who needs editors? / They're worse than creditors.' And then there was, 'Alice Quinn, Let Us In.' She was the..."

"Poetry editor," I said, dredging up one of a million pieces of trivia stored in my memory bank.

"Yeah, poetry editor," said Sparrow, visibly impressed. "So, anyway, we took our signs and occupied their offices. Well, actually, all we did was sit in the waiting room and very slowly get thrown out. Meanwhile, I wrote a series of twenty-three poems right on the spot to submit to *The New Yorker*. Poems like, 'Poetry / is easy / to write. / Why is it / so / difficult / to / publish?' A week or so later, I received a very warm rejection letter from Alice Quinn. She wrote, 'I realize this isn't your best work, dashed off on the spot as part of your merry—I know she used the word *merry*— 'spree, and I would like to read more.' I sent her some poems and never heard from her. Then, a year later, she called me and accepted four. Two have already been published."

"Why do you think she capitulated?"

"The Unbearables are united in the belief that we had terrified the ruling class and that she was operating out of fear that the Unbearables would never stop protesting her." He shrugged. "It's *possible.*"

"So, how did it feel to finally be published in *The New Yorker?*" I asked.

He thought for a second. "It's like winning the Academy Awards of poetry. It's like playing the Palace. At least, it's seen that way."

"I guess that was my point. I can't think of another high-profile consumer magazine that publishes poetry."

"People read *The New Yorker* but they don't read the poetry in *The New Yorker*," he said. "It's there so you can jump over it, get to the end of the magazine faster. So you can believe you're reading poetry without actually having to read it. It's more like a decoration. Like having a beautiful bad painting on your wall."

I laughed and glanced at my watch. It was getting late. "Well, I really should be going," I said. "Always a pleasure. And I'll be in touch about interviewing you."

"I'm going to put that on my résumé, you know—'Interviewed by *Element*.'"

I laughed as we turned our attention one last time to the stage, where Holman was introducing another contestant.

"Let's hear from our bartender Evan," he said. "I understand he's prepared something special for us."

Evan strolled into the spotlight and squinted through the curls and swirls of cigarette smoke for a few seconds. His face was completely serious but his eyes suggested that he might not be. "Shampoo, lather, rinse, repeat," he intoned solemnly, not breaking a smile till he was through.

"Wow!" yelled Holman, jumping from the sidelines. "Another example of *found poetry*! Found right on the side of a shampoo bottle!"

28

I FELT GOOD for having gone to the Nuyorican and even better about having spoken with Bob Holman and Sparrow. It was a step in the right direction, an affirmation that I *could* master my emotions if I set my mind to it. And if I did it one night, I could do it another. I had finally figured it out, I thought. I had finally gotten it right.

First thing at work on Monday, I called Jeffrey Posternak to check on the status of my request for an original Ginsberg poem.

"Oh, it's all set," said Posternak.

"It *is?*"

"Yes, he's working on it. You should have it soon."

"That's great," I said, trying to figure out how to ask my next question as tactfully as possible. "Jeffrey, can I ask you something off the record?"

"Sure."

"Allen realizes that *Element* is a mass-market magazine, right? I really want to be able to publish his poem."

"Oh, yes," he answered with a laugh. "He knows. There won't be any poems about handsome young men."

For the next few hours, I caught up on paperwork, heading to the art department at two to grab Jay for lunch. Donal, the managing editor was there, held captive by Ted, the art director, who said that Donal couldn't leave until he came up with a headline for a story about the current glut of made-for-TV movies ripped from real life. Ted needed the headline before he could begin designing the layout. Sitting on Donal's lap was the yellow legal pad he used to concoct headlines—he called it his "Pad of Precociousness"—but it was as blank as the expression on Donal's face. He was so deep in thought that he didn't even notice Jay and me till we were about to leave.

"Sil Kagen quit this morning," he stated almost mechanically.

"He got a job at the *Times*."

It took a second for the ramifications to sink in. Sil, the director of *Element Online*, was leaving. Sil, who wanted Jay to be his art director. I looked at Jay. He looked deflated.

"Why'd he quit?" I asked Donal.

"He got tired of all the machinations," Donal replied. "He was hired to be the editor-in-chief of *Element Online* but before it even got off the ground a new corporate-level Internet division was created with a publisher who's sort of an uber editor-in-chief at the top."

"Vivien," I said.

"Yes," affirmed Donal. "Vivien, who said she doesn't really care that Sil is leaving because she thinks he's boring."

"So, what's she going to do?" I asked. "She's in charge of creating digital versions of a dozen magazines. She needs an editor-in-chief for each one."

"You know Vivien," replied Donal. "I'm sure she has something—or someone—up her sleeve."

On that note, Jay and I turned to go, only to be intercepted by Cliff.

"Harry, can I see you in my office?" he asked, realizing as he did that Jay and I were on our way out. "It won't take long," he added.

"I'll wait for you," said Jay.

I had a feeling I knew what Cliff wanted to discuss. My yearly evaluation was due.

"Close the door," said Cliff as I followed him into his office. "Vivien's going to call you today and offer you the job of editor-in-chief at *Element Online*. I'd really like you to stay at the magazine—and, if you do, you'll get a raise and a promotion—but I'm not going to get into a bidding war for you with Vivien."

I was stunned, silently trying to process the unpredictable. If I stay or if I go, a promotion, a raise. Was his offer prompted by Vivien's offer? And what, exactly, was Vivien offering? "I'm really happy here," I said finally. "But I would like to look into it."

"I can't say I would blame you if you took it," sighed Cliff. "I've moved around a lot to get ahead in my career."

I returned to my office in shock. Jay was waiting at the door with his coat on, ready for lunch.

"What's *that* face for?" he asked.

"We have to talk," I said, grabbing my jacket just as my phone rang. It was Vivien. "I'm sorry, Jay," I said. "Can you give me a few more minutes?"

"No problem," he replied, sensing that something was going on. "I'll meet you out front."

"Vivien," I said as nonchalantly as possible. "What's up?"

"I'm calling to ask if you would be interested in being the editor-in-chief of *Element Online*. Sil quit today and when I thought about who should replace him, I immediately thought of you."

"Thanks."

"You've been at *Element* for a while now," she continued. "I'm not going to tell you how to plan your career, but it might be time to do something else, creatively. Think about it."

Over sandwiches at our usual place, I related the morning's revelations to Jay.

"Wow," he said when I'd finished. "This is great, Har. Editor-in-chief. We're talking six figures."

"We're not talking *anything*," I said, "until I decide what I'm going to do."

Jay sighed as we went for our after-lunch walk. "How the tables turn, huh, Har?"

I knew what he meant. Until the day before, *he* had been the one with the job offer at *Element Online*. With Sil gone, Jay's prospects were up in the air. "Ah, kid." I put my arm around his shoulder. Feeling self-conscious, however, I immediately removed it.

"It's okay, Har," he said. "I feel the same as Sil. Too much corporate maneuvering going on for my taste. I'm going to start looking for something else in the spring."

I didn't tell him that I had already decided to test my bargaining power with Vivien by informing her that I, like any new editor-in-chief, wanted to be able to choose my own art director and that Jay was at the top of my list. I didn't tell him because I didn't want to get his hopes up again if I couldn't help realize them.

As we walked along, I thought about how much I cherished our lunches together and how much I would miss seeing him every day should the day arrive, as it inevitably would, when we no longer worked together.

"Hey, do you think you could do me a favor?" asked Jay. "Last night, Zahra called to tell me that Ginsberg was on Channel Thirteen, talking about the Beat Culture exhibit with Charlie Rose. I only caught the last half, though. Do you think you could call and get a tape?"

"No problem."

I SET OFF TO MEET with Vivien the next day. The headquarters of the Internet division was located on the newly renovated twenty-third floor of the Flatiron Building in Chelsea, and as I stepped off the elevator I immediately experienced corporate culture shock. The space was enormous, a loft the size of a city block, filled with the smell of recent construction and the scent of something fresh and promising. A receptionist led me past a sleek mahogany wall embedded with a row of television monitors and then through a huge circular newsroom with several more televisions suspended on a high rail surrounding the perimeter. A vast cubicle farm lay beyond, with rows and rows of self-contained beige workspaces extending almost as far as the eye could see. Above them, the office's power supply coursed through color-coded cables that wove in and out of a horizontal track attached to the twenty-foot ceiling.

Vivien occupied an enormous office larger than many New York City apartments, right at the apex of the Flatiron's triangular shape, overlooking Madison Square Park. I found her sitting behind the exquisite rosewood table that had served as her desk at *Element*. The freedom to choose her own office furniture was one of the perks of her position.

"Harry, so *good* to see you," she began. "Do you know everything you need to know to make a decision?"

"Well, *almost* everything," I said. "I'd like to choose my own art director, if that's possible."

"Who did you have in mind?"

"Someone from the magazine, actually."

"Well, it would be good to have two people familiar with the *Element* brand in charge of *Element Online*. As long as it's not Ted. I can't go stealing everyone from the magazine or Cliff will hate me."

"No, not Ted. One of his designers, Jay Bishop."

"Jay Bishop? The fellow Sil wanted to hire? I saw his portfolio. Great stuff. He would have been my own pick if it were up to me. I'm glad we're in agreement. I'll have the director of HR call him. Anything else?"

"Salary?"

She threw out a figure that was lower than I'd expected and I immediately asked for another ten grand. She smiled and explained that I would be on a bonus system. If *Element Online* was financially successful at the end of the fiscal year, I would receive a bonus of up to twenty percent of my salary, which, she pointed out, was potentially more than the extra ten grand I'd requested. I wondered what chance any online operation had of being financially successful in its first year.

"I'd rather have the higher salary than the bonus option."

"*That*," she responded, "*is not* an option."

Though I'd already decided to accept her offer, I didn't want her to think that I'd give in so easily. "Let me think about it," I said. "I'll call you later."

Jay found me as soon as I got back to my office. "Well?" he asked. "Am I looking at the new editor-in-chief of *Element Online*? Because you're looking at the new art director."

"You got the call?"

"I got the call."

"Give me a minute."

Jay took a seat as I punched in Vivien's number and gave her my yes.

Jay could hardly contain himself when I hung up. He went to shake my hand but hugged me instead, so excitedly that he literally lifted me in the air.

"We're outta here!" he yelled.

He had just set me down when Mercedes materialized.

"Please tell me you're not leaving," she pleaded, searching my face for an answer when I failed to respond. "No, you're *not* leaving," she insisted, interpreting my silence as an indication that I was, in fact, on my way out.

"Actually," I replied, nodding toward Jay, *"we're* leaving."

She looked at Jay and wrung her hands. "Not you, too! What am *I* supposed to do?" she wailed. "What's going to happen to *me*?" She stormed out only to return a few seconds later. "Please take me with you," she implored. "Don't leave me here with Donal. *Please.*"

"I'll see what I can do," I offered.

Just then, as though her words had conjured him, Donal appeared in the doorway. "Harry and Jay!" he said with an exaggerated wink as Mercedes fled past him. "We have *got* to talk."

"How does everybody *know*?" I wondered aloud.

Cliff was next in line. "Like I said," he sighed, clearly disappointed, "I can't say I blame you." He looked at Jay. "Either of you."

Finally left alone, Jay and I talked excitedly about what had just happened. For my part, I couldn't believe that events had conspired to take us both to *Element Online* via a most unlikely set of circumstances. It was more than mere coincidence, I concluded. It was part of the unseen scheme.

ACCORDING TO TRADITION, everyone who left *Element* received a going-away present, tailor-made by Ted, the art director. He would select a recent cover, seamlessly insert a picture of the departing person's head onto a celebrity's body using Photoshop and present the result, matted and framed, at a farewell party. Ted excelled at matching cover and subject with a certain impertinence that walked a very thin line between reverence and ridicule and the results of his efforts never failed to provide a good laugh at the expense of the person leaving the fold. When the magazine's copy chief, Katie Galloway, quit, for example, Ted transplanted her head on to the body of Kate Mulgrew as *Star Trek: Voyager*'s Captain Janeway, because she had decided to "boldly go" without having another job lined up. When researcher May B. Shepherd split, Ted switched her noggin with Gillian Anderson's of *The X-Files* because May B. Shepherd, like Gillian Anderson, had red hair, and because May B. Shepherd had a crush on David Duchovny, who was also on the cover. And when Vivien left for greener pastures, Ted grafted her grape on to the bod of Danielle Steel, the queen of romance, because Vivien was off to become the queen of cyberspace.

When word got out that Jay and I were both going to *Element Online*, Ted started teasing us almost immediately.

"Let's see," he said, theatrically rubbing his chin with his thumb and index finger, "what should Jay and Harry's *cover* be?"

"*Cover?*" said Jay, alarmed that Ted had emphasized the singular. "Oh, *no.*"

"Oh, *yes*," said Ted, gleefully rubbing his hands together. "I looked through all the covers from the last several months and found just the one—or two. Jay and Harry are the first *couple* to leave *Element.*"

Jay didn't catch the word Ted had emphasized that time. I mulled it over for a moment and realized which covers Ted must have had in mind—the one plugging the will-they-or-won't-they relationship between Ross and Rachel on *Friends*, with David Schwimmer and Jennifer Aniston cuddling for the camera, or the one promoting the budding *ER* romance between Dr. Doug Ross and Nurse Carol Hathaway, featuring George Clooney and Julianna Margolies wrapped in each other's arms. I considered the implications of inserting Jay and me into either cover and I was not amused.

The day after Jay and I accepted our new positions, I arrived at work to discover a four-page fax on my desk from Allen Ginsberg's literary agent, Jeffrey Posternak. It was a moment before I realized that it was the poem I had commissioned, and Jay poked his head in my door just as I did.

"Jay!" I said excitedly. "Ginsberg's poem!"

"What's it called?!" he asked, rushing to my side.

I hadn't even looked. "*Is About.*" I recognized the title immediately. "Oh, it's not an original. He read this at MoMA. It's one of his unpublished poems. I guess I won't be the first person to commission an original poem from Allen Ginsberg after all."

"Still," countered Jay, "you'll be responsible for publishing it."

"Well, that's true."

Though we'd heard the poem once before, we read it again.

"It's great!" said Jay, with a long, low exhale. "Even better than I remember. And it's *perfect* for *Element.*"

"Yeah, it is," I agreed. "But I think we might have a hard time with *this.*" I pointed to the line about the Pope. "'The Pope is about abortion & the spirits of the dead.' A little too loaded, I think."

"Maybe he'd take it out if you asked," suggested Jay.

"No, I don't think so. That would be censorship and Ginsberg is no stranger to censorship—the 'Howl' obscenity trial, remember? If I asked him to delete or change the line, he'd refuse, and then every time he did a reading of the poem, he'd introduce it by saying, '*Element* asked me for a poem and then asked me to change it.'"

"Well, if Cliff doesn't want to publish it in the magazine, *we* can publish it online," said Jay conspiratorially.

"That's right!" I said, remembering that I would soon be in a position to make such decisions.

I made three copies of the poem, one for Jay, one for Zahra and one for Cliff, who said he would look at it later. Just after one o'clock, I received a call from Bob Rosenthal in Ginsberg's office who told me I could interview Ginsberg in person the following Thursday at his apartment on Twelfth Street.

"Maybe he'll make you oatmeal," said Rosenthal. "It's interesting. He puts seaweed in it."

I related the conversation to Jay over lunch. "And," I said as I finished, "you're coming with me."

He looked doubtful. "Won't he wonder why I'm there? You're the one doing the interview."

"We'll make something up," I said. He still wasn't convinced.

"Listen, you *can't* say no. How many chances are you going to get to talk to Ginsberg in his home?"

"All right," he said finally. "Yes, of *course* I'm going with you. What was I *thinking*?"

"You got me."

"So, Har," Jay continued, "Ted told me he's going to be relentless this week about our farewell cover. Have you figured out which one he's planning to use?"

"Yeah. I'm thinking it's either the *Friends* cover or the *ER* cover."

Jay thought for a second, remembering the photos on each. "Well, either one would be really insensitive," he said flatly.

"I'm glad you think so," I said. "I thought the same thing but I wasn't sure if I was overreacting."

"It's rude. I mean, I'll laugh along with everyone else when he presents it, but, afterward, it's going right in the trash. No offense, Har. It's just that some things…"

"I know, Jay, I know."

Bob Rosenthal called later that afternoon from Ginsberg's office.

"I'm sorry, but Allen won't be able to do the interview with you," he said. "He's in a hospital in Boston with congestive heart failure."

"I'm sorry, too," I said. "But not about the interview. How is he?"

"He's resting. He just needs to rest."

I broke the bad news to Jay, who was just as upset as I was, as we headed out to lunch. We didn't realize it at the time, but it would be our last lunch at our usual place. For the record, we both had the same thing—fresh turkey sandwiches on kaiser rolls—and the guy behind the counter said nothing about it.

At home that evening, I wrapped the first edition of *On the Road* I'd bought from The First Edition Finder in a map of the United States. Then I went through my journal on my laptop, located the entry I'd written the day I got the book and printed it out. I was all set for the day I had waited months to arrive, the day I would give Jay his book of dreams.

29

I AWOKE THE NEXT morning to an unexpected snowstorm. Four inches already on the ground and a whirl of huge white flakes still falling from a slate-gray sky with no sign of stopping. I made my way to the subway, leaning into a biting wind that sent tiny ice crystals into my eyes, thinking all the while that it would not be the best day to convince Jay to come by my apartment during lunch.

Jay stopped by my office around eleven, on a break from packing up his belongings so they could be shipped to the Flatiron Building. Like me, he didn't have much to do that week, our last week at *Element*.

"Do you have any special plans for lunch?" I asked.

"Actually, I was going to do some Christmas shopping," he replied. "Why?"

"I want to do something with you." He smiled and raised one eyebrow suggestively. "No, Jay, I'm serious."

"Okay," he said, giving in.

Later that morning, Bob Rosenthal called to tell me that Ginsberg was back in New York and feeling a lot better. If I still wanted to interview him, in person, at his East Village apartment, I could do so at four that afternoon, although in deference to his condition, I could only have an hour. I was ecstatic.

"Get your questions ready," I said excitedly to Jay. "Our interview with Ginsberg is back on!"

"All right!" he exclaimed. "When is it?"

"This afternoon. At four."

Jay's face fell.

"What's the matter?"

"I have to go to the Flatiron at four. The HR director wants me to come down to sign some papers before he leaves on vacation."

We looked at each other, both of us disappointed.

"Oh, well," said Jay. "At least one of us is going."

At twelve-thirty, he appeared in my office doorway with his coat on. "Ready?" he asked.

"Ready," I replied.

Downstairs, in the lobby, Jay pulled out a cigarette, obviously thinking that we were going to walk to wherever it was I wanted to go.

"We're taking a trip," I said as we headed to the revolving doors on the side of the building.

"Where to?"

"To my apartment."

"You mean on the subway?"

"Yeah," I said, already formulating an argument should he resist. But he didn't. Instead, he just looked at the cigarette in his hand. "Do you want to smoke that first?"

"Yeah." We went outside, where he lit his Camel Light and took a deep drag. "You finished your book?" he asked. "Is that what you want to show me?"

"Jay, I haven't even *started* my book. I just started thinking about it."

"Still waiting for something to happen?"

"Still waiting for something to happen. But I think it's going to happen soon."

He took another drag from his cigarette. "Har, I have so much to do for Christmas," he said, almost as though he were reading my mind. "This year, I'm telling everyone, 'This is my last Christmas.' No more buying things just for the sake of buying them. If I see something small that I know someone will like, I'll get it. But that's it."

I began to wonder whether I should call our whole trip off. But I decided to go for it. I'd waited too long to give him *On the Road*. And if this really was his last Christmas, at least *On the Road* would make it a memorable one.

"All set," he said, snuffing his cigarette out in a concrete ashtray.

We went back inside and took an escalator to the subway station below the building. "Let me pay," I said, sliding my Metrocard through the turnstile for him. "Since this is my idea." A near-empty northbound B train arrived after only a few minutes.

"So, Har, I wrote three more," said Jay as we took a seat. I realized he was referring to poems. "They're about Christmas."

"Maybe you could give them as gifts."

He laughed. "Not these."

"Not exactly in the Christmas spirit?"

"Not exactly."

We stepped off at Seventy-Second Street where a wicked wind was wailing down Central Park West, whipping the still-falling snow into a frigid frenzy and chilling us both to the bone on the two-block walk to my apartment. Flannery was in her usual cold-weather location, contentedly sprawled across the wooden radiator cover in the living room. Katie Galloway, the magazine's former copy chief and a fellow cat lover, had once observed that the first day landlords turn the heat on every fall was a feline national holiday.

Jay walked over to the radiator and scratched Flannery behind her ears.

"Nice place," he said, looking around.

"Thanks," I said as we removed our coats. "Have a seat."

He sat on the sofa, leaning forward expectantly. I sat next to him, not realizing how nervous I was till I began to talk. "Based on what you said about Christmas earlier, I'm not sure I should do this, but I got you something. And I wanted to give it to you in private."

I stood and walked to the bookcase in the hall and took out the package I'd put there the previous night.

"Here," I said. "Merry Christmas."

"A map?" he asked, eyeing the wrapping. Taking care not to tear it, he peeled off the tape, set the intact map aside and then opened the box. As he gently pulled back the tissue paper, I watched his eyes grow wide and his jaw literally drop.

"Oh, *wow*! Where did you *get* this?" He lifted the book from the box and held it in his hands, incredulous. "Har, *where did you get this?*!" he asked again, turning to look me in the eye.

"I'll tell you in a minute."

He ran his hands over the dust jacket and then looked inside. "It's in really good shape. Come on, where did you get it?"

"Here," I said, extracting several pages from a manila envelope. "I knew you'd want to know where it came from so I printed the journal entry I wrote on the day I got it."

He returned the book to the box and began to read the tale of my encounter with The First Edition Finder. I stared at the snowflakes swirling silently outside the bay window above the muted traffic on Columbus Avenue and then turned to study his face for a hint as to what he was thinking but I couldn't tell. When he finished, he looked down at the book nestled in the box filled with tissue paper at his feet, deep in thought.

"What a story," he said, finally. "That book has such a story." For a moment he was quiet and then he turned to look at me. "Har, I don't know how to say this, but I'm not sure I can accept it. It's overwhelming that you would give it to me. It really is. But the book means too much to me. It's meant so much to me for so long. I need to find it on my own."

"But I found it *for you*," I countered.

He smiled and then sighed. "Har, it's enough that you want to give it to me. The gesture is enough. This story is enough. Even if it ended *without* you getting the book, the fact that you went to all that trouble *for me* means as much as you giving me the book."

Though I knew there was probably no changing his mind, I

was determined to try. "Jay," I began, struggling to find the right words, "giving you the book means more to me than the book means to you."

He stared at the book in silence, also searching for the right words. "Har, hold on to it for a few days. Hold onto it for a few days and let me think about it."

I knew he was trying to let me down as gently as possible. "You won't accept it if I do."

A few soundless seconds passed. "You know me, Har. We know each other. I know you must have thought that I might not be able to accept it." He paused. "I need a cigarette."

I could tell he was anxious and that, in turn, made me anxious. I got him an ashtray and sat down next to him again. He lit up and inhaled. He was quiet, thinking.

"I really wish I could accept it, but I can't," he said softly. "Maybe if it was *The Dharma Bums* or one of his other books."

I wanted to say something but I didn't know what. "Jay..." I began, but I stopped when I heard my voice crack.

"Come on, Har," he said, his own voice trembling in a way I'd never heard as he put his hand on my shoulder.

"Jay, you've given me so much," I said. "You'll never *know* how much. I just wanted to give something to you. I know how much this means to you, and I wanted to be the one to give it to you."

We both stared at the box on the floor. "It's really beautiful, Har," he said. "I can't believe I'm seeing it. And holding it. You know how much *that* means to me? That's *enough* of a gift." He brightened suddenly. "I'll tell you what—why don't you give me the paperback and you keep this?"

"No, I want you to have the hardback. That's the one you really wanted."

"It's your copy," he said. "You wanted a copy, too."

"Yeah, but you wanted it more." I tried another approach. "It will be *ours*. It's in the family."

Another silence. And then I knew. It wasn't the book that was too much. It wasn't the book that Jay couldn't accept. It was the sentiment attached to the book, the sentiment that had prompted me to buy it and give it to him. That's what Jay couldn't accept. And that's what I had to accept.

"Jay, it's okay," I tried to assure him. "The last thing in the world I want to do is make you feel uncomfortable. It's okay."

"Har..."

"Jay, you don't have to say anything else. It's all right." He looked at me doubtfully. "It's all right," I insisted, scooping up the box and taking it to the kitchen where I left it, out of view, on the table. Jay was standing when I returned to the living room, awkwardly clutching the journal entry I'd given him. "Here," I said, picking up the manila envelope sitting on the sofa and handing it to him. He slid the printout inside and started to put on his coat. I did likewise.

"Please don't be disappointed, Har," he said. "I mean, I know you're disappointed. But don't be. You were really looking forward to giving it to me. And you *did* give it to me. That's the important thing. Are you all right?"

"Yeah," I said unconvincingly.

"You *sure*?"

I dropped my coat on the floor and put my arms around him, holding him closer than I ever had as I felt his arms surround me.

"I love you, Jay," I blurted out before I could stop myself.

"Yeah, Har," he said softly. "I know."

And there it was. After all this time, after everything we'd ever said to one another, after everything we'd gone through together, it all came down to that not-so-simple statement, to those three words. I loved Jay. I loved him. And no matter what I did, no matter how hard I tried, I couldn't stop loving him. I would never stop loving him. And now I had gone and said it. Now I had spoken what should have remained unspoken. Now I had gone and changed everything.

"Harry," said Jay, releasing me from his grip. "We've met before."

I looked at him, puzzled for a second before realizing what he meant. "In another life, you mean?"

"Yeah. We were brothers."

"Brothers?" I considered the implications. That *did* change everything. "And in this life?"

"Harry, like I said to you once before, we *are*, we *were*, we *will* be."

I wanted to hug him again, hold him with all my might, but I didn't. Instead, I reached out and touched his arm and then let my hand fall to my side. We put our coats on in silence and walked out. In the lobby, Jay paused to light a cigarette before we stepped back into the brutal snowstorm still raging outside.

"You know, Har, every time I come to your apartment, I'll want to see the book. It'll be a ritual."

I realized he was still trying to make me feel okay. "You can see it as often as you like."

We were quiet as we trudged down Seventy-Fourth to Central Park West, both of us contending with occasional vicious blasts that sent snowflakes sailing into our eyes, hampering visibility. Near the corner, where the wind began to border on unbearable, Jay suddenly grabbed my arm and yelled. "Hey, Har!" I thought he was going to ask if we could turn back but I was mistaken. "I'll tell you what—when I find a first edition of *On the Road*, I'll give it to you and you can give me that copy!"

I stopped in my tracks and stared at him. All this time he'd been trying to think of some way to set things right.

"You mean it?"

"Yeah," he assured me. "I mean it."

"It's a deal," I said, removing my right glove and holding out my hand.

Smiling excitedly, he did the same and we shook on it, standing like a couple of fools in the falling snow.

We boarded a downtown B train a few minutes later and got off at Rockefeller Center.

"A two-hour lunch," said Jay, glancing at his watch. "But what are they going to do? Fire us? Let's get a slice of pizza."

At a pizza place on Forty-Eighth we each ordered two slices and headed for a table in the back. On the way, we passed the only other person in the place, a striking, dark-haired and very pregnant woman sitting by herself and savoring every bite of an enormous slice of chocolate peanut butter pie. Jay smiled at her and she offered an awkward smile in return.

"I don't suppose you'd believe me if I told you *he* likes peanut butter?" she asked, patting her stomach.

"Maybe I'll ask him myself someday," said Jay as we slid into a booth.

"Well, I guess I won't be giving Zahra that first edition of *Howl*," I said.

Jay laughed.

"I'm only kidding."

"*That* I don't think you'd find anywhere," said Jay. "Except maybe in Ginsberg's apartment."

"Which is where I'm going at four o'clock!" I said. "I almost forgot! I'm interviewing Ginsberg in an hour!"

30

NUMBER 437 EAST TWELFTH STREET, the building in which Ginsberg lived, was a run-down red-brick apartment building crisscrossed by rusted fire escapes. As I stood in the small entranceway and pressed Ginsberg's buzzer, I remembered that Zahra and Jay's friend Bobby had also lived there at one time. Another coincidence in what had long ago become an endless string of coincidences, all suggesting the existence of some unseen scheme in which our collective destinies were incontrovertibly entwined.

A low-pitched hum in the latch signaled that I had gained admission. Pushing through the wood and glass entrance into a dimly lit musty foyer, I proceeded up four flights of stairs and rapped on a door to my right. I listened intently for sounds of life but all I could hear were sounds of my own life, the pounding of a heart pumping at twice its normal speed. Though interviews with celebrities had lost their mystique years earlier—and, consequently, their ability to induce apprehension—I wasn't sure whom I was about to meet: A compassionate dharma bum or a dismissive literary giant.

The door swung open with no warning. Ginsberg stood on the other side, bent but imposing, slowly eyeing me from head to toe. He was dressed in the simple unstylish uniform physicians wear beneath their white lab coats—gray slacks, a white shirt and a nondescript tie—although instead of the black penny loafers that would have completed the outfit he wore a pair of red and gold pointy-toed silk Indian slippers that were embroidered with tiny mirrors.

I cleared my throat after an uncomfortable silence. "Hello, Allen?"

"Yes," he shot back. "And you are?"

"Harry Charity. An editor from *Element*. I believe Bob Rosenthal..."

"Yes. Come in, come in." He waved me through the door and as I stepped into his apartment, I stepped back in time. We were in his kitchen, a kitchen that hadn't changed in forty or fifty years, with tall wooden cabinets covered by a hundred coats of paint, a white ceramic sink and matching enamel stove, a checkerboard linoleum block floor and a Formica table trimmed in chrome with yellow vinyl chairs. There was something cooking in an aluminum pot on the stove, filling the air with a steamy indistinct aroma.

"I'm just making oatmeal," announced Ginsberg. "Would you like some?"

"Sure," I answered.

"It's got seaweed in it."

I couldn't tell if his tone was challenging or merely informative. "Sounds good."

He squinted at me and smiled slightly. I had passed the seaweed test.

"Follow me," he instructed, leading the way to a large room in the back of the apartment where he deposited me on a couch covered with an Indian-print blanket. "We'll talk in here. I'll be right back."

I placed my coat next to me on the couch and looked around. Like the kitchen, this room showed no signs of modernization, with a well-worn hardwood floor visible around the edges of a thin Oriental, a single simple light fixture centered in the ceiling and two large wood-sash windows hung with bamboo shades that overlooked the snow-covered fire escapes of the surrounding buildings. The furniture was Salvation Army chic, an eclectic collection culled from the last few decades that included a shaded brass floor lamp, an overstuffed chair and ottoman upholstered in mahogany mohair, a Deco end table with a blue mirror top and a gunmetal-gray desk piled with books, magazines, papers, envelopes and file folders. Hanging on the white walls were large prints of his familiar black-and-white photographs, featuring Jack Kerouac, William S. Burroughs, Neal Cassady, Peter Orlovsky, Lawrence Ferlinghetti, Lucien Carr, Herbert Huncke, Amiri Baraka and Gregory Corso, as well as a few faces I didn't recognize.

Ginsberg returned in a minute, bearing two bowls of hot oatmeal. I tasted mine as he settled into the overstuffed chair and put his feet on the ottoman. Not something I would have ordinarily eaten, but, as I'd said to Jay, how many chances does anyone get to share a bowl of oatmeal with the man who wrote "Howl"?

"If you don't mind me asking, how are you feeling?" I began. "I understand you were in the hospital."

"Oh, my own matter of exhaustion, overwork," he answered as he started to eat. "Congestive heart failure, actually. I was waterlogged. So, are you *the* editor of *Element* or *an* editor?"

"Senior editor."

"Wow, big deal."

I laughed nervously. "Yeah, big deal."

"Mass-communication-brain-washer-commander-in-chief." Was he being genuine or sarcastic? "I guess you could put it that way."

"Yeah, well, use your power wisely."

Genuine. "Oh, I try to. Which is why..."

"How did that poem look?"

"I like it very much."

"Do you think it will pass through?"

"I gave it to the editor-in-chief but I haven't gotten his reaction yet."

"Actually," he said, setting his empty bowl next to a brass incense burner and several candles on the Deco table, "I had a better poem for that purpose. I don't know whether you saw it. It was in *The Nation*."

LARRY CLOSS

"Yes, 'Skeletons.' I loved it."

"That would have been better. We could have doctored it up and emasculated it a little but it would have been funny in that situation. But maybe too provocative."

I was surprised to hear him say he would have revised it. "Allen, since you mention that, I'm curious: You were involved with one of the most famous censorship trials in the country. What would you have done if you had submitted 'Skeletons' to us and we said, 'Sorry, Allen, we can't use it. It's just not right for *Element?*' "

"I would have said, 'Screw you in the face.' "

"Huh?"

" 'Said the Talkshow skeleton, *Screw* you in the face.' "

"Oh, right."

"Instead of '*Fuck* you in the face.' Maybe. It's worth getting it out. And *screw* and *fuck* mean the same thing. There was that and there was one other... 'Said the Big Brother skeleton, Jail the dirty pricks,' yeah. Well, 'Jail the jerks for kicks.' " He laughed. "Or something like that. So," he added without skipping a beat, "what's on your mind?"

"Uh, *The United States of Poetry*," I said, referring to my notebook after a second's delay. "Have you seen your segment?"

"I saw my segment, yes."

"Are you happy with it?"

"Well, the young boy's face is a little dark," he replied, resting his elbows on the arms of the chair and placing his fingertips together. "You can't quite see how handsome and pretty he was. But, yeah, pretty much so. That little flash of skin is nice. And the relationship is unusual and interesting and realistic in some ways. He's an old friend, actually. Not a boyfriend, just an actor. One of my secretaries. But he was willing to go through the motions." He smiled. "I have very *tolerant* secretaries."

"One of the clips features Johnny Depp reading from Kerouac's *Mexico City Blues*..."

"Actually," said Ginsberg, "I gave him my ideas on how to do

238

that particular poem 'cause I'd heard Jack do it. And we sort of collaborated on touching up his performance."

"Had you ever met him before?"

"No, but I liked him. He offered to take me home in his limo. And we came upstairs and we sat and talked for about three hours after that."

"Were you aware of his interest in Kerouac?"

"Oh, yeah, I already knew that. Depp had been in touch with the Kerouac family to buy some memorabilia from them."

"He bought Kerouac's raincoat."

"Yeah, for quite a bit of money. So then he invited me to do a show at his club, the Viper Room, in L.A. I thought it would be noisy and difficult but the stage had been arranged like a little book-filled private library. I did a two-hour reading with a guitarist. It was quite successful."

"You're so plugged in," I observed.

"Well, I have my likes, too," he said with a shrug. "I'm a fan. I'm a Dylan fan. I'm a Patti Smith fan. I'm a Beatles fan. I'm a lot older than most of them so a lot of them grew up reading me or Kerouac or Burroughs and it had quite an influence, apparently. And not only here but all over. China, Italy, Russia. There are a lot of people familiar with my poetry and that makes it easy for me to connect with younger generations. Like, right now, there's a young fellow named Beck…"

"Right," I said, recognizing the name.

"Not *Jeff* Beck, but Beck."

"Right. Beck. I know who you mean."

"I saw him on the Lollapalooza tour and had a long, long talk with him. We had mutual friends and mutual interests in blues texts. I think an online magazine is going to reproduce our conversation."

"Given the fact that so many people around the world continue to look up to you, do you feel responsible in any way for the current interest in poetry?"

"Well… *responsible?*" He shifted in his seat, crossing his legs on the ottoman. "I don't feel responsible for *directing* anything but I feel responsible to be lucid and candid with my own material, to represent my own consciousness accurately and precisely so that people use it as a mirror. I notice that when I go out and do a reading now, about a fifth of the people in the audience are fourteen, fifteen, sixteen—high school kids. Then there's a lot of twenty-year-olds, some thirty-to-fifty-year-old yuppies and some old sixties folk—alter kockers, white-haired like myself. So there's quite a spread but there is about a fifth that's really young, and very intelligent. Literate."

"To what do you attribute their interest in your work?"

"Candor. Being frank. To have an older person talk realistically about what it's like to be older or younger or some yearning on my own part for younger people. But I think mainly it's the frankness, including the frankness of language, frankness of thought. I'm willing to talk about anything that comes to my mind rather than what I think is appropriate, whether it's politics or drugs or lovemaking or the CIA. Partly because I don't know any better. I'm not smart enough to get away with anything."

"What do you think your greatest achievement is?"

"Oh, beauty in the language. Kind of massive, ecstatic, poetic oratory. It's a kind of transcendent visual quality plus a reasonable... buildup." He paused. "I hope I'm making sense."

"You're making perfect sense," I assured him. "Do you think there could ever be another Beat Generation?"

"Well, the Beat Generation was basically a variation of the old bohemian tradition. Whether you call them Beat or bohemian or the outriders or the marginal people or the avant-garde, they've existed all along and always will. It seems to me that there is a straight line from Beat to punk, grunge and slacker that encompasses certain spiritual elements."

I closed my notebook. "Would you mind if I asked you a personal question?"

"No," he replied. "Go ahead."

"This is related but sort of not related. What do you miss most about Jack Kerouac? What did you love most about him?"

He paused but only for a moment. "A kind of tender appreciation of language. *My* language and my poetry. And also a kind of basic sanity—despite his alcoholism—a solidity of mind."

"I was reading Gore Vidal's memoir recently and there's a whole section about Kerouac..."

"Yeah, I read that," he said, sitting up straight. "And he consulted me. But, you know, Vidal's a little mean. Boasts that he *had* Kerouac. There's a very funny section where he sees a young kid years later wearing a Kerouac T-shirt. And the kid says, 'I love Kerouac.' Vidal says amusingly, 'I used to.' He actually had a little heartthrob for him. But for somebody he had a heartthrob for he sure doesn't treat him respectfully."

"Not at all," I agreed. "What would Kerouac be up to these days if he were alive?"

"I always wonder," he said thoughtfully, sinking back into the cushions of the chair. "When I ponder over something, I wonder, 'What would *he* think about this?' He drives me a lot, sort of like an old guru. Because of a certain tenderness in him. I remember one of the last times I saw him he was listening to St. Matthew Passion by Bach and he had tears in his eyes because of the music. He had a very kind heart, ultimately. For all of his alcoholism and all the freneticism that went with it, his underlying nature was *extreme* vulnerability and tenderness."

Tenderness. A question escaped from my lips before I could stop it. "I suppose this would be a sweeping generalization, but Kerouac seemed very... to use your words, he was very kindhearted and he was very tender. Those aren't attributes I encounter very often."

"Well, that may be," he said, unfazed and unperturbed, "but the Buddha view is that our nature is not necessarily Malthusian, dog eat dog, but basic goodness. We all suffer by being born and having to die, and, since we are aware of our own suffering, we are also aware of others.'"

I felt like I could ask anything I wanted. "I think Kerouac's tenderness comes through in his writing."

"Very much so," he agreed. "A kind of brooding, melancholy tenderness. Really realizing that everybody's suffering, I think, and having a kind of compassionate attitude toward that."

"Just one more Kerouac question," I said, thinking I was pushing my luck.

But Ginsberg remained unruffled. "Sure."

"Hanging on the bulletin board in my office is a Gap ad I tore out of a magazine. It's got a picture of Kerouac standing outside a bar in the Village and underneath it says, 'Kerouac wore khakis.' Any idea how he would have felt about that?"

"I don't know if he would have really liked it. He didn't sign up for that, his family did. *I* signed up for one. I refused it for a long while but then I had a light bulb in my head and on the side of every ad it says all monies from this ad go to the Jack Kerouac School of Disembodied Poetics at the Naropa Institute in Colorado. That was a Buddhist way of turning waste to treasure."

"You were on *Charlie Rose* the other night..."

"Was I making sense on that? I had one good speech saying what I thought the themes of the Beat Generation were. That's really about the most coherent thing I've said on the subject. Plus the preface to the Whitney show catalog."

"Yeah, I saw that."

"Wow, you seem to be up on a lot. So why *is* the interest in the Beats continuing? What is *your* interest?"

"It's what we were discussing earlier. The Beats offer a fresh, compassionate take on humanity."

"Kerouac again," said Ginsberg. "It's actually there in Burroughs, though Burroughs is tougher."

"He's a little hard to get through," I said.

"But, you know," countered Ginsberg, "Burroughs ultimately has this great sticky sentimentality at the center, if you read *Queer*, or a few of the other books. Or his letters. The reason he's so externally dignified is that he's so vulnerable and sentimental, ultimately, underneath."

"It's also the honesty," I added. "To encounter complete honesty in this world is a rare occurrence and a completely unselfconscious honesty permeates all the Beat writings."

Ginsberg nodded. "We were lucky. Kerouac couldn't get anything published after his first book, *The Town and the City*. So, he wrote *On the Road*, *Visions of Cody*, *Maggie Cassidy*, *Dr. Sax*, *The Subterraneans*, part one of *Desolation Angels*, *Book of Dreams*, and all the books of poetry with no idea that they would be published but just talking to God or talking to us. I didn't expect to publish 'Howl,' even. I realized that once I got to the sex parts I couldn't show my family, so I was free to say anything I wanted. Burroughs never expected to publish *Naked Lunch*—it was just some letters to me with these wild routines. So, we were protected, say, for ten years, while we were hatching these monstrosities, and we were very candid 'cause we were just our own audience. And then once we began getting published we had all this work piled up. Kerouac's only problem was fame. I think fame was the tax he had to live with. He was really treated despicably by a lot of critics in his time."

"I often wonder," I said, "what would have happened if *The New York Times* had given *On the Road* a bad review, ripped it to shreds instead of calling it a landmark book. Would that have been the end of Kerouac's career?"

"No!" declared Ginsberg. "He would have written anyway! He was a *born* writer. He wasn't writing for the *public*. There's a very beautiful passage in *Visions of Cody*, in which he talks about his ideal…"

" 'Go moan for man,' " I said, repeating the words I'd heard Kerouac read a million times on the CD," 'and of this world report you well and truly.' "

" 'And of *Cody* report you well and truly,' " said Ginsberg. "That's the line in the book. He changed it for the recording, you know. He tinkered with a lot of his writing when he did a reading."

"Of *Cody*?!" I asked, thinking and talking at the same time.

"Of *Cody*?! But that changes…"

"Cody was Neal," continued Ginsberg. "His best friend. His

243

brother. 'Cody is the brother I lost.' Kerouac thought Neal could have been the reincarnation of his older brother Gerard, who died when Jack was four."

Visions of Cody blurred with visions of my own as I repeated the line to myself. "And of *Cody* report you well and truly." Of course. Best friends. *Brothers.* In *this* life.

"You know," said Ginsberg, "in *On the Road* and *Visions of Cody,* the most intriguing aspect is Jack's portrayal of Neal as Walt Whitman's romantic ideal, as a man who loved another man, as a man who believed that generous emotional intimacy was the ultimate communion of soul. *On the Road* and *Visions of Cody* were both love songs of a sort. Even though Jack and Neal were never lovers, they had a heroic tenderness for one another, a stirring and poignant love affection of the heart. It's an aspect of traditional masculine relationships that has been lost and all but eradicated from modern society. Unfortunately."

A heroic tenderness. Yes. That was it. "Allen, you loved Neal."

"Well, I was *in* love with him. And Jack, too."

"But Jack and Neal weren't *in* love."

"No, they loved each other very much but they were not *in* love."

"What's the difference?"

"The sex part."

"Right."

"Why do you ask?"

Ginsberg's openness prompted my own. "I have feelings for my best friend and I'm not sure what those feelings are."

"Do you want to sleep with him?"

"I don't think so. I wouldn't allow myself to think so."

"That's not exactly the same as..."

"I know," I said, looking away. "But it's all I've got."

I could feel his eyes on me. "Well," he said after a moment, "it might help to think of him as your brother, not your lover."

"Heh. He said we were brothers in a previous life. Just about an hour ago."

244

"So there you go. You're brothers in this life, too. Anything else you'd like to know?"

"How much time do you have?"

He laughed at that.

"How'd you deal with being in love with Neal and Jack? How'd they deal with you being in love with them?"

"I accepted that they loved me as best they could and they accepted that I loved them in a way they couldn't love me. It wasn't always easy, but we loved one another, that's what mattered more than anything, and it got easier, eventually. Over time."

Yes. Over time.

"I think," he added, "that it was Truman Capote who said, 'Just because someone doesn't love you the way you want them to doesn't mean they don't love you with all they have.'"

I nodded. "Got it." Finally.

"You know," he continued, returning to what we'd been talking about before I steered us off course, "the first ninety pages of *Cody* are all sketches, like, 'Sounds of Long Island in the Night.' Jacking off in his bathroom there. And 'Hector's Cafeteria.' 'The Third Avenue El Subway Station.' Someone suggested to Jack that he take his pen and sketch just like a sketch artist does but in words and he's got a hundred pages of that as the opening of the book. It's terrific. Like prose poems."

Or prosetry, I said to myself, experiencing another small satori.

"So, with all this interest in the Beats, do *you* write?" he asked.

"Yes, well, sort of. I have been working on an *idea* for a novel. Working on *starting* a novel."

"That's a lot of qualifiers. What are you waiting for?"

"Heh. I'm not sure. My best friend asked me that and I told him that when a reporter asked Kerouac that same question, Kerouac said he was waiting for God to show his face."

"Well," said Ginsberg, "consider that in *Les Misérables*, Victor Hugo wrote, 'To love another person is to see the face of God.'"

"Then I guess it's time to start writing."

Ginsberg nodded and exhaled audibly and I noticed for the

first time he looked a little tired. Glancing at my watch, I realized that we'd gone on for over an hour—longer than the limit set by Bob Rosenthal in the interests of Allen's health.

"I should go," I said, leaning forward on the couch and reaching for my coat. "I really want to thank you for talking with me. Especially given the circumstances."

"Oh, no problem," said Ginsberg as he led me out, shuffling along somewhat unsteadily in his silk slippers. "I hope you got everything you need," he added, opening his door.

"And then some," I assured him.

He closed his eyes, dipped his head and smiled a beatific smile.

"Ahhhhh!"

31

DARKNESS HAD ALREADY DESCENDED on the city when I left Ginsberg's apartment. At first I chalked it up to the still-falling snow but then I remembered that it was December twenty-first, the winter solstice, the shortest day of the year. On any other day, given that it was already after five, I would have headed home, but since I only had two more days left at *Element*, I decided to return to the office. It occurred to me that most people in my position would have used that as an excuse *not* to return to the office, but I was beginning to feel slightly sentimental—about the people, about the place, about the daily and weekly routines I would shortly be leaving behind—and I wanted to gather as many memories as I could in the final few hours of that phase in my life.

The office was nearly empty when I arrived. After depositing my coat on my desk, I walked to the art department where Jay was talking with Ted and Mitch. "Hey!" he said when he saw me. "How'd it go? Did you get to ask all your questions?"

"Yes," I replied. "And more."

A moment later, at six o'clock, the heating system shut off with a short hiss. Ted went outside to grab a smoke just as Cliff rounded the corner. He stopped in his tracks when he saw me. "Harry, what are *you* still doing here?"

"Just hanging out," I answered defensively.

Jay stood and stretched. "I think it's time to call it a night." He shut down his computer and started packing his backpack.

I went back to my office to grab my coat. Jay swung by a few seconds later and we left. Outside, the snow had stopped but not the wind. Jay lit a Camel Light and we headed to the subway entrance at Forty-Seventh, where he took a final drag and tossed his cigarette onto the ice. I followed him down the stairs and as we pushed through the turnstiles, he paused to say goodbye, or so I assumed, but he suddenly seemed deep in thought.

"So, Ginsberg was good?" he asked after a moment.

"Yeah, Ginsberg was good," I replied. "I'll tell you all about it when we have more time."

Again, he was quiet, thinking. "Har?"

"Yeah?"

He searched my eyes while he searched for words. I wondered what he could possibly want to say after everything we'd already said to each other that day. Finally, he held out his hand and took mine in his, holding on tightly for what seemed an eternity. "See you tomorrow."

We headed down the steps of our respective platforms. A downtown F train was waiting on the tracks between us and when it pulled away Jay was gone. A northbound B train arrived in a few minutes and whisked me away to the Upper West Side. I'd caught a chill that I wasn't able to shake and I shivered in my coat as I struggled up the icy sidewalk by the Dakota and the rest of the two-block walk to my apartment. In my mailbox, I found a Christmas card from Matteo. In my bed, I fell to pieces on my bed, overwhelmed by everything that had happened in the last few minutes, hours, days, weeks, months and years.

THE NIGHT AFTER MATTEO and I went home together following dinner, drinks and dancing at Elfreth's, everything returned to the status quo. Our night together was just that. One night. As much as I wanted to read something more into it, in the end, there was nothing more to be read into it. We would never spend another night together again. Matteo was just as frustrated as I was, frustrated that he didn't feel for me what I felt for him, frustrated

248

that we didn't want the same thing. What we had, he felt, was good. We lived in the same house together, we hung out together and every once in a great while we slept in the same bed together. For my part, I couldn't understand how he could want all that and not want the one thing I thought was missing.

Months passed. Seasons changed. But the situation between us did not. It only grew more unstable. Matteo had slipped away. Away from everything he had aspired to be when we first met. He was an unemployed drunk. An unemployed drunk who slept with strangers nearly every night. No amount of alcohol could make him forget it for a minute. As for me, I had slipped away also. Away from everything that I had ever been. I was the pathetic, dejected romantic who continued to look out for Matteo to the exclusion of almost anything else, still hoping for something that would never be. We were both on the edge, wound up and waiting to explode.

I came home from work one Friday to find him finishing the last bottle in a six-pack of Bud. He greeted me as I walked in the door.

"Hey, Har, happy hour started at home today!" he yelled, stumbling toward me as he jumped up from the couch.

I put my arms out to break his fall and he smiled as he fell into them, taking my hands in his.

"Shall we dance?" he asked, slurring his words and tripping over his own feet as he attempted an awkward two-step. "Anyway," he said, giving up and falling back on the couch, "get changed. The night is young and I need to get drunk."

I looked him over. He reeked from six feet away.

"How about dinner?" I suggested. "I think you need to eat."

His face contorted. "What I *need*," he said angrily as he stood up again, "is for you not to tell me what I need." He staggered for a moment, caught his balance and then looked at me with a huge grin. "Now, are you going to come with me or do I have to get drunk all by myself?"

Though I knew it was a mistake, I threw on a long-sleeve T-shirt and a pair of jeans and we headed out. It was raining steadily when we pulled away. Matteo had been flagged from the Car Bar and wanted to go to a place where nobody knew his name. He directed me to the turnpike and then to a club he'd heard about in New Hope, a small village of cafés and galleries an hour north of Philadelphia. I glanced at him as I drove. He was staring blankly out the passenger seat window and tracing the path of raindrops with his index finger as they slid sideways along the glass. He seemed very sad.

"Everything okay, Matteo?"

He didn't answer.

"Matteo?"

He looked at me like I'd just woken him up. "What?"

"Is anything wrong?"

"Nah," he replied unconvincingly. "What could be wrong?" He forced a smile, flicked on the radio and turned the volume up past the point of any further conversation.

At the club, Matteo ordered us two Buds and two shots of Jaegermeister, immediately downing his shot and then mine.

"Don't worry, Har, there's more where that came from," he said with a laugh when he saw the concern in my eyes.

He ordered another round and when the bartender had refilled the shot glasses, Matteo picked them both up.

"Cheers!" he said. He downed the first, held the second out to me for a moment and then pulled it back and downed that one, too.

"Matteo," I began, "maybe you should..."

But before I could say anything else, he picked up his mug of beer and cut me off.

"Don't tell me what I should or shouldn't do," he snapped. His face clouded over and then cleared. "Get yourself a shot, Har. I'm four up on you. I'll be back."

With that, he was gone. I stood at the bar not drinking my beer, wondering what the night would bring. I found out about twenty minutes later, when Matteo returned with a young guy on his arm. He told me the guy's name but I didn't hear it.

"Listen, Har," he said, "I know we just got here, and I'm awfully sorry to do this to you, but I'm going to hang with my new friend if you don't mind."

"Nah, I don't mind," I said, trying to sound indifferent. Matteo detected the undertone in my reply.

"Sounds like you do mind." He glared at me for a moment and then broke into an exaggerated smile. "Good ol' Har." He leaned over and whispered in my ear. "Do you have a twenty I could borrow?"

The last thing Matteo needed, I decided, was to keep drinking. Was it up to me to make that decision? I didn't know. I only knew he was hurting and I didn't want him to hurt any more.

"No, Matteo, I'm not giving you any money."

He studied me for a moment trying to determine whether I was joking or serious.

"Matteo, you've had enough to drink. More than enough. I'm going home. Come with me. We'll get something to eat."

He realized I was serious as I stood to go.

"I'm not going anywhere," he yelled. "I don't want to *eat*. I want to *drink*."

I knew there was no changing his mind in his condition and reluctantly I headed for the door. Just as I reached for the handle, however, Matteo grabbed me by the shoulder, spun me around and slammed me up against the wall.

"Are you going to give me some money or what?" he screamed. I stared at him, undone and unrecognizable, his ruggedly handsome face contorted by too much pain and too much alcohol.

"No, Matteo, I'm not going to give you any money," I said flatly, my eyes glazing over. "I love you too much to give you any money."

"No," he yelled. "You love me too much, *period*."

His eyes burned with a mixture of anger and frustration. He pinned me to the wall with his left hand as he raised himself up on the balls of his feet and cocked his right hand in a tight white-knuckled fist. He struggled to keep control and finally lost it. The last thing I saw as I closed my eyes was his fist coming at me. I braced myself for the impact but only felt his fingers graze my cheek as they slammed into the wall a half-inch from my head.

I opened my eyes as Matteo burst into tears, his bloody fist repeatedly and reflexively punching the air and his bloodshot brown eyes overflowing with an agonizing mix of hurt and horror, sorrow and self-loathing.

He blinked back his tears as he struggled unsuccessfully to regain control of himself. "Go... home!" he yelled, choking on his words. "Just...go...*home!*"

Shaking uncontrollably, he turned and headed back into the club, disappearing into the darkness. I stood there for a moment, finally able to breathe again but unable to move, frozen in place against the wall where Matteo had pushed me. For a split second I considered going after him. But I knew in my heart, just as he knew in his, those days were over.

I drove home through the pouring rain, barely able to see the roads ahead of me between the water on my windshield and the tears in my eyes. I had already decided what I was going to do. I had spent the last year trying to convince someone to love me. I had spent the three years before that trying to convince someone else. And I had failed. I was unloved. I was unlovable. There was only one thing to do.

I was awakened by my ringing telephone. I opened my eyes to see that the sun was up and that I was sprawled across my bed, still in my clothes. As I rolled over and reached for the phone, I struggled to piece together the events of the previous night but my mind was an utter blank.

"Huhlllo," I heard myself say. I was shocked by the sound of my voice, shocked that I had somehow managed to slur a single word.

"Harry? Is that you?"

I tried again. "Yeahhhh."

"It's Marlee."

I tried to place the name. Marlee. An old friend I worked with at *Rittenhouse Square*. I had forsaken her in my unflagging fixation on Matteo. She had never forsaken me.

"Is everything all right? You didn't come into the office this morning and you didn't call."

My head was spinning. Work? What was she talking about?

"Marlee, it's Saturday."

She paused. "Harry, it's Monday."

"Monday...?"

I glanced around the room and spotted the empty plastic prescription pill bottle on the floor. Next to it, an open notebook.

"Harry, are you okay?"

"I... think... so."

The phone slipped from my grasp as I stared at a page of illegible apologies I had scrawled three days earlier and in a single awful instant I realized what I had done, not only to myself but to all those who cared about me. My heart heaved in my chest and broke and I choked on a flood of uncontrollable and inconsolable tears, tears for time lost and time regained, tears for all that was still to happen in my life, for all those I would someday love, for all those I would someday love. For all those who would someday meet, for all those who would someday love me.

Downstairs, I heard the front door open and then a familiar voice.

"Harry?"

A moment later, Matteo appeared.

"Harry? You all right?"

I sat on the edge of the bed staring at the floor, unable to answer.

He sat next to me and put his hand on my shoulder. I caved at his touch, wrapped my arms around his waist and buried my face in his chest, trembling violently. Without a word, he pulled me close and held me for several minutes.

"I'm really sorry about what happened Friday night," he said finally. "And I'm sorry I didn't come home till now. I love you, Harry. I hope you know that. But not like you love me. I can't love you like that. I can't love *anyone* like that. I just... I just don't have it in me."

He paused and I felt his body shift as he reached for something. From the corner of my eye I saw him pick up the notebook on the floor before I could stop him.

"What's this?"

A moment later I felt his breathing stop. He pushed me away from his chest, held me tightly at arm's length and stared at me hard, noticing for the first time just how horrible I looked and that I was still wearing the same clothes I had on when he'd last seen me, three days earlier. In his eyes I saw the reflection of the tender anguish in my own. And I realized—he knew.

Matteo and I parted ways shortly after that. We agreed that it would be best if we saw each other less, for a while, at least, until the wounds had healed. His and mine. After he moved out of my house, however, I told him that I couldn't see him at all. I tried to explain that it wasn't something I wanted to do but something I had to do. It was the only way, I said, that I could ever fall out of love with him. He got mad at me. Or he pretended to be mad. Despite what had happened, he still thought of me as the one person in his life he could depend on to always be there for him, to always help him out of all the jams he got himself into, and I think he felt that he had screwed that up for reasons that were beyond his control.

He wrote me a letter a few months later and confessed that his heart had broken the day I walked away, that he couldn't stop crying. But he said he had come to understand and he wanted me to know that he, too, had walked away—from drinking, from one-night stands, from the awful life he'd been living. He'd returned to his studies and passed his test. And he'd also returned to work. He said the two twenties he'd slipped into the letter were just the beginning. In time, he would repay every penny he had borrowed from me. Even so, he said, he would always owe me much more. I wept as I read his words.

While we were a part of each other's lives, he was never able to tell me what I meant to him. He still tries. He sends me a Christmas card every year. And he calls every so often. To apologize over and over again for the way he treated me. For taking me for granted. For never being able to express his appreciation for everything I did for him. And to tell me that he's still haunted by what he did to me one awful night in a bar when he'd had too much to drink, something he can never take back, something that my forgiveness will never undo.

But I too am sorry. Sorry that I ever let my judgment become so clouded I would hurt someone who cared so much. Sorry that I didn't recognize that he loved me as best he could, the only way he was able. Sorry that was never enough. And I'm still haunted by what I did to him one awful night, something that I can never take back, something his forgiveness will never undo.

It was a terrible love.

AN HOUR AFTER I SAID goodbye to Jay in the subway and collapsed on my bed, I awoke to find Flannery curled up in the crook of my arm, warmly pressed against my chest. She was always there for me. Always there. I wrapped a blanket around her, pulled myself together and got up to work on my journal, recounting the day's momentous events on my laptop. I was only at it for a few minutes, however, when the phone rang.

"Hi, Harry," said a familiar voice I hadn't heard in a while.

"It's Zahra."

"Hey, what's up?"

"Jay and I were sitting here talking and we decided to give you a call. I wanted to thank you for making a copy of Ginsberg's poem for me."

"No problem."

"I also wanted to congratulate you on your job. I haven't talked with you in so long. Not since you got it, anyway."

"Yeah, we've both been so busy."

"Well, school was finally over today," she said. "I still have a few things to wrap up but I'll see you tomorrow night at the going-away party for you and Jay."

"Really? You're going to come?"

"Yeah, I have a Christmas party I have to go to first, but I'll come by later. We also invited Zeus and Marilyn."

"Great. It'll be like a real party for Jay and me."

"Yeah," she agreed. "Actually, Jay has something he wants to say to you."

My heart started beating faster as she handed him the phone.

"Har?"

"Hey, what's up?"

He cleared his throat. "Listen, I was talking to Zahra about the book and if the offer still stands I'd like to accept it."

I couldn't believe what I was hearing. "What? Are you sure? No, why am I asking that? Of *course* the offer still stands. Why did you change your mind?"

"I thought it over," he said slowly. "I thought of everything we talked about today at your apartment. And I realized a few things. About me. About you. About us. I know how much you want me to have the book and that means a lot to me. Maybe more than I'll ever be able to say." He paused. "It was a great gift. You have a good heart, Harry."

A good heart. A *good heart?* I repeated his words to myself, over and over. The last thing I'd ever felt through all my misplaced, inappropriate affection for Jay was that I had a good heart. Silent tears streamed down my face, not for the love I didn't have, but for the love I did.

"Let me talk to Zahra again," I said. He laughed and handed her the phone. "What did you say to him?" I asked. "I was all right with how we left it earlier."

"No you weren't," she said, laughing.

"Yes I was," I insisted. "I really was."

"No you weren't."

"Well, I was okay with how we left it, but I'm happier about this."

"Tell Jay that," she said, handing the phone back to him.

"What'd she want you to tell me?" he asked.

"I said I was really okay with how we left it earlier, but I'm happier about this."

"Yeah, well," he said laughing and embarrassed.

"But we still have a deal," I added. "You owe me a copy when you find one."

"You got it."

I heard Zahra say something in the background and laugh. Then Jay laughed.

"What'd she say?" I asked.

"She says she wants that first edition of *Howl*."

"Did you tell her about that? I told you I was kidding."

"No, man, I didn't tell her about that."

"You *didn't*? And she just *said* that?"

"Yeah." I heard Jay explaining that I had joked about giving her a first edition of *Howl* over lunch in the pizza place. "So are you ready for tomorrow night?" he asked. "Ready for our covers?"

"You mean *cover*, don't you?"

"No, I asked Ted not to embarrass us. He did a cover for each of us. I've actually seen yours."

"You have?"

"Yeah, and it's really funny. It's appropriate. But I had to swear I wouldn't tell you what it is."

"Am I in drag?"

"No."

"Well, that's all I need to know. So, do you want me to bring your book in tomorrow?"

"Yeah, bring it in tomorrow."

I heard Zahra say something in the background again. Jay laughed. "What'd she say?" I asked.

"She said, 'One day it will be mine.' Well, I'll see you in the morning."

"Jay?" I said hesitantly.

"Yeahhhhh...?"

I paused. He knew what I wanted to say and we both knew there was no need to say it. "Never mind."

He laughed. "Later, bro."

"Yes, that's right," I said. "Later, *bro*."

I hung up and went back to my laptop, the glowing screen still empty except for the date, which was as far as I'd gotten on my journal entry when the phone rang. I thought back to a day years earlier, back before Jay and I had met, in this life, anyway. I was without hope. Hopeless. Unable to foresee a time when I would ever be hopeful again. Unaware that Jay was out there, surprised by joy in this obscure space of life and scribbling a poem about it in a sketchpad.

And I suddenly realized I had finally found that last thing, that last thing we keep on living in hopes of catching once and for all. It arrives when you least expect it, in ways you never imagine, from a place you never thought it could come, in a form you never thought it could take. And though it may not be what you hoped it would be, or exactly how you pictured it, to accept it for what it is, and for what it isn't, to *live* with what it is, and what it isn't, is the greatest gift of a good heart.

"There are two mistakes one can make along the road to truth," Buddhists say. "Not going all the *way*, and not *starting*." I knew I still had a long way to go but I had started. I had finally started. Finally, I was on the road.

I sat there staring at my laptop, with only the date staring back at me, the date when something happened, and I typed from memory the words Jay had written in his sketchpad, knowing that those were the only words that could end this book, the book Jay and I promised each other we'd write together but lived together instead.

Today love abounds. There is nothing but extreme, unselfish, undying love. Yesterday was black and death was in the air. Today love abounds....

AFTERWORD

AND THEN WHAT HAPPENED? In the ten years since Harry, Jay and Zahra discovered boundless love in the final few pages of *Beatitude*, more than one reader has asked that question. Strange as it might seem, I have, too. You would think that, as the author, I would be in total control of my protagonists' fates, but at some point during the decade I spent writing *Beatitude*, Harry, Jay and Zahra took on lives of their own. They became Real. And as anyone who has ever read *The Velveteen Rabbit* knows, "once you are Real you can't become unreal again. It lasts for always."

How do I know they became Real? Because I saw Harry and Jay once, on May 21, 2001. How do I remember the date? Because I was at Christie's New York for the auction of Jack Kerouac's original scroll manuscript of *On the Road*. I was in the third row in a large, noisy, windowless room packed with nearly two-hundred literary agents, librarians and booksellers, along with Beat Generation royalty—Kerouac's literary agent Sterling Lord and Kerouac biographer Ann Charters, among them—and at least a few millionaires and their emissaries. Along one wall, a dozen men and women in suits sat shoulder to shoulder at a long table lined with telephones, staring anxiously at a stage in the front of the room. In the back, a cluster of news cameras were trained on the same subject. Scanning the crowd around me, I spotted two familiar faces in the first row: Harry Charity and Jay Bishop, the protagonists of *Beatitude*, looking a little rough around the edges and endearingly out of place in a room full of high rollers.

The room grew quiet as the man at the podium on the stage cleared his throat. "Up next, lot number three-o-seven... Jack Kerouac's original typescript scroll of *On The Road*... I'll start the bidding at six-hundred-fifty-thousand dollars on this."

Immediately, a hand holding a paddle shot up. And then another. And another. The row of men and women along the wall sprang into action, yelling excitedly into telephone receivers and thrusting paddles into the air as the bids ticked up in fifty-thousand-dollar increments.

"One million dollars in the front row!"

The tension reached a fever pitch as successively higher bids—now at a hundred thousand dollars a pop—ping-ponged frenetically around the room. Harry and Jay tried to keep up, their eyes darting from one corner to another at whiplash speed. There was a lull as the bidding topped off at one-million nine-hundred-thousand dollars and an expectant silence descended.

"Last call... Two million dollars!"

And then, just under the two-minute mark, the final bid, from a dapper man with a silver goatee and longish slicked-back salt-and-pepper hair who was sporting a dark gray wide-pinstripe suit.

"Two-million two-hundred-thousand dollars! Are we done? Sold!"

The high bidder was Jim Irsay, owner of the NFL's Indianapolis Colts and new owner of the legendary scroll manuscript of Jack Kerouac's *On the Road*. Christie's had estimated the scroll would fetch between one and one-and-a-half million dollars. The final price of two-million four-hundred-sixty thousand dollars (two-million two-hundred-thousand dollars plus a buyer's premium of two-hundred-twenty-six-thousand dollars) set a new world record for a literary manuscript. "I was willing to spend a lot more!" Irsay told reporters afterward with a laugh. The sale came exactly fifty years and one month after Kerouac finished the scroll on April 22, 1951, following a three-week frenzy of typing.

As the exuberant audience slowly scattered, I watched as Harry and Jay made their way out, before finally losing them in the crowd. Six years earlier, in 1995, they had bonded over a private viewing of the scroll only six blocks south of Christie's, in the basement of the New York Public Library. Now they were off, no doubt, to discuss what they had just witnessed—what in the world would

Jack Kerouac think?—over cappuccinos at some downtown cafe.

At that point, they were still wandering the pages of my recently completed seven-hundred-fifty-page first draft of *Beatitude*, two characters—and one author—in search of a story. I was struggling. I knew there was a story somewhere in those seven-hundred-fifty pages but I had yet to zero in on it. In my desperation to do so, I had even thought of making my own scroll and typing on a vintage portable Royal typewriter I'd bought at a flea market. But Jack Kerouac had been there, done that. He above all would encourage me to find my own road, not travel his. And, eventually, I would.

But, yes, Harry and Jay—and Zahra—were already Real by then. And in the years of writing *Beatitude* that followed, as I went from creator to chronicler, their fates were out of my hands. All I did was decide where to leave them at the end of the novel. I know their story continued, because I wrote an epilogue that I decided to leave out. In it, Harry and Jay go to the Nuyorican Poets Café on an open-mike night, Jay reads a new poem and they plan their next adventure. Some might have found that a more satisfying ending because it's less ambiguous. But, to me, the most powerful moment, the moment the entire book leads up to, is the actual ending, when Harry accepts that Jay can't accept the first edition of *On the Road* and the sentiment attached to it, when Zahra convinces Jay to accept it and when Jay finally does. Harry, Jay and Zahra's ultimate insight is to put themselves in each other's place, to view the world through another's eyes and heart, and in so doing, evolve. They each take a step forward. They each discover true empathy.

That might be why, when a friend finished reading *Beatitude*, he emailed to congratulate me for writing a "modern Beat novel." At the time, I wasn't sure what he meant, because I certainly hadn't set out to write a modern Beat novel. Looking back now, however, on the tenth anniversary of *Beatitude*'s publication, perhaps I did.

SET IN NEW YORK CITY, 1995, *Beatitude* follows two young men fascinated with the unfettered lives of Jack Kerouac, Allen Ginsberg and the Beat Generation, and explores how intense passions can confuse the sometimes thin line between friendship and love. In *Beatitude*, the Beats themselves appear in sequences that illuminate the main story and Ginsberg inspires the ultimate insight.

But even with all the Beats running around the pages of *Beatitude*, I didn't consider it a Beat novel, modern or otherwise. In fact, I had taken steps to ensure that it wasn't. I am a Beat aficionado, as is obvious to anyone who reads *Beatitude*. I've read and absorbed nearly all the literary output of the holy Beat triumvirate of Jack Kerouac, Allen Ginsberg and William S. Burroughs, in addition to works by fellow Beats Neal Cassady, Gregory Corso, Gary Snyder, Amiri Baraka, John Clellon Holmes and Diane di Prima. I've read even more books about them.

On the Road by Jack Kerouac made the biggest impression. And, it seems, not only on me. Author Crawford Kilian, a columnist for the British Columbia online magazine The Tyree, once listed ten modern literary classics he believes are harmful to aspiring writers—"more hazard than inspiration"—because "their readable styles look so easy they might seduce a young writer into imitating them." *On the Road* was one of the ten.

As William S. Burroughs famously remarked, "Kerouac opened a million coffee bars and sold a million pairs of Levis to both sexes. Woodstock rises from his pages." Kerouac's influence on would-be writers is even more profound. I had wanted to be a writer long before I read *On the Road*, but when I did, it had the same effect on me as it does on nearly every aspiring writer. Kerouac made me believe that I *could* be a writer. And that it was easy. After all, in April 1951, he wrote *On the Road* in a single, nonstop caffeine-and-nicotine-fueled creative marathon on a one-hundred-twenty-foot scroll of Teletype paper. Employing a new "wild form" of writing he dubbed spontaneous prose, Kerouac produced a perfectly polished and publishable manuscript in a mere three weeks that became an instant and enduring bestseller.

That's the legend. The truth is that Kerouac had been preparing to write *On the Road* for years, starting and shelving several drafts, scribbling endless observations in stacks of small notebooks and searching, searching, searching before finally finding the "fast, mad, confessional" style that would evoke "the holy contour of life." He equipped himself with all of those resources when he sat down to write what would become his most famous book, and the resulting effort entailed as much editing, curating and collating as actual writing. Though Kerouac swore that no one would edit the scroll—"first thought, best thought"—they did. He did, in fact, as revealed by his own revisions and copy-editing marks on the scroll and the subsequent versions of the manuscript he typed in a more traditional format.

Still, it's the legend that endures, and despite Kerouac's own advice that "It ain't whatcha write, it's the way atcha write it," it's the legend that sparks every aspiring writer's dreams, prompting naïve imitations of Kerouac's jazz-inspired cadences. My own were on exhibit in the first half-dozen drafts of *Beattitude*. But I eventually realized that emulating Kerouac was pointless. Kerouac's style was a response—and a reaction—to all that had come before, including his first novel, *The Town and the City*, an homage to his own literary hero, Thomas Wolfe, that was greeted with general indifference. My style also had to reflect all that had come before—and, more importantly, *after*—*On the Road*. For me to try to replicate Kerouac's spontaneous prose, I would have to forget or ignore the last fifty-some years. It made no sense.

I started over, searching for my own voice, and I finally found it several versions later. One element I kept, which I shared with Kerouac but had nothing to do with style, was *Beattitude*'s real-world setting. *Beattitude* takes place in the real New York City of 1995, where my fictional characters occasionally interact with versions of real people, including Allen Ginsberg. I live in New York City and I was fortunate to be able to set *Beattitude* there. New York is instantly familiar to nearly everyone on the planet and instantly epic at the same time. Nearly every book, movie or television show that's set in New York has an air of verisimilitude, which is something I wanted to convey. Naturally, New York would play a starring role.

I've always loved books that blend fact and fiction, especially in New York, to create a sort of hyper-reality—*Winter's Tale* by Mark Helprin, *Forever* by Pete Hamill, *Time and Again* by Jack Finney and, yes, *On the Road* by Jack Kerouac. You want to believe that they really happened, or could have happened, and that makes the story and the characters more identifiable. The real-life Beat Culture exhibit at the Whitney Museum of American Art, for example, aligned with *Beatitude*'s timeline and provided the perfect backdrop for Harry, Jay and Zahra's first encounter with Ginsberg. My three protagonists also attend a 1995 Ginsberg poetry reading at MoMA which I based on a recording of the reading and which in turn led to my discovery of the two unpublished Ginsberg poems featured in *Beatitude*.

When I wrote the scene at MoMA, I selected excerpts from a few of the poems Ginsberg read. After Rebel Satori Press accepted *Beatitude* for publication, I had to clear the rights to the poems and I contacted Peter Hale at the Allen Ginsberg Estate. In the course of his research, Peter discovered that two of the poems—"Like Other Guys" and "Carl Solomon Dream"—had, surprisingly, never been published. I initially thought that I would have to rewrite the scene with other poems but Peter put me in touch with Ginsberg's literary agent at The Wylie Agency and, long story short, I was able to include the two poems—using excerpts in the scene at MoMA and the full text in an Appendix. Needless to say, I was overwhelmed that two previously unpublished poems by Allen Ginsberg would be featured in my first novel. Beatitude, indeed.

The nods to reality have actually spawned the question I am most frequently asked: How much of *Beatitude* is true? My standard reply to that question is: If I made you believe it's true, then I succeeded in what I set out to do. However, I will add that it's a first novel and I think nearly everyone who writes a first novel is inspired to some extent by their own life, the people in their life and all they've experienced. Also, I think if you poke at something too much, it can fall apart and lose whatever magic it might hold. There's a story on the back of a Harry Nilsson album, a fairy tale written by a six-year-old, in which she slowly realizes a lamp she found is magic. "But," she writes at the end, "when somebody knew it was magic, it wasn't magic anymore." On the cover of *Be-atitude*, it says "A novel," and I'd like to leave it at that so the book retains as much of its magic as possible.

In the end, Kerouac as well as a hundred other authors inspired me—not to write *like* them but to *write*. Consequently, I would argue that reading *On the Road*, or any great book, does aspiring writers more good than harm. As author Samuel Delany proposes in *About Writing*, "It is almost impossible to write a novel any bet-ter than the best novel you've read in the three to six months before you began writing your own. Thus you *must* read excellent novels regularly."

Is *Beatitude* a "modern Beat novel"? I've come to realize that it is. Not because Kerouac and I share a similar style but because we share a similar sensibility—a belief in the basic goodness of human nature. As one reviewer pointed out, "The antagonist of *Beatitude* isn't a person, it's a situation... The enemy, if there is one, is society's conventions. An idea that falls right in line with the Beats' message." In *Beatitude*, I quote from an interview Kerouac did with television talk show host Steve Allen in 1959. "What is the meaning of the word *beat*?" asks Allen. Kerouac pauses and replies, "Sympathetic." In that sense, Jack and I are on the same page. We're both beat.

SO, WHAT HAPPENED TO HARRY, JAY AND ZAHRA? We may never know. But, on the tenth anniversary of *Beatitude's* publica-tion, twenty-seven years after the events chronicled in *Beatitude*, we can imagine: Harry is a celebrated novelist, Jay an acclaimed poet and Zahra the darling of the downtown art world. They fre-quently collaborate with each other across media, continuing the artistic endeavors of their Beat gurus. Despite their success, their notoriety eclipses their wealth—because, let's face it, novels, poems and art rarely pay the bills—and they remain bohemians at heart. Jay and Zahra parted amicably many years earlier and are now both married with children. Harry is happily partnered. Everything is bliss. Or maybe not. Because in life, and in literature, it rarely is. And also, per *The Velveteen Rabbit*, becoming Real sometimes hurts. So there's that.

And then what happened? We may never know. But when I consider the twists and turns my own life has taken, and those who have remained steadfast by my side, I think of what Jack Kerouac said on *The Steve Allen Show* about Neal Cassady at the conclusion of the adventures he chronicled in *On the Road*: "We're still great friends but we have to go into later phases of our lives." I'd like to believe that's true of Harry, Jay and Zahra. In fact, I know it is.

Larry Closs
March 2022

APPENDIX

Two previously unpublished poems by Allen Ginsberg, read at MoMA on November 14, 1995, appear in *Beatitude* for the first time.

LIKE OTHER GUYS
(Identified by AG at MoMA as "After Ted Berrigan")

I'm too serious, I should be feminine marvelous & tough
like other guys, I should fall in love with chicks.
I should get a tattoo on my ass and raise two kids.
I should move. Shouldn't grow old, shouldn't climb stairs.
Make a million dollars, give it away to Antler, Bremser, Clausen.
Stop publishing poems, they chop down trees.
My biodegradable books should be printed on hemp paper.
I should take care of stepmother Edith, Marie, Lafcadio
Julius Orlovsky, go to A.A. meetings with Peter
Move to Woodstock & inspire fresh air grass
I should take it easy, avoid stress, breathe
to the bottom of my lungs eat a little meat,
I should stop jacking off. I should jack off more
Make friends with myself and my laptop computer power
book. I should write more poems stop farting around
with rock & roll, I'm rock star automatically.
I shouldn't give famous autographs, meditate instead.
I should be so lucky I should live a thousand years
like Methuselah. I should read the Bible again, & Lankavatara
Sutra. Give away possessions & enter Clear Light,
Answer old letters from old boyfriends, I should
get my hemorrhoids fixed by laser, a colonoscopy
a chest x-ray, I should eat more rice, get more sleep. It's 9:49 AM

Saturday, I went to bed 4 AM last night done reading
NY Times at the kitchen table. Did I say I should get more
sleep? I would if I could but I can't so I won't.

CARL SOLOMON DREAM
(Identified by AG at MoMA as "Dream of Carl Solomon, January 1955")

I meet Carl Solomon
"What's it like in the afterworld?" I ask
He answers, "It's just like in the hospital. You get along if you
follow the rules."
"What are the rules?"
He answers, "The first rule is, 'Remember you're dead.' The
second rule is, 'Act like you're dead.'"

1995

ACKNOWLEDGEMENTS

Just as I was finishing the manuscript for this book, I came upon a quote by Antoine de Saint-Exupéry, author of *The Little Prince*: "Perfection is achieved, not when there is nothing more to add, but when there is nothing left to take away."

No one helped me take more away from *Beatitude* than my very dear friend Mindy Kitei, who just may be the greatest editor on Earth. Mindy read more versions of this book than anyone, making suggestions about what should stay and what should go, patiently waiting for me to see the light until she wisely *demanded* I see the light. Tough love. And the book is all the better for it.

I am fortunate to have not one but two families who provided immeasurable support: My mother (Eleanor), father (Jack), Kathy, Marilyn and Johnny from my biological family, and John, Richard, Al, Sandra and Al Barrow from my adopted family.

One of my very closest friends, Tina Bibars, was also always there for me, a loyal, loving supplier of considered, calm wisdom (and very happy holidays).

The encouragement of other great friends helped me along the way, even if they didn't always know exactly what I was working on: Brian Laguardia kept me honest (no snowflake ever falls in the wrong place), Ben Ahrens told me to have faith in the words I wrote, Kerri Griffith negotiated my idiosyncratic use of commas, Eric Swenson connected the dots, Michael Kimball translated contracts, Tammy Lakatos Shames offered seasoned insights, Jody Weston Brake sent love and enlightenment from afar, Valerie A. Reeves and Valerie Showan found a lost hero and the heroic Dan Billany and David Dowie reminded me what really matters ("You can't call it life if you're alone").

I'd like to extend my warmest wishes to Naz Shahrokh, who

LARRY CLOSS

was present at the moment of creation, a beatific soul who sees the extraordinary in the everyday.

My friend, colleague, Nepal travel companion and Next Generation Nepal founder Conor Grennan, author of the wondrous *Little Princes* (which is and isn't related to *The Little Prince*), was an enthusiastic advocate and sounding board who told me that he had once asked poet Allen Ginsberg about the "Ah" after his signature, just like a character in this novel. "It's the perfect occupation of space," explained Ginsberg.

For creating a book cover that exceeded my wildest dreams, I am in awe of artist extraordinaire Anthony Freda, who read between the lines and delivered a design that's not only intriguing and evocative but an unexpected homage to the real Flannery, a gentle spirit who kept me company for twenty-three years.

A special thanks to every agent and publisher who ever rejected me, for helping me write a better book, to my agent, Michael Harriot at the Folio Literary Agency, for his wise counsel, and especially to my publisher, Sven Davisson at Rebel Satori Press, for seeing something no one else saw.

Thanks also to Deanna Kirk, Sparrow, Hal Sirowitz, Bob Holman, Bob Rosenthal and Jeffrey Posternak, for allowing me to include some version of themselves.

For easing the daunting process of obtaining reprint rights and permissions, I am deeply indebted to: Peter Hale at The Allen Ginsberg Trust, Alexandra Levenberg and Jeffrey Posternak at The Wylie Agency, Dwight Curtis at Sterling Lord Literistic, David Grossman at DG Management, John Antonelli, producer of *Kerouac, The Movie*, and Anthony Elia, intellectual property lawyer.

Many thanks, too, to Allen, Jack, Neal, William and their Beat comrades, for inspiring the search, and to Joyce Johnson, for helping me distinguish between the essence and the facts.

Lastly, I was inspired to write this story by John Barrow, whom I am blessed to call my best friend, my brother and my roadmate. The two words that matter most in this book are on the dedication page. Always.

272